Commonwealth. Every planet is l
them, they just borrow them. Flag
away when someone else takes the world. That's the nature of the
Inner Sphere. Anyway, the Falcons sent one of their fancy frontline
Clusters to wrestle it away this time. You know the ones I'm referring
to, all Trueborned-up. They must have wanted it pretty bad, because
they fought like savages.

It took a lot of work for me to get a copy of Jamison's battleROM.
I called in some favors, burned some karma, but I had to see it. He
was piloting an *Enfield*...a good 'Mech. I watched the images for hours,
over and over. Jamison squared off outside of the domed city of Kanda
against a Star Commander named Kincaid. Arrogant pus-bucket.
Kincaid was piloting an older *Flamberge*. It had seen better fights, that
much was evident. You could see the replacement armor didn't fit just
right, signs of structural damage even the Clanner techs couldn't fix.

Kincaid toyed with him, like a cat playing with a mouse. My boy
held his own, but didn't see that his enemy was luring him away from
his company...away from fire support. I could see it in the battleROM,
and I understood.

They say the Clans don't like using physical attacks with their
'Mechs. That's mostly true—except for the Jade Falcons. They seem to
like it. Kincaid got in close and jabbed one of that *Flamberge*'s clawed
fists right into the cockpit. On the battleROM, you can hear Jamison
scream—but only for a millisecond. Then it thankfully goes to static.

He survived the fight...for a while. Crushed spine in two places,
open head injury, lost an arm and leg. It was a miracle he didn't die out
there, outside the dome. He was in a coma for six months. We were
at his side day and night, Martha and I.

You always hear about the MechWarriors that get bionics and live
on to fight. Those are the rarities. Jamison died with us at his side. They
disconnected his life support when his brain activity dropped off. A
man shouldn't die that way, but in many ways he had been dead long
before that...them pulling the plug, that was the final act.

Martha took it harder than I thought. Maybe I was too wrapped up
in my own grief to notice. She didn't want me touching her, that was
the real clue. There were days in the house when neither of us spoke.

I never heard her go upstairs one day about a year afterward. She
got my service pistol out and stuck the barrel in her mouth and went
to join Jamison. I had her buried next to our boy because I knew she
was with him in heaven.

I contemplated joining them. Her suicide left me alone. I didn't
have any family. For hours I held that gun in my hands 'til the metal was
the same temperature as me. What did I have left to live for? I was old,
58 at the time. If I died, no one would notice. The VLCAF (Veterans of
the Lyran Commonwealth Armed Forces) would fold the flag over my

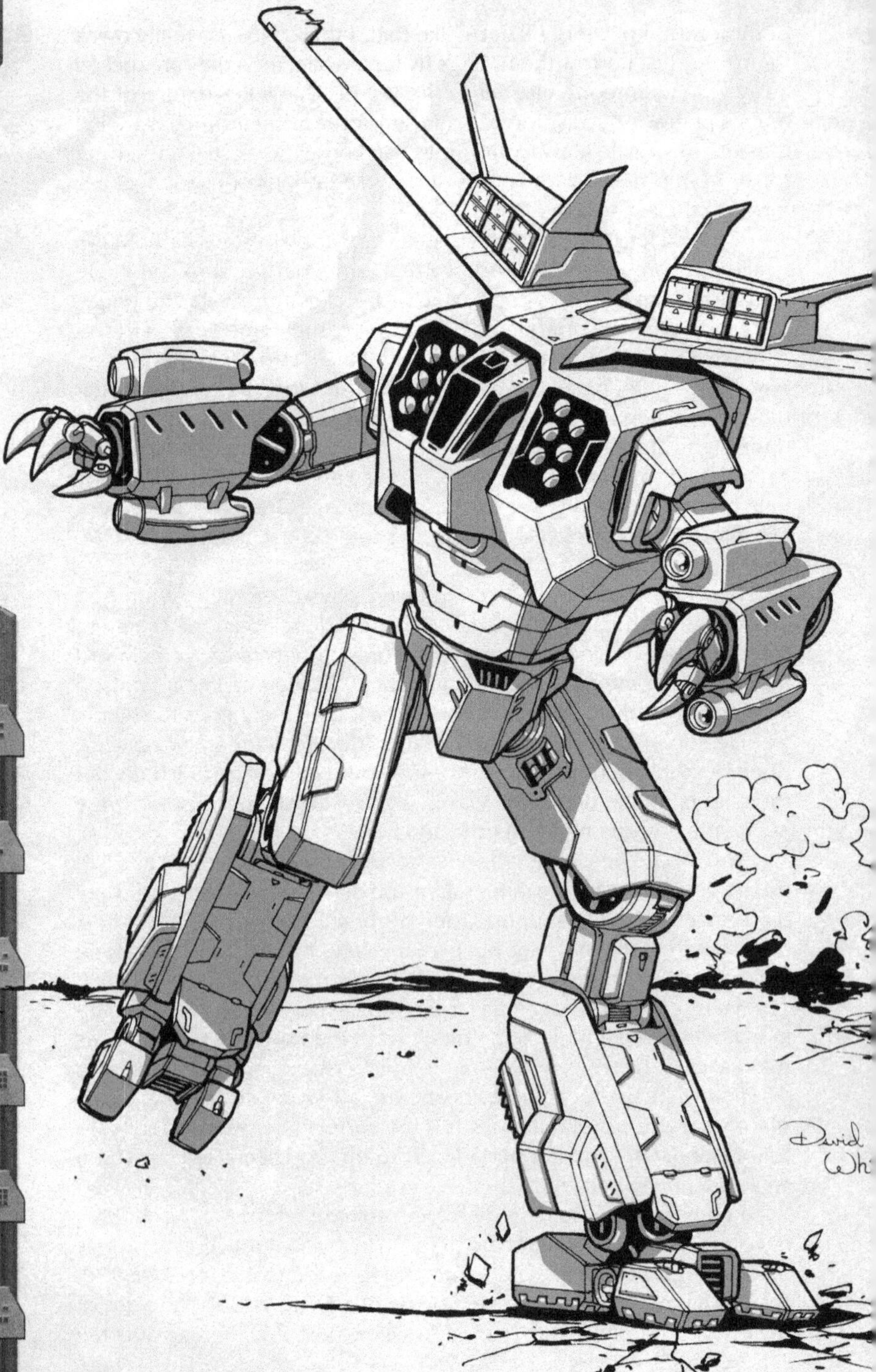
David
Wh

coffin, play taps, talk about honor and duty and a life well-lived. My death would mean nothing.

There was something in me that couldn't do what Martha did. Maybe I just wasn't brave enough. I don't think that was it. It was the knowledge that that filthy Jade Falcon had killed my boy. Kincaid had killed him, and was still alive. My life had no value, but I couldn't let him get away with what he had done. He had taken two people from me. He had taken almost everything I had. The thought of him sitting around with his comrades, continuing to live, well, that ate at me. If I was going to die, it should be to set things right. I needed to see Kincaid dead.

I studied his battleROM, every reading, every nuance of it. I watched it over and over again, analyzing every move he made, every taunt Kincaid threw at my son. There was a point when it felt like I almost knew him, though his face was a mystery to me. My mind filled in the blanks. I saw him with chiseled cheeks, arrogantly cropped hair, with a murderous gleam in his dark eyes. In my mind, Kincaid was young, the Clans favored young warriors. With youth came a cockiness, an arrogance, only made worse by being a Jade Falcon. In my thoughts, he was always smiling, not a happy smile, but a mean smile like a bully that has just beaten up someone. Anger tempered my obsession with him, that and a cold logic that I could not escape. He had taken everything from me, I was going to do the same to him.

I was going to kill Kincaid.

It wasn't anger. There was a reasoning to it, a mental process that was difficult to articulate. Killing that Jade Falcon was not retribution, it was justice in my mind. To do it, I would need a BattleMech and the means to get to Dustball. Somewhere between all of that, I would need to learn to be a MechWarrior. It sounds crazy now, especially at my age, but I was determined, and determination is often enough. I had a reason to live for.

The first part was easier than it sounds. I sold everything—our house, my worldly possessions; I even cashed in my pension and retirement savings. The only things I kept were a couple sets of clothes and my service Mauser.

The insurance policies on my wife and son helped as well. There was no planning for the future any more. I didn't give much thought of what would happen if I succeeded, or what would come after that. There was no future other than facing that bastard and killing him. That was my retirement plan now. Days went by when I envisioned his 'Mech exploding, or his body lying dead at my feet. I didn't even know what he looked like, but those hate-filled images consumed me.

I met with Klaus Kolberg, who ran a shop that custom-built BattleMechs for mercenaries. It took me weeks to find him...I had never purchased a BattleMech before. Klaus was a tough man, all muscles and grit. He too was a vet, his green-shield and axe tattoo from the Arcturan Guards said a lot about his past.

"So, you wish to purchase a BattleMech? Aren't you a little old for trying to join a mercenary unit?" When he spoke, the words rolled out of his mouth with a heavy Germanic accent.

"I am not joining a merc unit. I'm going to kill the man that killed my son."

Kolberg stared at me for a moment, as if he were reading every wrinkle and age spot on my face. His eyes almost stared right through me. Then he said, "You have a story to tell, then. Sit, and we will talk."

He invited me into his office and poured me a drink, a tall glass of Northwind Scotch, not the black label shit they sell to tourists, this was the tartan label, the good stuff. The aroma of it nipped at my nostrils, conjuring up memories of friends long-forgotten.

I had not spoken to anyone about my plan. I had hardly talked to a soul since Martha's funeral. Kolberg said nothing for a long time, he just nodded and sipped his drink. The scotch flowed in, and the words flowed out from my mouth. I barely stopped to breathe. I told him everything—the name of Jamison's killer, what I saw on the battleROM, the death of my beloved wife.

When I finished, Kolberg leaned back in his creaky chair and for a few long moments, said nothing. Slowly his eyes narrowed, and he gulped down all but a trickle of his drink.

"You will die there on Dustbowl if you go. You know, that don't you?"

"Dustball," I corrected. "And I don't care. Just as long as I take that Falcon-bastard with me."

He nodded with understanding. "If you face the Jade Falcons, you will need a good machine, very good. Most of my stock is lights and mediums. I have a *Zeus*, one I refit and rebuilt myself. A former 'Steiner Scout 'Mech,' or so he claimed, modified 5S model." He flashed a grin. "She has medium pulse lasers, salvaged Clan ones. I armored her up myself. This one, she mounts an LB-X autocannon—good for gutting your enemies. She is a beast, but one that can hang in a fight. If you are going against the Jade Falcons, you will need that."

A *Zeus*, that sounded about right. "How much?"

He chuckled. "You cannot afford it."

"I have five-mill," I offered.

Kolberg said nothing for a long moment, and I feared the deal was off. I was holding back some money for training and some for transport. It would do me no good to have a BattleMech and no way to get to Dustball.

Finally, the massive man shook his head. "I lost my niece to the Jade Falcons. Many of my comrades in the Guards fell to them as well. They almost got me in one fight." He held out his arm and pulled back the tee shirt to reveal a bullet hole scar. They are a soulless people. They spit out words like 'honor,' but what they bring is death and chaos."

"Five-mill is all I can afford. Perhaps you have something else?"

"Nothing that would stand against a Jade Falcon *Flamberge*."

I was disheartened. Kolberg had come highly recommended. "Is there anyone you can recommend that might be able to help me?"

"None whose work compares with mine," he said, pride ringing in the air. "You will not go anywhere else. You will take the *Zeus*."

"But you said I can't afford it."

"You cannot. That is why I am giving it to you for your price."

I had a hard time processing what he was saying. "I don't understand."

"You will go and kill this Jade Falcon. His last minutes will be looking at you as he bleeds out. As it should be. When you do, it will be as if I was there killing him with you. You will avenge my niece and my comrades. When you return, you will bring his BattleMech back. That will pay the difference."

"You are taking a big risk. As you pointed out, I am old. He may very well kill me." I didn't like making the concession, but I also did not harbor any illusions as to the odds against me.

Kolberg shook his head. "He won't. You have a fire in you, I see it in your eyes when you talk about killing him. Metal can be defeated. It can be blasted and burned. The spirit of good men, that cannot be crushed with ease. You kill someone of spirit, and it merely inspires another."

We shook hands, and he took me out to see it. Age oozed from every seam of its armor. The olive drab paint had steaks of yellow crisscrossing it. The smell of coolant and lubricant mixed in the air around it like an invisible fog.

"She *is* a beast," I said, more to myself than to my new friend.

"She is at that. Her serial number is low, one of the real old timers. She has brought back many a MechWarrior from a fight. She will serve you well."

I nodded. I had a 'Mech—now I needed to learn to pilot it.

Getting time in good simulators was only a little tricky. The military made them available for youngsters, to see if they had the aptitude for being MechWarriors. It gave them some hands-on before they applied to the LCAF or to one of the academies. The parents usually footed the bill, making sure their young daughter or son was prepared. When I strolled up, I got a puzzled look from the veteran operator. I slid him my credit stick and he set me up in a simulated *Zeus*. "Looking to relive your past glories, eh? We get a few old-timers in here doing that."

I shook my head. "No. I was a tanker. A damn good one, too."

"Why are you here then?" he asked, running his hand through his salt-and-pepper hair, slicking it back.

"I am going to kill the Jade Falcon that killed my son."

I expected him to ask questions, but instead he nodded. "Good luck then," was all he said. No doubt he thought I was mad or drunk or both. He showed me the changing area and gave me a rundown on how to use the pods.

The simulator was problematic at first. It was a pit-style, old school. The coolant vest was snug on me, years of not working out were showing. I had it configured for my *Zeus* and went up against a *Flamberge*. I thought I was doing well, until I was gutted with a salvo of advanced tactical missiles. The next round I was roasting under the heat from the pod's blowers, simulating cockpit conditions.

For five hours, the battle between me and the simulated Jade Falcon raged, and for five hours, my death replayed over and over. When I finally stopped, I was wet with sweat and tired...tired of dying, tired of failing.

Popping open the pod, I was surprised to see a young girl standing there. "Can I help you?"

"Wow, you're old," she said.

I did not need that reminder. Every day the mirror reminded me of who I was and the kilometers I had put on my body and soul. She continued before I could attempt a rebuttal. "I was watching you on the monitors out here. You're going about it all wrong."

"And how would you know?"

She balled her fists and planted them on her hips in a quasi-heroic pose. Pride rose in her face, I could see it. "Second year at Coventry Military Academy," she said proudly.

"If you're so good, why are you not at school?"

"Jade Falcons came. Trashed the school, killed most of my classmates," she said flatly, her hands lowering to her sides. "They almost got me if it hadn't been for the Stormhammers. They sent us on leave for a year or so while they rebuilt." The pride in her eyes seemed to fade as she spoke.

"You have a name?"

"Roxie Gulledge," she said.

"Waylon Frake," I replied. "So, can you help me, teach me what I'm doing wrong?"

She crossed her arms in thought and said nothing for a minute. "I hang out here, hoping to get some sim time. You front me for the time, Mister Frake, I'll help you."

"Deal," I extended my hand and we shook on it.

I learned a lot about her in a short period of time, she spoke so fast. Roxie's real name was Roxanne, but no one called her that, no one that didn't want a knee to their groin. She hailed from Skye, a proud family that had been sending sons and daughters to fight for centuries. Roxie used wild hand gestures when she spoke, and shifted in her stance as if she was nervous. Eventually she stopped talking about herself and asked why I was there. I told her, and she got quiet, real quiet.

"Don't take this wrong, but you're old, Mister Frake."

"Don't take this wrong," I shot back, "but I am aware of that. And call me Waylon."

"This isn't like piloting a tank. Tanks are hard on you. BattleMechs are worse. They'll toss you around, slam you forward and backward with every hit. A tank can't fall over and throw you down so hard that your restraining straps snap bones. You can't roast alive in a tank by pushing it. A BattleMech conspires to kill you while you try and kill someone else."

She spoke as if she had years of experience. I knew from my own time in the service that Roxie was right. That was the moment I respected her. She didn't talk down to me, or patronize me. She was poetic and blunt all at the same time.

"I am not fighting a war. I am killing one warrior. Help me do that."

Roxie did just that. "The AI is good on these sims, but you need to go up against a thinking person, someone that can adapt like a human being." She mounted up on a pod against me, speaking to me over the headset as we fought.

And boy, did we fight. Hundreds of battles were waged over the next two weeks, hundreds of times I died. I was beginning to think I would never beat her. And if I couldn't beat her, I couldn't kill Kincaid. Roxie became a temporary obsession for me. She killed me a lot in those early days, and each time I got more resolved to beat her.

She told me her rules, and they were good ones. "First, stop thinking like a tanker, move, twist your torso more. Second, watch your target display—aim for where you've already done damage. Third, he's going to want to get in close—so make him play by your rules, keep him distant as long as you can." They were all good words that I took to heart.

At night, when we were done, I went for runs and worked out. I say I ran, but those days were in my past. Now it was a quick jog, and afterward my hips and knees ached. Roxie was right though, I needed to be in physical shape to fight, not just mental. Slowly, my muscles came back online. The paunch around my stomach became a small flap of extra skin. Each day my reflexes got better, because she pushed me.

In the third week, I killed her in the simulator. The excitement felt great. She beat me, but I beat her in the next round. Slowly, methodically, I began to develop the skills I would need. After I defeated her three times in a row, she brought a friend to fight me. He fought differently, but I quickly figured him out and after four defeats, I flipped the tables on him and took him out three times in a row.

There was something more happening to me. I felt happiness again. It wasn't much, but each victory seemed to make me feel more human. Since Martha's death, nothing gave me joy. Smiling was more of a reflex than a reflection of my feelings. Roxie didn't just teach me how to pilot a BattleMech, she taught me to be a person again. She almost made me whole.

We met one morning but she was not wearing her coolant vest. "I don't need it today. You are as ready as I can get you."

Nodding, I thanked her, shaking her hand. "You really going to do this, Waylon? You're going into the Occupation Zone and find this guy and kill him?"

"He took everything from me," I said. "It's the only way to set things right."

She nodded quickly. "You know, I could go with you. I mean, classes aren't going to started for some time. You may need the help."

Shaking my head, I put my hand on her shoulder. "I already lost one child to the Jade Falcons. The OZ is no place for you. With Malvina Hazen there, it isn't safe for anyone that isn't of their blood. I have to do this alone. I can't be responsible for what might happen to you there."

Roxie surprised me with a sudden hug. "Then make damn sure you come back, old man," she said, wiping a tear from her eye as we separated. "I want to hear everything that happened."

"I will," I said. It hit me as she left that this was the first time I had considered even coming back. Klaus Kolberg had talked about me coming back, but at the time, I hadn't believed it. There was nothing to come back to, no one. Roxie was a friend, as was Klaus, but they were not my kin. I had always assumed it was a one-way mission. But with Roxie telling me to come back, I realized it might happen. She had given me one more gift—a ray of hope.

Booking passage into the Occupation Zone was a little tricky. Most merchants weren't keen on making the run. One told me that trading with the Jade Falcons was as tricky as swimming a pool full of sharks carrying a bag of angry weasels, only to get bitch-slapped by the lifeguard at the other end. I'm not sure I fully understand that analogy, but I got the general gist of it.

I was advised by several captains to seek out one of the Lyrans that worked for the Lyran Free Traders Association, that one of them might be willing. It took five months of inquiries and meetings before I found the right man for the job.

One merchant made regular runs there, so I went to him at the spaceport in Slavhold, about six hours away. His name was Jackson Sachse. A willow of a man, he had spent a lot of his life in space. Sachse was the epitome of a Lyran merchant, right down to the name of his ship, *Anything for a Buck*. Even so, he wasn't keen on me bringing a BattleMech on the voyage. "The Falcons have some pretty tight restrictions on military hardware. Just showing up with a BattleMech, well, it's going to do more than just raise eyebrows. I'm not sure that's a hassle I want to deal with."

"The responsibility is mine. If anything goes south, I will own it."

He agreed, but bumped up the price by 20 percent. It would leave me penniless, but that wasn't important to me. What mattered was getting to Dustball and finishing what I started.

Backing the *Zeus* into the bay was something I hadn't trained for, and I have to admit I was surprised I pulled it off on the first run. Roxie would have been proud. All her time with me in the sims hadn't been wasted.

Captain Sachse and I spoke often on the outbound trip to the JumpShip. He asked why I was willing to risk so much to go to the OZ—and I told him.

He didn't say anything for the longest time, and I let the silence hang in the DropShip air between us. I'd learned long ago not to speak when another man is thinking. "You know you may very well die there, just like your boy."

I gave him a single slow nod. "I know. I'm already dead on the inside. I have to try."

"Every time they take a world, I lose money," he replied. "They're like locusts, these Clans. Ever since they showed up, all they want is to conquer. And for what? To reestablish a Star League? What would that solve? More bureaucracy, less profit, I say. We've spent far too much time looking back fondly at the Golden Age, if you ask me."

Sachse paused for another moment, seeming to think again. "I'll wait for you at the spaceport. If you somehow pull this off, I'll get you home again."

"That's not necessary."

"I disagree. Waylon," he said, "this is bigger than you. If you pull this off, you'll be doing it not just for your boy, but for everyone who lost a son or daughter or husband or wife to these Falcons. If you do kill this warrior, people need to know about it. I won't leave you stranded."

That was the basis of our relationship. I tried to pry anything from him about his family and past, but the good Captain was wily on such matters, and kept his secrets to himself. He opened up to me some, but never really shared all that much; that was his nature and I respected it.

I spent most of the rest of my time on the journey working out, not wanting to lose any of the muscle tone I'd managed to regain.

We jumped to Dustball with little incident, though as soon as we arrived we had aerospace fighters maneuvering around our ships. The Jade Falcons were not taking any chances, and escorted to the spaceport some eight days later.

We landed outside Tristin, one of the domed cities,. The spaceport had its own small dome with tunnels that were pressurized out to the berths. When the doors of *Anything for a Buck* opened and my *Zeus* was revealed, the number of Jade Falcon warriors seemed to increase almost instantly.

It was hotter than balls there, stifling, and the air was a little thin for my liking. One of their *Black Hawk*s moved into a position, its lasers trained on my 'Mech. An officer came forward and spoke with Captain Sachse, who pointed to me.

She then marched over in front of me, looking me squarely in the eyes. She looked me over as if I were a slab of spoiled meat before she spoke crisply. "You have brought a contraband BattleMech here. Who are you, and what are your intentions?"

I stood tall and let my chest puff out slightly. "I am Waylon Frake. I have come here to find and fight one of your warriors."

My answer seemed to catch her off guard. "You have come to fight a single warrior, *quiaff*?"

"Yes."

"Who is this warrior?"

"His name is Kincaid, Star Commander Kincaid." It wasn't until I said his name out loud that I realized how deep my voice was. Good. It sounded serious.

"Wait here," she said, nodding to a trio of Jade Falcon infantry who eyed me as if I had a target on my chest.

She was gone for nearly two hours, with me standing there in the airlock, wondering if these troopers who had come in with me were my firing squad. They glared at me, but I gave them nothing in response. I've played enough poker in my life to know how to put on the expressionless face.

She returned shortly with a man in a Jade Falcon jumpsuit at her side. He stood before me, just slightly taller than me. His eyes were a piercing blue. His hair—what was left of it—was black with streaks of gray except on the left side of his head where a nasty old scar prevented any hair growth. On his chin was another scar, this one vertical, running like a crack up to his lip. His eyebrows were grayer than the rest of his hair on his head.

Up to that point, the idea of an old Clanner had never entered my mind, but here was one right in front of me. I'd always believed they died off. The Clans didn't have use for old warriors that I knew of, but here was one, staring me down.

"I am Kincaid," he said slowly, with a gravely tone to his voice. "Who are you to seek me out?"

This was not the man I had imagined. He was not quite as old as me, but was not at all like the Jade Falcons I'd seen on holovids. This was the man that killed Jamison. This was the warrior I was going to have to kill. All of this time, the passage of years, had led to this meeting, and despite the rush of blood in my ears, I couldn't help but be disappointed by who I saw.

"I do. Waylon Frake."

"I do not know you," he said studying my face.

"No, you don't. You knew my son, though. He was Hauptmann Jamison Frake. You killed him when you took this world from the Commonwealth."

"So?"

"I came here to fight and kill you. I aim to make you pay for what you did."

Kincaid paused, averting his eyes in thought. "I believe I remember that battle. Your offspring fought with honor. He died, *quiaff*?"

"Yes, after suffering for six months."

"He died with his honor intact, then." He turned and took a step away. For a moment, I thought it was over.

"Where do you think you're going?" I demanded.

He pivoted, like only a trained military officer can. "I have no time for such games. Your son died with honor. That is more than he deserved as a freebirth." He said "freebirth" as if the word burned in his mouth.

"What about your honor?" I asked.

"My honor? Explain."

"I challenge you to a fight...to the death. I have come here for justice. I intend to pay you back for what you did to my boy. You took everything from me. I will take your life. Doesn't your stupid little honor system demand you fight me?"

I got him with that, as sure as if I had fired a shot into him. "There is no Trial for revenge. That concept is beneath a Clan warrior. Go home, *solahma*. Go home and wither into old age."

"This is not revenge," I said coolly. "This is justice. Surely your code of honor addresses that."

The female warrior who I had spoken with was standing nearby. I had all but forgotten her until she spoke up. "There is the Trial of Refusal, Kincaid. He can refute using that." I wasn't sure, but I thought she might be enjoying pointing that out.

Her words clearly pissed off the older warrior. He shot her a fierce glare, then turned to me. "Star Commander Francesca has a point, but it stretches our rede. Refusals are for decisions. There is no precedent for such a Trial."

"Is that because you're afraid you will lose?" I asked.

His eyes narrowed even more. He didn't hide his contempt or his anger, and I liked that.

"I fear nothing from you. You are *solahma*. You are not worthy of my time."

"Watch the name-calling. I'm willing to bet I'm only a few years older than you. I think you are worried I'll beat you. I think you are a coward."

He sucked in a long breath and sighed heavily. "Very well, Waylon," he said avoiding my last name as if it would burn on his lips. "If you wish to join your son, I will gladly send you on your way. I agree to this Trial."

I grinned. "Good! You pick the place. I have a BattleMech. I will face you just like Jamison did. This time though, it will be you that dies."

"Augmented. Very well. We will form the Circle of Equals outside of the cities. No one will hear your cries for mercy as I slay you out there, where the heat will roast your carcass."

"When?"

"Tomorrow, at dawn," Kincaid said grimly. "I will have Star Commander Francesca send you the coordinates."

He walked away, and suddenly I felt very alone. I was in enemy space, fighting the killer of my son, and no one would know if I failed. They would dump my body somewhere or burn me to ash, but no one would know what I had tried to do here.

My stomach ached as the Jade Falcon warriors took up guard around my BattleMech in the DropShip bay.

That afternoon, I ran through every checklist I had for checking out the *Zeus*, twice. Captain Sachse brought my dinner to the cockpit. He sat at the hatch while I ate it. "Is there anyone I need to inform...you know...if you don't make it?"

"No. I lost everyone," I said. "If I do die, see if the Falcons will let you take the 'Mech back. If so, deliver it to Klaus Kolberg."

"I will. Anyone else, any family at all?"

"They are all gone," I said solemnly. Memories of Martha drifted to my mind for a moment. I remember thinking it was harder and harder to remember the details of her face. Time had blurred my memories. She would not approve of this course of action. Then again, if she were still alive, I would not be here. "There's a young girl, Roxie Gulledge. Let her know what happened to me, and tell her I appreciate all that she did."

Captain Sachse nodded and left me alone. I managed to drift off there, in the cockpit, around three times. There was no point in going to my bunk on the ship. The *Zeus* was my home now. Every time I woke up, it was with a sudden jerk. The last nap was the best, the deepest. I dreamt of the simulators with Roxie. In my dreams she talked to me, telling me what to do.

When I awoke the last time, it was just before dawn. I stretched, and heard the crack of my joints, a reminder of my age. My comm system had the coordinates flashing bright green, the location where my last battle was to take place.

Dustball was well named. Outside the domed cities it was a bleak world, light tan sand whipped into tiny tornadoes every so often. The sun crawling skyward was dulled in a yellow-tinted sky, with hints of deep purple on the horizon at all times.

The Jade Falcons, about a dozen of them in 'Mechs, formed a large circle to mark the perimeter of our fight. I chuckled at seeing them. I had come so far and so long, the thought of running made me laugh.

The old *Zeus* moved slowly, carefully under my control. Far away, nearly two kilometers, was a lone transponder signal marking Kincaid. He was piloting a *Flamberge*, no doubt the same one he had used to kill Jamison. People don't think the Clans have a flair for the dramatic, but I think they do.

Star Commander Francesca's voice filled my neurohelmet as I came to a stop. "*Trothkin*, we gather to stand witness to this Trial of Refusal. As has been our custom for centuries, we mark this Circle of Equals with honor, and stand ready to ratify the outcome of this battle."

In the swirls of dirt blowing by, my enemy was difficult to see. My sensors told the story though, Kincaid was moving in, closing with me. He came in on a jagged running path, jerking hard to the right and left. A rain of ATMs came at me first, plowing into the *Zeus*'s right side. Each explosion rattled my body, but I ignored it. My old muscles flexed to meet the challenge, and thanks to Roxie, I had them.

My own LRMs rained down on him, half of them blasting at his left side. I could make out the crimson explosions of the warheads through the sand and dust blowing between us.

Before he could respond, my LB-X autocannon tagged him back, sending a lone slug into his right arm. I kept my pace slow and steady, just as I had trained to do. I knew he was a jumper, and I didn't want to give him a chance to get in close, so I continued drifting in a wide arc to the right.

More missiles pierced the windblown sand, slamming into my legs and arms. My extended range large laser hit dead-center, and I could see the hot glowing mark where it had left a scar on his torso armor. As another wave of missiles came in, I swung around at the last second, letting them hit my rear armor. I responded with a rack of my own long-range missiles, which all seemed to plow into his *Flamberge*'s upper body, several twisting the metal of his wings.

I had watched Jamison's battleROM so many times I suddenly felt like it was in it. Kincaid drew closer, and with him came more ATMs, chewing up my armor. My lasers and autocannons blazed back at him. My forward pulse laser missed its mark, but the missiles and large laser bore in on his left flank again. Sparks sprayed out from the damage on his arm there, which I took as a good sign.

Sweat rolled down my brow in the neurohelmet as his ATMs once more rocked my *Zeus*. I had been a tanker my whole career, but I had never felt as one with the tank. It is different with a 'Mech. In a fight, it is like a second layer of skin, you bond with it, move with it, take damage with it.

My eyes darted to the tactical screen, and I knew he was closing the distance between us. Memories of Kincaid jumping and punching Jamison filled my mind. He would do it again, I knew he would, especially in front of these other Jade Falcons!

Roxie's rules came to me, reminding me to stay focused. I did not let her down. My autocannon blazed away, sending its deadly slug right into the *Flamberge*'s cockpit. It wasn't enough to penetrate it, but was enough to throw off his lasers and the incoming wave of missiles as he staggered backward a few awkward steps.

My LRMs filled the air between us again, the explosions sending several large plates of his armor flying into the air. I could see him regaining his composure from the head-shot in the way his 'Mech moved. He charged forward, a full sprint right at me. I fired my medium pulse lasers, hitting with one, the emerald bursts of energy blasting his left side and arm, leaving blackened holes in their wake.

If you have never been in a BattleMech that is being charged at 65 kph, I will attempt to describe it. He struck my *Zeus* like a pile driver...the only saving grace was that I outmassed him by 10 tons. Even so, I was tossed hard, as if in a car accident, twisting slightly in my command couch. I heard a *crack*, and felt a hot, stabbing pain in my side...a broken rib. My balance was off, but the sound of crunching and grinding metal was all around me.

I felt *the Zeus* sway to the right, and I compensated, almost over-compensated. Lights flickered amber and crimson on my damage display. Twisting back to keep balance, I felt my breath get ragged as I somehow kept my footing.

Turning at the waist, staggering slightly, I saw his *Flamberge* stumble back from the impact, one piece of armor on its torso peeled up, almost blocking his cockpit view. Instinctively I dropped my targeting reticle on the Jade Falcon and fired—unleashing my ER large laser and autocannon. The laser bored deep into his crumpled and mangled front armor, while the autocannon hit his left side with a *whomp*, some of the shrapnel glancing off of my *Zeus*.

My eyes burned from the sweat stinging them as he sent a wave of short-range missiles into my legs. Every explosion made the pain in my side flare, but I ignored it. This was what I had been living for, this battle.

He was going to jump—I knew that probably before he did. I waited for a second and saw the brilliant orange plumes of flame light up from his jets, kicking up their own tornados of dust. I did not lose my track of him as he rose, I kept the reticle on target—my medium lasers furrowed deep into the torso of the rising 'Mech as he flew toward me. My large laser cycled and I fired, hitting his left side, setting off the remaining missile ammunition there. The *Flamberge* quaked mid-flight from the blast, but he kept coming at me, soaring through the air, relentless.

I knew what was coming—death from above. I waited, listening to the roar of the jets. The millisecond they cut off, I reversed the battered *Zeus* as fast as I could.

He dropped right next to me—I heard the *crunch* of his legs hitting the ground only a few meters away. Swaying, off balance, I saw him with perfect clarity in that moment.

I punched at him, he did the same to me. It was as if I was suddenly in Jamison's BattleMech. The clawed arm came at me, hitting my right torso hard. I was thrown forward again, the safety harness digging into me, the searing pain on my side shooting up.

My own punch landed in the internal guts of his mangled center torso, going through the last fragments of armor and hitting his gyro with a grinding sound that made the *Zeus* reverberate with the impact. Kincaid had been injured, he had to be, by the way his 'Mech moved. The *Flamberge* swayed and fell on its right arm, twisting it under the impact and weight of the 'Mech.

I also could not fight the pull of Dustball's gravity. I fell as well, landing on my left side, right across his 'Mech's legs. It was hard to tell who was more damaged, but his 'Mech was pinned under mine. Every agonizing move I tried to make further crippled both of us. My targeting systems flickered on and off so fast I could not hope to aim.

This was it, I was going to die here—just like my boy.

From my cockpit, I could see his. He hit the explosive bolts on the canopy and blew it out with a *pop*, raining armored glass all over my 'Mech. He staggered out, his arm bleeding and bone poking through. With an angry snarl, he twisted off his neurohelmet and tossed it aside. Coolant oozed down his legs as he stood in the cockpit.

"It is over, Waylon. Your BattleMech is crippled. You cannot stand. I have defeated you as I did your child. Yield, and you may live. Refuse, and I will kill you as I did him."

There was a dark voice in my head that urged me to agree with him, but I suppressed it. Kincaid stood just inside the cockpit and it hit me, as clear as anything: *He can't fire either, not from there!*

I hit the release button on my own cockpit, blasting it clear. Dust and cooler air hit me as I unplugged my coolant vest and threw my neurohelmet to the side of the cockpit with a *thunk*. Just removing the restraining strap, I nearly passed out. I struggled to get enough air. I remember thinking my lung was probably punctured from the rib. It didn't matter. Kincaid had nothing but his bravado. He was trying to bluff me into submission.

I half-stood, half-leaned in the open cockpit and faced him, some twelve meters apart. The heat from our fallen 'Mechs radiated all around me. I remember hearing a strange hissing sound, too. Clarity comes to you in a moment like this. You remember the strangest little details.

"Do you stand down, Spherer?" Kincaid demanded. "I grow weary of this waste of the Jade Falcons' time."

"That won't be a problem for you anymore," I called back as my hand fell to the holster at my side. Then I felt the butt of my Mauser pistol in my hand. It hurt like hell to raise it, but my aim had to be true.

The shots made my side throb with each *crack* as three bullets blasted into Kincaid's body, with the last shot hitting his throat. The spray of blood out of the back of his neck said it all to me—he was dead. He fell backward into the cockpit.

I don't remember holstering the gun or even climbing down from my 'Mech, though I must have. I do remember Star Commander Francesca coming over and inspecting Kincaid's body. She declared the Trial over.

I was surprised that a Jade Falcon med tech came over and helped me as Francesca came over to me. "You defeated him fairly," she said flatly. "I trust this puts this matter to rest, *quiaff*?"

"It does," I said with a ragged breath as the med tech checked my side. "There is one more thing, though."

She cocked her right eyebrow at me, as if daring me to speak... so I did.

"I claim his BattleMech. If I remember right, you people do that sort of thing."

"*Isorla*," she said. "And as the victor, it is your right to do so."

"Thank you."

Francesca waved her hand. "Thanks are not necessary. Kincaid was *solahma*. At his age, his greatest hope was to die in battle. In redeeming your son's death, you have honored him with his own release." She stood at attention before me, out of respect. It hurt having your enemy look at you with respect.

Her words stung me deep and hard. Kincaid had not suffered like Jamison, he had just died. I didn't want to honor him, I wanted him to feel the pain I felt. Francesca's words hurt me more than the damage to my lung.

In fact, I wondered if, in that instant, he had deliberately popped his cockpit and stood there knowing I would kill him. That was the thought I would struggle with for the rest of my life. Had I actually done him a favor? It was the kind of twisted thought I had to suppress.

I secured my pistol in its holster, almost unconsciously, then closed my eyes. "I did it for you, Jamison—and you, Martha." Then the darkness took me.

I awoke two days later to find we were already burning out of orbit back to the jump point. Captain Sachse told me I had two broken ribs and a

dislocated shoulder. It was my right arm. I shouldn't have been able to lift the gun, let alone fire it—but somehow I had. I guess adrenaline does that to people—makes them not feel pain that should cripple them.

True to her word, Francesca had overseen the loading of my *Zeus* and the *Flamberge.* I kept to myself for the weeks it took to get home. Some of that was the time to heal. Some of it was recalling the battle and replaying it in my mind. The guilt over Martha's death, which had seemed to smother me for years, faded a little every day. What I was left with was something else, a strange calm. I had my life back...but I didn't know what to do with it.

When I arrived back on Lyndon, I invited Captain Sachse, Klaus Kolberg, and Roxie Gulledge to dinner. I sold the mangled *Zeus* back to him and gave him the *Flamberge*, per our agreement. Klaus was amazed, not just that I had survived, but that I had made it back.

I regaled my friends with the story of the fight on Dustball and the death of Kincaid. It hit me that night, that the only family I had was the people I had around that dinner table. They hung on every word, and Captain Sachse confirmed much of the story, as he'd been watching from a viewport on the bridge of *Anything for a Buck*.

"You should have seen it, I watched with binoculars. He pulled out his gun and took down this Falcon, one-on-one, one of their Trueborns!" As the drinks flowed something happened, something I could not explain, I started to laugh. I hadn't done that in a while. I don't even remember what it was over. I laughed and laughed, and while I did, tears ran down my cheeks. Each tear seemed to take some of the weight off of my soul.

I worked it out with Klaus right there at the dinner table over glasses of the good stuff, that Northwind Scotch. I used some of my remaining money after I sold the *Zeus* back to him to purchase a beat-up *Panther* for Roxie. I could afford that. It needed some work, but if she was going back to the academy soon, she would need a ride.

Klaus promised to get it ready for her. "You will be a star on campus with this old girl," he promised Roxie. She hugged me so hard it made my barely healed rib ache, but I didn't care. I hugged her right back.

The news media contacted me for the story, and I gave it to them in a series of interviews. I was shocked by how many families reached out to me. Most said I was a hero; that I had done what they had only dreamed of. The veterans offered to throw parties and have me come speak to them. I can't go into a bar and buy myself a drink any more, there's always someone there to make sure my glass is filled. Even in my own town, they wanted me to be Grand Marshal in a parade. I declined that offer. There was nothing to celebrate. I don't like being a symbol of anything. I sought justice and got it, nothing more or less.

I didn't feel the part of hero that they wanted me to be. I think Kincaid wanted to die that day on Dustball. The more I think about it, the more I came to realize that he *let* me kill him. Oh, I got my justice, but even in death, he had somehow taken something from me. That does not make me a hero or a fraud. It just makes me a father who tried to do the right thing. He's dead, so we will never know what he was thinking.

You may say this story is fiction, some propaganda piece created for the LCAF, but it is the truth, every word of it. I wrote it down so that Roxie would have it. You need things like that so that people don't forget.

After all, she is part of my family.

THE GREAT REAVINGS

ERIC SALZMAN

THE COLISEUM
SOLARIS CITY, SOLARIS VII
WOLF EMPIRE
22 JANUARY 3146

Solaris VII had never been a stranger to spectacle. The Game World had seen it all—from scrapheaps duking it out for the entertainment of logging camp yokels to elaborately produced elite duels in ultramodern arenas, not to mention gang wars, the Solaris Home Defense League's anti-Blakist crusade, and the Great UrbanMech Uprising of 3122. But in all his years as a holovid operator on Solaris, Marko had never seen anything quite so...alien.

Wolf Empire warriors filled the arena stands, each group in their own section down by the front, just behind the detonator grid. Freshly painted names adorned the walls of the arena: Kerensky, Fetladral, Ward, and more. Nearly a hundred in all. What got to Marko wasn't their exotic leather uniforms or ceremonial masks—you'd see stranger things at Zelda's Palace of Scorn any given Tuesday—but rather their expectant, almost reverent, silence, a sharp contrast to the raucous screaming of the typical audiences.

The status light on Marko's holocamera went green, and he made a final check to ensure the figure on the central dais was in focus before switching to the live feed. A twenty-meter-high projection, twice the height of a BattleMech, arose in midfield, and Khan Alaric Ward spoke.

"Trothkin, hear me! We have completed the first step of our long journey and carved out a new home among the stars. Your skill and sacrifice, your courage and honor have brought this Wolf Empire into being."

Marko adjusted the controls to slowly rotate the image, making Alaric seem to face each Bloodhouse in turn.

"Some of your lineages have been with us since the days of the Founder on Strana Mechty. Others joined us as bondsmen or rose from the ranks of *the freeborn. Know you this—all Wolves who bear a Bloodright have an equal place in my Clan Council..."* Alaric smiled wolfishly, a glint in his eye. *"...for so long as you can keep it. Let the Great Reaving commence!"*

The Clan Council's deafening roar filled the arena, sending a cold shiver down Marko's spine.

SEA FOX WATCH REPORT
ANALYSIS OF THE 3146 GREAT REAVING
27 MARCH 3146

After fifty years of Great Reavings, it is worthwhile to consider not only this year's outcomes, but the long-term impact of the tradition on our eugenics programs, intercaste relations, combat effectiveness, and territorial administration.

OVERVIEW

As has been our practice since the Council of Six developed the concept in 3095, each Clan holds a series of combat trials toward the start of the calendar year, with the goal of adjusting the number of active Bloodrights within the Clan. Bloodhouses that performed well the previous year in the eyes of their Clan Council are given the opportunity to fight Trials of Propagation and, if successful, are able to add to their numbers, up to a maximum of twenty-five Bloodrights. Bloodhouses that failed to distinguish themselves or were responsible for failure and defeat may be challenged by another Bloodhouse in a Trial of Reaving, which decreases the defender's Bloodright count if they fail. This is not entered into lightly: a successful defense entitles the challenged Bloodhouse to engage the opposed Bloodhouse in a counter-Reaving.

Finally, as the highlight of each Great Reaving festival (for this is, in truth, what the practice has become, replete with a level of pageantry and artistic spectacle rivaling the Martial Olympiads of old), the Khan may nominate freeborn bloodlines to be elevated to Bloodname status in a Trial of Founding. The Clan Council votes on the proposal, and the outcome determines the force ratio for the ensuing trial. If the freeborn champion fails, their bloodline may never again be nominated. Success results in the formal creation of a new Bloodhouse with ten Bloodrights, which may increase or decrease in future Great Reavings. Bloodhouse Magnusson of the Ghost Bears was the first Founded Bloodhouse to expand to full size, Propagating their twenty-fifth member in 3111. Such elevations have served to bind our Spheroid populations to their ruling Clans by elevating their best to join the ruling caste, and they encourage skilled freeborns to strive for distinction in hopes of one day Founding their own Bloodhouse. Given the impact seen on the battlefields, the results of this fresh infusion of elite genetics speak for themselves.

The Council of Six's other key decision on Bloodhouses, the 3095 Edict of Severance, reflected the monumental shift in how Bloodhouses from other Clans had been treated under the laws and precedents set down by the Founder. Prior to the Edict, warriors taken as bondsmen into the Clan could, upon restoration of warrior status, be eligible to compete for a Bloodname of their lineage when it became available, temporarily returning to their Clan of origin to compete in the Trial of Bloodright. Even Bloodrights taken in Trials of Possession were still administered by the heads of the originating Bloodhouse. The loss of contact with the Homeworlds and the Bloodhouses based there left such warriors in legal limbo. Given the large number of volunteers for the Harvest Trials, each seeking a chance to join the fighting in the Inner Sphere, nearly every Homeworld Clan Bloodhouse had members serving among our Clans.

Per the Edict of Severance, these warriors, cut off from their Bloodhouses, were given the right to undertake a Trial of Founding and begin a new Bloodhouse to oversee an initial ten Bloodrights, should their trial be successful. These Trials of Founding were the centerpiece of the Great Reavings of 3095-3100, and enabled these isolated Bloodhouses to begin anew—often diversified using genetic samples harvested from any warrior whose codex showed sufficient matrilineal or, in a radical departure, patrilineal connections through ancestry. Should contact be restored with the Homeworlds and the original Bloodhouses, this matter will have to be addressed, but for now it has allowed the scions of N'Buta, Telinov, Dinour, Boques, Holliday, and hundreds more to fight with pride (and vote in Clan Councils) alongside the Hazens, Kerenskys, McKennas, Cobbs, Jorgenssons, and Senders.

The relatively stable borders of the Pax Republica era limited opportunities to earn honor on the battlefield, allowing Reavings to outpace Propagations. By the 3130s, some Bloodhouses had dropped to single digits of active Bloodrights, but Gray Monday changed everything. The ensuing conflict and vast territorial gains provided ample justification for Trials of Propagation, swelling the ranks of nearly every Bloodhouse to levels not seen since Operation Revival.

THE GREAT REAVING OF 3146

A full accounting of Reavings, Propagations, and Foundings may be found in Annex C, but the following highlights reflect how each Clan used their event.

Ghost Bear: The Miraborg bloodline, distantly related to the famed Tyra Miraborg, undertook its Trial of Founding with the Khan's support. In an aerospace duel, champion Svenga Miraborg defeated two OmniFighters to establish the new Bloodhouse.

Hell's Horses: In celebration of Fulk Lassenerra's appointment as saKhan, the Lassenerra Bloodhouse fought and won a Trial of

Propagation, adding a twenty-third Bloodright. Khan Amirault sponsored the Techus bloodline for Founding, citing the family's martial tradition (including significant actions by an ancestor during the Battle of Luthien) and their exemplary adherence to the modern Mongol Doctrine traditions. Family champion Ilnay Techus proved unable to overcome the odds against him and was shot out of his *Arcas*. He expressed regret for having failed both his ancestors and children, and performed seppuku immediately after the trial had concluded, with Khan Amirault serving as his second.

Jade Falcon: Chingis Khan Malvina Hazen personally led the Trial of Reaving for the Bloodright held by Beckett Malthus, who had attempted to assassinate her on Hesperus II. Though tradition dictates such trials are Star vs. Star, Malvina ordered her Star to stay back while she dueled and destroyed each of the five Malthus 'Mechs, taking pains to kill their pilots in the process.

Sea Fox: Khan Mori Hawker put forward a motion to revert the Fowler Bloodhouse to a ProtoMech breed (as the Horses did when creating TankWarriors), arguing that a relaunch of ProtoMech production could lead to substantial profits in the current seller's market). Council voting went heavily against the motion, and the Fowler champion was swiftly defeated, tabling the motion and retaining the Fowlers as a lesser line of aerospace pilots.

Snow Raven: The Cooper and Howe Bloodhouses, embroiled in a feud stretching back to the Pentagon, once again battled each other to a draw in a Trial of Reaving that left both Bloodrights intact. Over the past fifty years, five Coopers and six Howes have been Reaved in these annual clashes. Having fallen behind in the 3138 Great Reaving, the Howes had hoped to even the score this year.

Wolf: Alaric Ward hosted the Wolf Empire's Great Reaving on Solaris VII for the first time, using its many arenas as trial venues. He rewarded the Bloodnamed of Alpha Galaxy for their victory over the Golden Ordun on Hesperus II with Trials of Propagation for each of their Bloodhouses.

THUNDER STALLION 4 ("AVENGING ANNIE")

Mass: 85 tons
Chassis: Type QMA Standard (Quad)
Power Plant: Fusion 255 Extra Light
Cruising Speed: 32 kph
Maximum Speed: 54 kph
Jump Jets: 3 Model KJ Boosters
    Jump Capacity: 90 meters
Armor: Forged Type HH32
Armament:
    1 Type Mu LB 20-X Autocannon
    1 Type AA4 Gauss Rifle
    1 Series 44h Large Pulse Laser
    2 Series 14a Medium Pulse Lasers
    1 Series 7N Extended Range Large Laser
Manufacturer: Arc-Royal MechWorks
    Primary Factory: Arc-Royal
Communications System: CH3V Series Integrated
Targeting & Tracking System: Version Kappa-III TTS

The *Thunder Stallion 4*'s origins are not with the Hell's Horses, but with a determined MechWarrior by the name of Ann-Marie Dalmas.

Ann-Marie was the XO of Gerrson's Ghosts, working a contract on Biuque in the Lyran Commonwealth. In October of 3135, a raid by the Hell's Horses shattered the Ghosts, and Ann-Marie found herself facing off against a *Thunder Stallion*. The Clan 'Mech's autocannon forced her to eject from her exploding *BattleMaster*.

After landing, she noticed the *Thunder Stallion* was not moving. The Clan MechWarrior was dead, killed by shrapnel from a single SRM round to the cockpit, but the 'Mech was otherwise undamaged. Ann-Marie took control of the *Thunder Stallion* and piloted it back to the Ghosts' assembly area, where she discovered that the Horses had wiped out the Ghosts' support staff and dependents. Gathering up a few survivors, she left Biuque, vowing vengeance on all Clans and Hell's Horses in particular.

After paying off the Ghosts' debts, Ann-Marie was left with the *Thunder Stallion* and little money. Undeterred, she approached Arc-Royal MechWorks with a deal: in return for rebuilding the *Thunder Stallion*, ARM would get unrestricted access to the 'Mech (a model that had not been seen much in Commonwealth space) for a period of two years. ARM agreed.

Once that period expired, the *Avenging Annie* walked out of ARM's assembly hangar in 3138.

Capabilities

Officially designated the *Thunder Stallion 4*, the *Avenging Annie* turns the support 'Mech into a front-line fighter. While it keeps the Type Mu LB-X autocannon, the rest of the standard weapons loadout is replaced with a Gauss rifle, a large pulse laser, two medium pulse lasers, and a rear-mounted ER large laser. In addition, the *Avenging Annie* has extra mobility from jump jets. To gain the space needed for all these improvements, the *Avenging Annie* mounts a XL engine and forfeits a half ton of armor.

In addition, the biggest flaw of the original *Thunder Stallion*—the autocannon storage and feed through the head and central torso—has been removed, placing the autocannon and Gauss rifle ammo and their feeds into the front legs. While this could lead to a crippling ammo explosion, it gives the MechWarrior a greater chance of survival.

Deployment

As of now, the *Avenging Annie* is the only *Thunder Stallion 4* in existence. However, reports claim the Hell's Horses' on Csesztreg are trying to duplicate the model for their own use.

Ann-Marie, now the commander of Annie's Avengers, was on Arcadia in December of 3140. It was here that the Clans first noticed *Avenging Annie*. Elements of Clan Wolf's Gamma Galaxy struck Arcadia and the First Steiner Strikers. The Avengers were part of an auxiliary mercenary force assigned by Roderick Steiner to defend DeSota City, and Ann-Marie was placed in charge of the defense.

When Wolf forces were sighted approaching the city on December 10, Ann-Marie deployed her forces inside the city, then strode out into the Wolves' view in her *Thunder Stallion*. She fired her Gauss rifle, decapitating a Wolf *Blood Reaper*. As she retreated into the city, the Wolves charged in.

For the next two days, Ann-Marie and *Avenging Annie* were in the thick of the brutal fighting, claiming twelve Wolf 'Mech and vehicle kills. By the time a Steiner Strikers force arrived, the auxiliary was reduced to a third of its original size, but they had held. By the time they left Arcadia on 22 December, Ann-Marie had seventeen 'Mech and vehicle kills and *Avenging Annie* had become a legend.

Notable 'Mechs and MechWarriors

Ann-Marie Dalmas: Now rebuilding the Avengers into a battalion, Ann-Marie has become a celebrity at a time the Commonwealth needs one. She turned down an LCAF commission, preferring to keep her independence. The *Avenging Annie* is a popular subject for local photographs, and Ann-Marie has been interviewed several times. The Avengers are expected to be sent close to the front as a garrison to free up LCAF units for other missions.

Type: **Thunder Stallion 4 (Avenging Annie)**
Technology Base: Clan
Tonnage: 85
Role: Juggernaut
Battle Value: 2,643

Equipment		Mass
Internal Structure:		8.5
Engine:	255 XL	6.5
Walking MP:	3	
Running MP:	5	
Jumping MP:	3	
Heat Sinks:	12 [24]	2
Gyro:		3
Cockpit:		3
Armor Factor:	272	17

	Internal Structure	Armor Value
Head	3	9
Center Torso	27	34
Center Torso (rear)		19
R/L Torso	18	20
R/L Torso (rear)		15
R/L Front Leg	18	35
R/L Rear Leg	18	35

Weapons and Ammo	Location	Critical	Tonnage
Ammo (LB-X) 10	FRL	2	2
LB 20-X AC	RT	9	12
Medium Pulse Laser	H	1	2
ER Large Laser	CT (R)	1	4
Large Pulse Laser	LT	2	6
Medium Pulse Laser	LT	1	2
Gauss Rifle	LT	6	12
Ammo (Gauss) 16	FLL	2	2
Jump Jet	RT	1	1
Jump Jet	CT	1	1
Jump Jet	LT	1	1

Notes: Features the following Design Quirks: Cramped Cockpit.

LAWS ARE SILENT

CRAIG A. REED, JR

When arms speak, the laws are silent.
—Cicero

LUVON MOUNTAINS
BREMEN, THARKAD
LYRAN ALLIANCE
5 MARCH 3068

"It's peaceful here," the blond woman said. "You wouldn't know the planet was occupied by a bunch of robe-wearing techno-fanatics, would you?"

This high in the mountains, the air was still cool, and the snow still very much in evidence, despite the clear sky and sun overhead. Leaning against the foot of his *Zeus*, holding a cup of coffee, Ansgar Shurasky felt the sun's warmth and wished he could stay in its glow a while longer. "No," he muttered. "You wouldn't."

"Want to talk about it, Gar? You've been moody recently."

Shurasky looked up at the woman sitting on top of the 80-ton 'Mech's foot. She was dressed in a LAAF jumpsuit too light for the environment, but didn't look cold at all. She had pale blue eyes and shoulder-length platinum-blond hair.

"I thought ghosts didn't come out during the day," he said softly.

"When did you become an expert on ghosts?" the woman replied, folding her arms as she looked down on him.

He sighed and looked up at the *Zeus*. *Thirteen* was the thirteenth *Zeus* ever built. It had been in a noble's private collection, now part of the Lyran resistance against the Blakist occupation. The tech who had been maintaining *Thirteen* told Shurasky the 'Mech was haunted.

Shurasky, who had his own ghosts, had taken it anyway, and found it did have a ghost—his sister Shana, who had died in the FedCom's waning days.

Or it was his mind, still recovering from an emotional breakdown, projecting his dead sister as a quirk in his current state of mind? Shana said she was a ghost, but was she really?

Shana rolled her eyes. "You're the one who decided I was a ghost, remember? We had this debate the first time I manifested in *Thirteen's* cockpit. It was either that, or thinking you were crazy. So, we both agreed I was a ghost."

"How did you know what I was thinking?" Shurasky asked.

Shana sighed. "You've always had a bad poker face. I can *always* tell what you're thinking." She looked in the direction of the camp. "Here comes O'Toole."

Shurasky pushed himself off the *Zeus*'s foot as Senior Sergeant Major Felan O'Toole reached him. "Sir," he said, not bothering to salute. The veteran NCO had been retired when the Blakists had invaded Tharkad, but any retirement rust had been scoured away by four months of guerrilla warfare. His lean face was leaner than the first time they'd met, and only a few wisps of white hair were visible from under his cap.

"What is it, Irish?"

"Message from someone claiming to be someone you know. It came through a dozen resistance stations, bouncing all over the planet."

"What's it say?" Shurasky asked.

O'Toole took a sheet of paper from his coat pocket, opened it and read out loud, "*Wolfsjäger*, this is Rook Two. In trouble, need help. Jackals at the door. Please respond."

"May I?" Shurasky asked holding out his hand for the message. O'Toole gave it to him. Shurasky read the note, then closed his eyes.

"You know this Rook Two?" O'Toole asked.

"I know the callsign. Rook Two was Staff Sergeant Liam Tremmel."

"That's a name from the past," Shana said.

"And Tremmel is?" O'Toole prompted.

"He was a member of my battalion during the fight in the Stahlwurzel," Shurasky replied. "He piloted an *Axman* during that disaster until it was blown out from under him and he lost a leg. Last I heard, he'd retired to his hometown."

"And where is that?"

"A little town called North Emden. There's a couple of skiing complexes up there."

"What does he want?"

"Help, obviously."

"Can you say 'trap,' boys and girls?" Shana said brightly. "Sure you can!"

O'Toole frowned. "You realize this is probably a trap."

"I know, but I can't ignore it if it isn't."

"What are you going to do?"

Shurasky thought for a few seconds. "Send this reply: '*Wolfsjäger* to Rook Two. How is the leg, you old pirate?'"

O'Toole raised an eyebrow. "You want to send *that*?"

Shurasky nodded. "It's something only he and I know about. It should at least rule out if someone's faking Tremmel. Send it just before we move out."

"Which way are we heading?"

"I'll tell you before we move out."

"All right. I'll tell Sparks."

After O'Toole left, Shurasky climbed the ladder to the *Zeus*'s cockpit and climbed in. Shana was waiting for him as he secured the hatch, arms folded. "It's probably a trap."

"Yeah," Shurasky replied.

"So, why bother answering? You know the Word has a hundred thousand C-bill price on your head!"

"You know why."

"Guilt over what happened in the Stahlwurzel?"

"No, a bond of blood. I have to find out why he's in trouble."

"You don't know he's in trouble, or if it's even him!"

"My mind is made up." Shurasky lowered himself into the command chair. "Depending on what the answer is, I'll decide what to do next."

"All right," Shana said. "But I still think it's a trap."

LUVON MOUNTAINS
BREMEN, THARKAD
LYRAN ALLIANCE
9 MARCH 3068

The Lucky Strike Mining company had gone bust in the late 2990s, leaving a mining complex with plenty of places to hide a FedCom-era weapons cache—and now *Kampfgruppe* Shurasky—deep in the mines' tunnels and caverns.

Shurasky was sitting in what had once been a supervisor's office, drinking a cup of coffee and looking at a map laid out on the desk when there was a knock at the door. "Enter," he said, not looking up from the map.

The door opened and O'Toole entered. "You have a message, sir," he said. He handed Shurasky a piece of paper.

Shurasky looked at it. *ROOK TWO TO WOLFSJAGER. LEG IS FINE. DON'T YOU KNOW PEGLEGS ALWAYS GET THE GIRLS?*

"It's Tremmel," he said, handing O'Toole the paper.

"And you know this because?"

"Because that's what he told me when I visited him in the hospital after the Stahlwurzel. We were the only two in the room, so only he and I know what was said there."

"Well, it may be Tremmel, but it doesn't mean he's not dancing to the Word's tune."

"It doesn't. Which is why after you send a message to Tremmel setting up a meeting, we're moving out. Have a pencil?"

"Yeah."

"Transmit this: 'Wolfsjäger to Rook Two. Meet five days after this message received, midnight. Location is Purgatory. One vehicle, no weapons, sign and countersign the same as the Stahlwurzel.'"

"All right," O'Toole said, jutting down the words, "but it still sounds like a trap."

"It may be, but in case it is..." He motioned to the NCO to come over to the map. "What do you see?"

O'Toole looked at it for a few seconds. "Map of the area."

Shurasky pointed at one corner. "This is where we are right now. He pointed to an area on the other side of the map. "Here's North Emden. and most of this is the Kisiel Valley." He pointed to a location near the top of the map. "And that is the Steiner family's private ski chalet, known among the Royal Guard members as Purgatory."

"Why is that?"

"Because until a few years ago, the chalet was guarded by members of the Royal Guard as a punishment. It's thirty kilometers from the nearest town, primitive conditions, and almost always cold. A month guarding it was known in the Royal Guard as a 'Term in Purgatory.' It was never called that in any official documents, so only us Royal Guard should know."

O'Toole stared at the map. "It's going to take at least five days to reach the chalet from here, and though a number of narrow passes."

"That's what I want them to think," Shurasky said. "But this mining complex has a secret only a handful of people know about. There's a tunnel that goes through the mountains and out the other side." He pointed to an area near the chalet. "We can be here in less than twenty-four hours."

"Can the tunnel withstand us going through it?"

Shurasky gave O'Toole a smile. "When I was assigned to set up this cache before Peter's invasion, I also had the tunnel reinforced by LAAF combat engineers for such an eventuality."

"So if the Word is involved and knows of the meeting, they'll expect us there in five days, not in one."

"Exactly. The forest is thick enough to hide us from overhead observation, and we can ambush any Word force that comes calling."

O'Toole shook his head. "This still could be a trap."

"True," Shurasky said. "Which is why I'm sending Kivi and Pekka Deremer to North Emden and have them look around. They have enough furs to sell to make their presence plausible for a couple days."

O'Toole rubbed his chin. "Aye, that would be reasonable, and no one's going to see them as anything more than a couple of fur trappers."

"All I want them to do is look and listen when they're in town. I want to know what the townspeople are talking about and what their mood is."

"That shouldn't be a problem."

"Good. Officers' meeting in one hour. I want the Deremer brothers moving out in two, and the rest of the command in three. Have Sparks send the message to Tremmel right before we leave."

"Yes, sir."

KISIEL VALLEY
BREMEN, THARKAD
LYRAN ALLIANCE
14 MARCH 3068

"Groundpounder to *Wolfsjäger*."

The voice of Leutnant Nadia Christiansen, the *Kampfgruppe*'s infantry commander, woke Shurasky. He tapped the headset his was wearing. "Go for *Wolfsjäger*."

"I have one snowcat on the road to the target location. ETA, seven minutes."

"Copy Groundpounder. How many in the snowcat?"

"IR shows three heat signatures."

"Any sign of a tail?"

"Negative. It's quiet."

"Keep your eyes open. *Wolfsjäger* out." He switched radio channels. "Rook Two, this is Knight Six. Huntsman Nine."

"Rook Two to Knight Six. Trapper Five."

"Copy. Come ahead slowly."

"Understood. Rook Two out."

"Still could be a trap," Shana said.

Shurasky pushed himself out of *Thirteen's* command chair. "I know. But so far, so good."

"Stay alert, Gar. No telling what's going to happen."

"I will."

After climbing down the *Zeus*' ladder, Shurasky started for the chalet, a hundred meters from where his 'Mech sat. The *Zeus* was hidden by trees in one of several prepared 'Mech-sized berms designed to defend the chalet from enemy attack.

The last four days had been the quietest the *Kampfgruppe* had spent since the war started, and it had been needed. The trip through the tunnel was as Shurasky had expected. and they reached the objective only five hours behind schedule. After that, it was deploy and wait for the meeting. The techs had taken advantage in the down time by repairing technical problems that had accumulated in the last four months, and most of the troops had rested and attended to their own list of repairs and cleaning.

Shurasky reached the chalet's back door and knocked. The door opened, and Staff Sergeant Derick Cormier, the senior NCO of Shurasky's infantry contingent, stood there. Shorter than his commander, he was thick-bodied, with most of his face hidden by a visor.

"Sir," he said softly as he stepped aside to allow Shurasky to step inside.

"Coffee ready?" Shurasky asked.

"Yes, sir."

"All units, this is Irish," O'Toole said over the radio. "Snowcat is approaching the location. Shift to Alert Status Alpha."

Shurasky looked at Cormier. "You know what you have to do?"

"Yes, sir."

"Go. I'll wait here until you give me the all-clear."

"Yes, sir."

Cormier left, leaving Shurasky alone in the kitchen. The decor was rustic, but Shurasky knew from experience that the windows and doors were reinforced against small-arms fire, and there was a sophisticated security system in place. The chalet had its own fusion reactor, located under the garage, and Shurasky had ordered it to be brought up to five percent power, supplying just enough energy for the security system and a few lights.

He heard a door open, and low voices in the hall, the sound muffled by the closed kitchen door. From the sounds, one of the newcomers objected to being searched. The voices stopped and after a couple of minutes, Cormier opened the kitchen door. "We're ready."

Shurasky nodded and followed him across the hall and into a large sitting room. As with the kitchen, the decor was rustic, mostly wood and stone, with a large fireplace and several overstuffed chairs. Only a couple lamps were on, illuminating the room and little else. The curtains were closed and the fireplace was cold.

Cormier and two of his soldiers stood in the room's corners, their weapons not quite pointing at three people sitting in chairs. One was an older woman, mid-fifties, with short blond-gray hair, and ice-blue eyes. The second, a slightly younger man with thinning dark hair, hazel eyes, and a dozen kilos overweight. The third man was taller and younger than either of the others, with short dark hair and grey eyes. His face was paler than Shurasky remembered, and there was a gauntness that hadn't been there the last time he'd seen it.

Liam Tremmel rose to his feet and brought his hand up as if to salute, but Shurasky waved him down. "No need to salute, Liam."

"Is this Shurasky?" the man asked.

"It is," Tremmel said with a weak smile. "Kommandant, this is Karl Varis and Elke Folger. Karl, Elke, this is Kommandant Ansgar Shurasky, the man the press called the *Wolfsjäger*."

Varis snorted. "He doesn't look like a hero."

"What were you expecting?" Shurasky asked, his tone mild. "I left my dress uniform and medals at home."

Varis growled. "Listen here, soldier boy, if—"

"Enough, Karl," Folger said, her tone cutting through Varis' voice like a knife. "Liam, sit down. You too, Kommandant."

Shurasky sat in a chair. "Call me Gar," he said. "Would you like some coffee?"

"If it's not too much trouble," Tremmel said.

One of Shurasky's soldiers came in with a tray with large mugs full of coffee. The three civilians each took one and for a couple of minutes, no one said anything. Finally, Folger said, "Thank you, Kommandant."

"You're welcome. Now, what's the problem?"

"Bandits," Varis spat.

Shurasky nodded. "I'm listening."

"I'm the head of the Kisiel Valley Council," Folger replied. "Karl is a council member."

"And I'm against hiring a bunch of bandits to fight bandits!" Varis growled.

"Careful how you address the Hauptmann-Kommandant!" Cormier snarled.

"Oh, so you're fighting the Word?" Varis shot back, turning to face the NCO. "How's that working out for you?"

"Better than cowering, you yellow-bellied bastard!"

"Karl!" Folger snapped. "Shut up!"

"Cormier, quiet," Shurasky said calmly. He looked at Tremmel. "What is your assessment, Liam?"

The former sergeant exhaled slowly, holding the mug with both hands. "Pre-invasion, the Kisiel Valley was a quiet place, known for skiing and nature walks. Usually, the population is about five thousand year-round, and maybe quadruple that during winter. But right now, the valley's population is about fifty thousand, mostly refugees."

"Bad?"

"It's tough, but we make do. That's not the problem. The problem is bandits have been hitting the camps and towns across the valley."

"Bandits, or the Word?"

"Doesn't matter," Tremmel replied. "What matters is they're terrorizing the population and taking what they want."

"Bastards," Varis muttered.

Shurasky nodded. "You should have enough arms and military to drive off a few bandits."

Tremmel shook his head and looked at Shurasky. "Not that easy, sir. The head of these bandits is calling himself 'The Baron of Kisiel Valley,' and demands that we submit to him and his people. He has two 'Mech lances, a couple of armored platoons, and several platoons of armed thugs. If it was just the thugs and armor, we could handle them, but we can't handle 'Mechs."

"Sergeant Tremmel is the head of our militia," Folger said.

"There's several low-tech ways to take down 'Mechs," Shurasky said. "You should know most of them, Liam."

"I do," Liam said. "But the baron has spies among the refugees. Every time we set a trap or move to reinforce a town, the bandits either strike somewhere else, or bypass our traps and planned ambushes and hit their objectives even harder."

"Did you try tracking them back to their camp?"

"Tried more than once, but they're good at covering their tracks. They use rivers to throw us off, and ambushes to stop us from following. Besides, the survivors are usually too stunned to follow them."

"I see." That was matching up with what the Deremer brothers had found. They had reported about the bandits and how people in the valley were losing hope. Shurasky couldn't let it happen, not if he could do something about it.

Not all of Tharkad's citizens had risen up against the Word. Some had fled from the Word-controlled areas, while others collaborated with the enemy. But a few had taken advantage of the chaos and became bandits, preying on anyone they could find. Two of the prisons near Tharkad City had been damaged in the first days of the invasion, permitting prisoners to escape, and rumors said the Word had emptied several other prisons, allowing the criminals to run free.

"I know you have enough on your plate dealing with the Word," Folger said. "But we desperately need your help."

Shurasky looked at each civilian for several seconds before he said, "All right, we'll help you, on two conditions."

"I knew it!" Varis growled. "He's no better than the bandits!"

Shurasky shifted his gaze to Varis. "First condition: I run things my way. That means that no one outside of this room knows my *Kampfgruppe* is here—no one."

"But—" Varis began, but Shurasky's calm voice overrode his objection.

"You said you had spies. The less people that know we're here, the better chance of nailing these bastards."

Folger pursed her lips. "Your second condition?"

"I want Liam Tremmel as your liaison officer from this operation. All requests and intelligence will go through him."

"That can be done," Folger said.

"Good." Shurasky stood. "Mister Varis, Miss Folger, good night. Sergeant Trammel and I need to have a discussion."

Varis shot to his feet. "That's it?"

Shurasky looked at him. "Yes. We'll help you, and the sooner we start, the quicker we can stop these bandits."

Varis opened his mouth to say something, but Folger said, "He's right, Karl. Leave it to the soldiers. Good evening, Hauptmann-Kommandant." She walked to the front door, and after a final glare at Shurasky, Varis followed her.

Shurasky waited until they had left before sitting down again. He looked at Trammel. "How are you doing, Liam?"

The retired sergeant shrugged. "As well as can be expected." He tapped his left leg. "Damn artificial leg stiffens up when it's really cold." He gave Shurasky a level look. "The last I heard, you were in a hospital, suffering from a 'mental collapse'"

"I was released the middle of last year," Shurasky replied. "I was home when the Word invaded."

Tremmel nodded slowly. "Hell of a few years, sir," he said. "First Peter shows up with Clan support and hands us our asses, then the Word shows up and does the exact same thing. if the situation wasn't so serious, I'd be laughing."

"It's no laughing matter."

Tremmel leaned forward. "No sir, it isn't. If my tin leg was a more advanced model, I'd have found a ride and gleefully killed as many Blakies as I could. As it is, I can barely run, and climbing a ladder is damn difficult."

"You're doing what you can."

Tremmel slumped back in his chair. "I should be doing more. We should *all* be doing more."

"We do what we can." Shurasky looked up at Cormier. "Officers' meeting, here in ten minutes." Comier nodded then walked away, speaking softly into his radio.

"What are you going to do?"

Shurasky pulled a paper map from his pocket. "First, you're going to give me the lay of the land, then when my officers get here, you're going to tell us everything about this so-called Baron and his thugs—their equipment, where they've hit, when, and how."

"You have a plan?"

"The beginnings of one." Shurasky stood and walked over to the dining room table, unfolding the map as he went. "Now, I need to know what's *not* on this map."

KISIEL VALLEY
BREMEN, THARKAD
LYRAN ALLIANCE
22 MARCH 3068

"Some people would say this is stupid," Shana said.

Shurasky shrugged. "If it works, it isn't stupid."

"We've been sitting here for two days!"

"And we'll sit here until they show up."

The pit was one of ten dug inside the tree line surrounding the town of Braunsberg, located in the upper end of the Kisiel Valley, and the site for Shurasky's trap.

He glanced at his viewscreen, which showed the view aboveground via a camera. The snow didn't hide the series of earthen berms, topped with cut logs, surrounding the town. From this distance, he couldn't see the construction, but knew that most of the town's residents were working from dawn until nightfall. The dirt for the berms had comes from these pits, which now doubled as hiding places for the *Kampfgruppe's* 'Mechs.

Inside the town itself, the *Kampfgruppe's* armor and infantry were hidden in several warehouses, having infiltrated with Tremmel's militia force.

Shurasky had decided that bandit chasing was a waste of time and energy. Instead, he decided to give the baron and his ilk a target challenging their "authority."

A defiant town, building defenses against them, was something the baron couldn't ignore. If he did, other valley settlements would follow suit. Bandits were lazy; they didn't like anything threatening their power, and they would come.

Only to find the Wolf Hunters waiting for them.

The *Kampfgruppe's* 'Mechs had moved into the pits in the middle of a moonless night. Covered by a tarp, and subjected to two days of snow, the 'Mechs were invisible.

Shana folded her arms. "I hate waiting."

"You always did," Shurasky replied. "But we have only one shot at this."

"I know, but doesn't make it any easier."

He sat back and closed his eyes. He rarely slept more than four hours at a time, and sleep wasn't something that came easy to him—too many bad memories would surface. The hell of the Stahlwurzel, where the Wolves-in-Exile had ripped into the Second Royal Guard, the bitter street fighting in Tharkad City, where every block, every building had become a battleground, and the last four months up here in the mountains as guerrillas. Most LAAF soldiers could go an entire 30-year career without seeing as much combat as he had in the last five years.

And the soldiers he had lost over those years. Too many young faces, dead on the battlefields, or shattered in minds and body. How many people had died under his command? Fifty, a hundred, two hundred people? They called him a hero—the *Wolfsjäger*. How big was the pile of bodies that legend was built on? And how high would it be before he was done?

"Gar," Shana asked, cutting into his dark thoughts. "What was the first thing Colonel Von Halman always said on the first day of Battlefield Tactics class?"

His mind shifted to a tiered lecture hall, and a lean man in an Armed Forced of the Federated Commonwealth uniform with a shaved head and an eyepatch over a scarred face. In a military known for its social generals, there was no doubt Colonel Van Halman was anything but. With one cold blue eye, he had looked around the room and said in a cold, rough voice, *"If you remember anything I teach you, let it be these two rules. Rule Number One: In combat, people die. Rule Number Two: No matter how high in rank you get, or how brilliant you are as a battlefield commander, Rule Number One will never change. If you can't get past that, you are in the wrong line of work, and you had best serve the AFFC by leaving it."*

"He was a bastard, wasn't he?" Gar said softly.

"But he knew what he was talking about," Shana replied. "Soldiers die in war; that is a given. The best that can be hoped for that the price in lives was worth the outcome."

"Was your life worth it?"

"In the overall scheme of things, no. But you have made a difference in the last five years. The Wolves-in-Exile could have wiped out the Second Royal Guard, but you saved lives in the Stahlwurzel. Sergeant Tremmel, for one."

"I lost more lives in Tharkad City."

He could feel Shana shrug. "Fighting and being beaten by an overwhelming force is no disgrace, and the people under your command fought for you because they knew you would not spend lives needlessly. And you didn't waste lives, Gar. You only surrendered after everyone else had. You could have fought to the last man, but you didn't."

"And the people I've lost in the last four months?"

"Against a bunch of religious fanatics? You may not like Peter Steiner-Davion, but he is better than the Blakists sitting in Tharkad City. Even in the worst fighting, Peter never used nuclear weapons, nor did he use torture on his enemies under the disguise of 'interrogations.' Your people are following you because they would rather die on their feet than live on their knees. Yes, you've lost people—it's war, damn it! If you didn't feel anything, you would be no better than those chrome-covered bastards down in Tharkad City!"

Shurasky opened his eyes and stood up. He walked behind his chair and stretched. By the time he was finished, Shana was sitting on the arm of his chair, watching him. "Feeling better now?"

"Not really."

"What was the last time you ate?"

He looked at the clock in the cockpit bulkhead. "Eight hours?"

Shana rolled her eyes. "Try sixteen. Get something to eat, then take a nap. You always get moody and question yourself when you're hungry."

Shurasky nodded. "I suppose you're right. Thanks."

"All part of the service to keep you sane." He frowned, but before he could say anything, she said, "Don't think about it. As long as you stay sane, who cares if I'm a ghost or mental quirk? Eat, nap and when this baron shows up, we kick his teeth in. Psychoanalyze yourself later."

The night passed quietly. The sun was ascending over the horizon when the radio came to life. "Rook to Knight. Black is on the board. Five clicks out, from the northwest."

Shurasky slipped on his neurohelmet. and activated the radio. "Knight here. Message received. Sound the alert." He switched channels. "*Wolfsjäger* to all Hunters. Jackals are on their way in. Diamonds and Clubs, can you ID incoming Jackals?"

"Diamond Four here!" said one of his infantry scouts. "One Alpha, one Beta, two Gammas and two Deltas, four-pack of armor, half a dozen cracker boxes, and at least two dozen visible crunchies."

"Understood. Stay alert."

Shurasky quickly brought *Thirteen* to full power, but didn't switch on the active sensors, relying on his 'Mech's passive systems to track the incoming enemies. As he did so, he heard the town's sirens go off, signaling the residents to take cover. His passive sensors indicated the presence of the Baron's 'Mechs closing on the town from the northwest. Carefully, he adjusted the camera's view until he saw the first bandits come out of the forest.

A *Grasshopper* was first, followed by a *Firestarter* and a *Hatchetman*. All three looked roughed up, with mismatched armor panels, faded paint, and dents and scratches all over. The *Grasshopper* stopped, but the other two continued toward the town. A few seconds later, a *Hauptmann* strode out of the forest, flanked by a *Banshee* and a *Cataphract*.

Flanking them was an armor lance consisting of a Rommel, a Patton and a pair of Typhoon urban assault vehicles, all looking as beat-up as the 'Mechs. A half-dozen APCs followed, all carrying armed bandits on the outside, and stopped when they reached the *Grasshopper*.

The *Hauptmann* came to a stop near the *Grasshopper*. Over both Shurasky's radio and from the *Hauptmann*'s loudspeaker: "Attention,

residents of Braunsberg! I am disappointed in your pathetic attempts to defy my authority!"

"Blowhard," Shana muttered.

"Agreed. *Wolfsjäger* to Diamond Four, any more Jackals?"

"Negative, *Wolfsjäger*. No one else."

"*Wolfsjäger*," another voice cut in. "Heart Three here. I have movement from the Southwest. Three Alphas, two Betas, a Gammas and a Delta, with an armor four-pack, five cracker boxes, and two dozen crunchies."

"I am the ruler of this valley!" The voice continued. "In this state of emergency, my word is law!"

"Piling it high and deep, isn't he?" Shana said.

Shurasky ignored her. "*Wolfsjäger* to all elements. Change of plan. Black Lance, Coyote and Dingo Platoons, we'll hit the blowhard baron and his thugs. Grey Lance, White Lance, intercept the band coming in from the southwest and put them down as quickly as you can. Groundpounder, keep your people in their bunkers and the civilians safe. All card suites, expand your circle by three hundred meters. Pick off any stragglers on foot, but let the armor go. Move on my word."

"By this defiance, you risk your life and the lives of your loved ones!" The baron was silent for a few seconds. "I demand that you take down these defenses and recognize my authority!"

Shana frowned. "Wait, doesn't that voice sound familiar?"

Shurasky nodded. "As does the *Hauptmann*."

"Didn't he die in the Stahlwurzel?"

"He was declared missing, presumed dead." Shurasky's hands tightened on his controls. "Actually, I hoped he was dead. Bastard got three-quarters of his company slaughtered in the Stahlwurzel due to his incompetence."

"If you do not," the baron said. "I will be forced to take action myself and tear down these barricades!"

"Hauptmann Schäfer," a voice snarled on the radio. "You bastard!"

"Damn," Shurasky muttered. "I forgot that Tremmel served under him."

The *Hauptmann* shifted slightly, as if surprised by the reply. "Who is this?" the baron demanded.

"You don't remember me, do you?" Tremmel's voice was cold with fury. "I'm Staff Sergeant Liam Tremmel, Rook Lance. First Leutnant Alice Bedrosian's lance. Remember her? Remember running away, leaving her and rest of your company to be slaughtered by the Wolves?"

"You are mistaken," the baron said, but Shurasky heard the worry in his tone.

"Hauptmann Edel Schäfer, I accuse you of cowardice in the face of the enemy, disobeying lawful orders in the face of the enemy, desertion in the face of the enemy, and the murder of six members of the LAAF."

Schäfer barked a laugh. "You're a fool, sergeant. I'm still in control, and when the smoke clears, I will be hailed as a hero!"

"Sounds like the right time," Shana said.

Shurasky nodded and turned his radio on. "No, you won't."

The *Hauptmann* shifted again. "Who's that?" Schäfer demanded.

"Really, Edel?" Shurasky said. "You disobeyed my orders in the Stahlwurzel. You ran like the coward you are."

"Shurasky?" Schäfer said. "No...it can't be. You're dead!"

"I'm very much alive, and I'm giving you one chance for you and your men to surrender."

"Surrender?" Schäfer replied with a laugh. The *Hauptmann* twisted from side to side. "Do you see what you're up against? I have the largest force in the valley!"

"He really is stupid, isn't he?" Shana said.

"Last chance, Hauptmann," Shurasky said softly. "Surrender or die."

"Bring it, Kommandant," Schäfer snarled.

"*Wolfsjäger* to all Hunters, Bring the hammer down."

The *Zeus* rose out of its pit, the tarp falling away and revealing itself to the bandit force. Other forms rose, revealing themselves— O'Toole's *Awesome*, Rabbikowski's *Victor*, and Walliser's *Catapult*—and the heavy armor of Coyote Platoon rose from their revetments as the six hovercrafts of Dingo Platoon raced out of the town.

The *Awesome* fired first, all three particle beams ripping into the *Grasshopper*, shattering torso and right arm armor. The 70-ton 'Mech staggered, but stayed upright.

Both of Coyote's Rommels cut loose with their Gauss rifles. Both rounds slammed into the *Firestarter*, one destroying the 'Mech's right knee, the other striking just under the cockpit. As the 35-ton 'Mech reeled, it was struck twice more as Coyote Platoon's three Pattons added their heavy autocannons to the attack. What was left of the right leg from knee to mid-shin exploded into fragments. Without a leg, the *Firestarter* fell over, dirt and snow flying into the air as it crashed into the ground.

The *Banshee* and *Cataphract* surged forward, intent on closing in on O'Toole. Shurasky starting running, raising his ER PPC and firing at the *Cataphract*. The actinic blast caught the 70-ton 'Mech in its side, shattering most of the armor there.

The bandit 'Mech turned to shoot at Shurasky, but the *Victor* fired its Pontiac autocannon first. The volley slammed into the *Cataphract*'s other side, ripping into the armor and finding something inside to wreck. A salvo of short-range missiles, twisting and weaving around each other, hit the *Cataphract*, opening its left side even more. Stumbling, the heavy 'Mech tried to stay on its feet, but an eruption of fire ripped through the rear armor as the CASE system blew the force of the exploding ammo out the back, saving the pilot but toppling the now-powerless 'Mech.

Shurasky saw the *Hauptmann* backing up. "Schäfer!" he said. "Surrender!"

"No!" Schäfer snarled, turning toward Shurasky and firing. One large laser beam struck *Thirteen* in the left leg, leaving a vertical scar on the armor, while the other one was high and to the right.

"Looks like a *Hauptmann* Prime!" Shana said. "It's a brawler, so don't get too close!"

Shurasky raised *Thirteen*'s arms and fired all three of his long-range weapons. The PPC blast struck the *Hauptmann* full in the chest, while the laser melted armor on the assault 'Mech's left arm. The missiles landed in and around Schäfer, not doing any damage to the BattleMech, but making it uncomfortable for the bandit leader.

The *Grasshopper* went down under the combined firepower of the other three members of Shurasky's lance, four months of fighting making the three work together like a well-oiled machine.

The bandit *Banshee* hammered Walliser's *Catapult*, ripping away the left missile launcher and large chunks of the 65-ton 'Mech's left leg. The *Catapult* staggered and fell over, smashing down on its wounded side and kicking up snow and dirt.

Before the *Banshee* could take advantage, triple particle beams smashed into its chest, forcing it to take a step back. As it did so, Rabbikowski's *Victor* moved closer and cut loose with its massive autocannon, the slugs slamming into the *Banshee*'s chest, though the armor and deep into its torso. The step became a stagger, but somehow the assault 'Mech stayed on its feet.

One of the bandit APCs exploded as it was struck by a Gauss round that punched through its thin armor and found something volatile inside. Dingo Platoon charged through the APCs, firing lasers and SRMs at point blank range. In one pass, all but one of the APCs were destroyed or damaged, and the bandits who had been riding in or on them were dead or dying.

The *Hauptmann* began backing away. "Stay away!" Schäfer snarled. He fired the large lasers again, both missing Shurasky by several meters.

"He's rattled!" Shana said.

Shurasky fired again, saving his missiles for a better shot. The PPC shattered a tree to the right of the *Hauptmann*, but the large laser melted more armor on the bandit chief's broad chest. Schäfer continued backpedaling, closing on the illusional safety of the woods.

"No closer than four hundred meters!" Shana said quickly. "Wear him down from long range!"

Shurasky suddenly shifted right and ran for the trees. Schäfer's shot missed *Thirteen* by even more than the previous shot had. As he crashed through the trees, his said, "Irish! Sit-rep!"

"One moment, sir," O'Toole replied. The sounds of PPCs being fired was followed by, "*Cataphract* and *Hatchetman* are down. Bandit

Rommel is detracked, and a Typhoon's on its side. *Banshee*'s taking a pounding and—*Banshee* pilot has ejected."

"Keep on them," Shurasky directed.

A Hunter *Commando* charged the *Hauptmann* from the other side, firing a volley of short-range missiles at the heavier 'Mech. Several struck Schäfer's 'Mech, doing little damage, but the *Hauptmann* spun and unleashed everything at the lighter 'Mech. Most of the volley struck the trees or fell short.

Shurasky fired again. "Sledder, back off! I got him!" *Thirteen's* PPC and larger laser smashed or melted away more of the *Hauptmann*'s armor

The *Commando* danced to the right and fired it's laser at Schäfer, leaving a glowing scar on the assault 'Mech's leg. "But, sir—"

"Help Irish," Shurasky said, angling *Thirteen* so he could cut Schäfer off. "I'll drive him back into the open."

"Yes, sir." The *Commando* ran off at an angle, placing trees between him and the *Hauptmann*.

Shurasky changed channels. "Schäfer," he said. "You can't escape. Your men are being slaughtered again, just like the Stahlwurzel."

"You don't understand!" Schäfer snarled. "Those damn Wolves were killing us!"

"And we were killing them," Shurasky replied. The *Hauptmann* spun toward them, firing at Shurasky and missing, the weapons ripping into the trees in front and around the *Zeus*. "You ran, Edel," he continued. "Ran and left your company to be slaughtered. I told you I was on my way. I told you to hold for two minutes. *Two minutes*!"

"But—"

"No 'buts,' Hauptmann," Shurasky said, his voice becoming cold. "Despite you, your company held in spite of everything the Wolves threw at them, held until I ripped into the Wolves' flanks and drove them back. They died, but they died as soldiers. You're going to die as a common criminal."

"I've got money! I'll give it all to you if you let me go!"

"Uh-oh," Shana said.

"Money?" Shurasky said, his voice dropping several more degrees. "How much of that is blood money, Edel? Your company gave the most valuable thing they had in the Stahlwurzel—their lives. No amount of money is going to change that."

He saw the *Hauptmann* through the woods and fired his PPC. The blast somehow lanced through the trees and stuck the bandit 'Mech in the head, slicing through the armor and leaving the interior open to the weather.

Shurasky switched to the *Zeus*' loudspeaker. "Right now, if killing you would bring them back, I'd do it without a second thought. You're a disgrace to the LAAF. You're everything I hate, everything I worked against as a Lyran officer."

"You can't kill me!" Schäfer howled. "I know things! I know where there's caches of ammo and equipment!"

"I already know most caches in the area," Shurasky said, continuing moving *Thirteen* toward the road that marked Schäfer's best escape route. "I'm the one who established them. Try again."

"I can release people! I have a hundred of them locked up!"

"You're going to be doing that anyway."

Thirteen reached the road. The *Hauptmann* was closer to Braunsberg, running toward Shurasky with a run that seemed off-kilter. Shurasky spun, planting the *Zeus'* feet in the middle of the road facing the fleeing bandit.

"Give it up, Edel. Even if you escape, your power is broken. None of your men are going to escape mine. Unlike yours, mine are soldiers who fight for the people of Tharkad. Yours preyed on the citizens. Not anymore."

The *Hauptmann* fired, but the volley missed the *Zeus*. Shurasky's one-two-three punch of particle beam, large laser and missiles ripped away more armor, knocking the 95-ton 'Mech off balance. Schäfer tried to regain control, but overcompensated, and the *Hauptmann* fell forward, striking the road surface with an echoing *clang*.

Shurasky walked *Thirteen* forward, weapons pointed at the downed *Hauptmann, who* struggled to stand up. Shurasky fired his PPC, aiming for a spot ten meters from the struggling BattleMech's arm. The particle beam slammed into the road's surface, sending chunks of it flying in every direction, pelting the *Hauptmann*.

"Surrender," Shurasky said over the loudspeakers. "Or I will kill you here and now."

He saw movement in the *Hauptmann*'s damaged cockpit and a figure dropped to the ground. With a flick of a finger, Shurasky increased the viewscreen's zoom so he could see the figure. The man staring at him was ten kilograms lighter than the chunky Schäfer he remembered, but it was clearly the same man.

"Irish to *Wolfsjäger*," O'Toole said, sounding pleased. "I am proud to report that the gaggle of nearly talentless amateurs pretending to be bandits is no more. Dancer's *Catapult* is messed up, she has a broken arm and is cursing up a storm about being taken down by these pathetic wannabes. Other than that, we have some armor damage and Corporal Marlowe sprained his ankle. What's your status?"

Schäfer stumbled away from his 'Mech and ran into the forest. Shurasky swung the *Zeus'* toward the running man, his targeting reticule centered on Schäfer's back. All it would take would be—

"Gar," Shana said. "Don't do it."

"Bastard deserves it," he growled. "He ran. He ran while the rest of his company died fighting. He's a coward, and he should die."

"Who made you god?" Shana asked. "The world has gone to hell, Gar. It's easy to excuse killing him because of that. Then the next time, the excuse becomes easier, and the next, and the next and when does it stop? You're a better officer than Schäfer ever was. You're not fighting for revenge, Gar. You're fighting for the people of the Alliance."

"Irish to *Wolfsjäger*, are you hearing me?"

Shurasky aimed, then relaxed. "You're right, damn it. Irish, send some infantry support to my location. The 'baron' is on foot and trying to escape."

"Tremmel and three truckloads of town militia are on their way."

Shurasky switched radio channels. "*Wolfsjäger* to Rook. Schäfer's 'Mech's down, but he's fled into the woods. What's your ETA?"

"Twenty seconds!" Tremmel replied. "We can see you!"

Shurasky looked up and saw three trucks rolling toward from the town. "Sergeant," he said. "I want this made clear. I want Schäfer taken alive."

"Are you sure?" Tremmel growled.

"Whoa, he sounds pissed," Shana said.

"I don't think he's armed," Shurasky said, twisting the *Zeus* in the direction the fleeing bandit was taking, "but in case he is." He raised *Thirteen's* right arm, aimed at a spot ten meters in front of the running man and fired. The man-made lighting blast erased several meters of snow-covered ground, leaving a smoking crater and sending chunks in every direction. Schäfer slid to a stop and lost his footing, falling onto his back.

He desperately scrambled to his feet, but Shurasky said over the loudspeakers, "Stay right there, Edel. If you're armed, get rid of it now. The people coming to get you want an excuse to kill you. Your days as the 'Baron of Kisiel Valley' are over."

KISIEL VALLEY
BREMEN, THARKAD
LYRAN ALLIANCE
15 APRIL 3068

The judge, a retired Tharkad City superior judge, rapped his gavel on the table in front of him. Inside North Emden's only courtroom, the crowded room was silent, all attention on the judge. "The defendants will all rise."

The five defendants, the last of the fifty-five captured bandits to be tried, rose slowly, each one flanked by two militia guardsmen acting as bailiffs. Edel Schäfer stood on the end, looking as miserable as he had when Tremmel's men had captured him.

Next to them stood three defense lawyers, their expressions one of relief. They hadn't wanted to defend the bandits, but they had put up a spirited defense for their "clients." Across from them, the prosecutors also stood, waiting to see the results of their case be decided, the last of six the courtroom had seen in the last three weeks.

Behind them sat Shurasky, O'Toole, and Tremmel, watching the proceedings. There was no doubt in Shurasky's mind what the verdict would be; the evidence was overwhelming. Some witnesses' told stories of loss, while others told of their time as slave labor for Edel Schäfer. The bandit base, located in caves thirty-five kilometers from Braunsberg, had been taken quickly and quietly by Shurasky's infantry and valley militia right after the bandits' defeat. In addition to a small fortune in valuables, they'd found 145 captives.

Shurasky had informed the valley council that he wouldn't get involved with the trials, except as a witness. But he had attended every session and had given his testimony when asked. He noticed, that despite the general air of hostility toward the defendants, the judge had ruled the courtroom with a firm but fair hand, running the trials as if they were taking place in Tharkad City. Shurasky thought the trials would stand up to a judicial review, whenever there was a planetary superior court that could take the time to review it.

"I will make this simple," the judge said. He had the weathered look of an outdoorsmen and his white hair fit the image of a senior judge. "You five have committed some of the worst crimes I have ever had the misfortune to preside over. In order to give you trials in a speedy manner, you have only been charged with offenses arising out of the last three raids. At the current time, there are investigators who are investigating and taking witness statements from other raids. Those charges will be compiled and brought against you at a future time, most likely when the current emergency is over. As to the current charges, let us start with Edel Schäfer. On the first charge, murder in the first degree of Harold Farrow of Mount Holstein, this court finds you guilty. On the second count, murder..."

It took the judge over an hour to work his way through the charges, which ranged from major theft to willful destruction of an entire hamlet and the deaths of over a hundred people. Each bandit was sentenced to life without parole. When he had finished the judge looked around the room. "Does anyone wish to address the court at this time?"

Shurasky rose to his feet. "Your honor," he said. "At this time, I wish to state that Edel Schäfer is a LAAF deserter, and once the emergency is over, he will be taken into LAAF custody, court-martialed, and if found guilty, will serve his sentence in a LAAF prison facility."

The judge nodded. "The court wishes to thank the hauptmann-kommandant and his unit in bringing these criminals to justice. However, as the Archon has declared martial law, the court feels that you could easily try him yourself."

"I could," Shurasky said. "But as I am the officer bringing the charges against him, it would be a breach of the LAAF uniform code of conduct. The court-martial should be conducted by a neutral third party of officers. Until such a time arises, I believe that leaving him in the court's custody is the best and most logical choice."

"Very well. I—" The judge's comments were broken by the sound of laughter. Everyone stared at Schäfer, who was leaning on the table, his body shaking. "I fail to see the humor," the judge said angrily.

"You're all assuming I'll be spending the rest of my life behind bars." Schäfer shook his head and his face became serious. He looked back at Shurasky, who was still standing, then back at the judge. "Your honor, I wish to speak to the Hauptmann-Kommandant alone. I have some information for him."

The judge looked at Shurasky. "Do you accept?"

"I do."

"The bailiffs will take the defendant to the consulting room across the hall. As for the rest of the defendants, they will be taking to the holding cells until such time transportation can be arranged to take them to the newly named Black Rock Detention Facility. There, you will stay in the same cells your captives were housed in until the emergency is over and the courts can continue the process." The judge rapped his gavel on the table. "The session is adjourned."

The consulting room was small and gray, with wire-mesh windows facing out into the hallway, allowing conversations to be private while allowing the bailiffs to keep an eye on the prisoner from outside. With the exception of a table fixed to the floor and two chairs, the room was bare.

By the time Shurasky entered, Schäfer was sitting in one chair, his right hand cuffed to a steel bar attached to the table. The blaze orange and red-striped overalls were worn and dirty, and Schäfer had several days' worth of beard covering his weak chin.

"What do you want?" Shurasky asked.

"What do I want?" Schäfer said in a mocking tone. "You know what I want."

Shurasky walked over to the wall facing the prisoner and leaned against it. He folded his arms. "You're not getting it from me."

"Didn't think so." Schäfer shrugged. "Doesn't matter. I won't be in custody for long."

"You planning an escape?"

"Not the type of escape you're thinking of. I'm not in on the planning, and I don't want to be."

"Stop with the smart remarks, Edel. What did you want to talk to me about?"

Schäfer looked outside at the people in the hallway, then back at Shurasky. "I'm not going to be around for a court-martial," he said, his tone somewhat distant. "Because court-martialing a dead man is not going to happen."

"You want to explain?"

Schäfer nodded. "Three months ago, I was in a village tavern way up in the mountains, staying drunk and cursing my fate. Suddenly, I'm surrounded by armed cyber thugs and hauled outside to some woman whose face was more chrome then flesh. She told me I had a job to do, and if I did, I would be rewarded. If I didn't..." He pulled open his jumpsuit to show a large burn on his chest.

"You're trying to tell me the Word told you to terrorize the valley?"

"Yes."

"Did she tell you her name?"

"She said her name was Jehoel." Schäfer refastened his jumpsuit and shook his head. "After our talk, she ordered the entire town destroyed and every man, woman, child, pet, livestock—every living thing in that village was killed except me. That isn't someone you willingly cross."

"Where did you get the men from?"

"She gave me a bunch of guys the Word had gotten from somewhere, told them I was the leader, and to follow my orders. When one of them objected, she broke his neck with as much effort as you would take to break a twig. She also gave me the weapons and 'Mechs."

"What were your orders?"

Schäfer looked down at the table. "I was to set up in this valley, establish my fiefdom, and make it impossible for any resistance groups to get a foothold here. If any resistance groups came into the valley, I was to pretend to be another resistance leader, gain their trust, eliminate them and keep their weapons and equipment. If the resistance group was too large or we couldn't gain their trust, I was to alert Jehoel, and she would take care of them." He looked up at Shurasky. "I never knew you or your people were here until you ambushed us."

Shurasky nodded. "That was the plan."

"Anyway," Schäfer said. "She knows what happened here. I don't know how, but she knows everything I've done. She'd radio me with critiques after every raid."

"She had spies inside your gang."

"Of course she had spies!" Schäfer snarled. "But I never found ouy who, or how they communicated with her." He stared out into the hallway. "That's why I'm warning you about her. Jehoel got inside my head and she stayed there, but since I'm useless to her now, I'm a dead man walking. She won't let me live."

"You're being melodramatic," Shurasky said.

"Well, we'll find out." Schäfer folded his arms and leaned back in his chair. "That's all I have to say."

"All right." Shurasky walked over to the door and rapped on it. Two bailiffs came in and hauled Schäfer to his feet after unlocking the chains holding him to the table.

"Remember what I said, Kommandant," he said. "When she comes for you, they'll be no place on Tharkad you can hide."

"We'll see," Shurasky said as the bailiffs escorted Schäfer out of the room.

O'Toole was waiting for him when Shurasky walked out. "What did he want?"

"To warn me about a Blakist," Shurasky replied. "Claims a woman calling herself Jehoel told him to cause havoc and gave him the manpower and material to do it with."

"That does sound a bit far-fetched."

"Let's get back to camp," Shurasky said. "I want us ready to leave before dark."

"Which way?"

"I'll let you when I know myself."

The walked out of the municipal building and into the late morning sun. On the street, the town was busy with people moving here and there, with a few fortunate people riding on horses and in vehicles.

One of those vehicles was a battered-looking bandit APC, now part of the valley's militia. Today, it was transport for the convicted criminals to the prison in the former bandits' hideout. Shurasky had turned over the majority of the small arms and vehicles over to the militia, but had kept two of the bandit BattleMechs, either for new MechWarriors or when they needed spare 'Mechs. The rest were taken to the bandit base, where they would be either repaired for the militia's use or for spare parts for the valley's LoggerMechs and MiningMechs.

Shurasky watched the prisoners being loaded into the APC. Schäfer was the last one in line, and he kept looking around. Shurasky noticed a flash of light between two buildings on the other side of the street. Even as his mind registered the flash came from a second-story window in a building on the on the next street over, he was yanking O'Toole down while yelling, "Sniper!"

The first round hit Edel Schäfer in the chest and knocked him down. The second bullet slammed into the wall a few centimeters over Shurasky's head, wood slivers showering him. As the sound of the first round reached him, Shurasky quick-crawled to cover behind the APC, O'Toole on him like a second shadow. Around them, people were screaming and running for cover as the report of the second shot reached them.

Shurasky rose to a crouch, drew his pistol, and faced the rear of the APC. He could feel O'Toole's back against his. "This is a fine how-to-do!" O'Toole said.

"Guard my back," Shurasky said, moving forward but staying low. There were no more shots, but he kept the APC between him and the shooter's position as he moved to the rear edge of the vehicle.

Schäfer lay still less than a meter away, lifeless eyes wide open and his chest a mass of spreading red. "Schäfer's dead," he called to O'Toole.

"Good riddance to bad rubbish!" the older men replied. "Tremmel's here."

Shurasky looked back and saw Tremmel moving toward them from the front of the APC. "Any bead on the shooter?"

"Next street over, two-story with a store on the bottom floor. Whoever it was, they shot between the two buildings on the other side of the street."

Tremmel nodded and spoke into a headset he was wearing. "I'm sending militia to check it out, but I bet the shooter's long gone."

"Probably."

Ten minutes later, the militia signaled the all clear. Shurasky stepped out and stood over Schäfer's body. He felt Trammel's presence at his shoulder. "I can't say I'm upset about this," Tremmel said.

"You didn't have anything to do with this?" Shurasky asked, his tone mild.

Tremmel was silent for a few seconds. "No. If I wanted him dead, I would have pulled the trigger myself. But I'm not the only one who wanted Schäfer dead, and enough people around here are hunters to make tracking down who did it impossible."

A pair of bailiffs came out of the municipal building with a stretcher. They loaded Schäfer's body onto the stretcher and carried it away.

Around Shurasky, the citizens were coming out of hiding, some going back to their business, others standing around and quietly discussing what had happened. Shurasky didn't hear the conversations, but the tone told him Schäfer's death hadn't generated any sympathy.

"Irish," Shurasky said. "Let's get back to camp."

"What are we going to do next?"

"Find a way to fight this Jehoel. If Schäfer's right, the Wolf Hunters will become her quarry."

"You believe him?"

"He was too scared to lie. Jehoel is a cold-blooded killer who ordered an entire village destroyed in order to make her point. People like that need to be—" He stopped as the thought hit him.

"Sir?" O'Toole asked.

Shurasky turned to look back at the bloodstained snow. "A test," he said slowly. "This was a test."

"A test for what?"

"To see if we were a true threat to the Word." He looked back at his NCO. "The Word just kicked things up a notch. We'd better do the same, or we'll end up like Schäfer. Let's get going."

SCENARIO: REINDEER DOWN

DANIEL ISBERNER

SOME BACKWATER PLANET
24 DECEMBER 3149

Christmas... Every year it's the same. Your superior officers are off-duty, celebrating with their families and everyone else does the same. Well, everyone except your lance.

Staying on duty at the base is boring, but you try your best every year. Hang up some lights, decorate a Christmas tree, and try to have some fun with your lancemates and nonalcoholic beverages. You would never drink on duty. Never!

And now, this... Pirates jumped in at a pirate point and are already descending to the surface. As if that wasn't enough, they started shooting at an unidentified DropShip none of your radar techs has ever seen before. It almost looked like a sleigh pulled by reindeer.

Yeah...right...

The unknown ship got damaged, and twenty-four very big crates fell down while it was crashing to the surface.

You tried to reach your superiors, but no one answered, and since they are up in the mountains, reaching them on foot or by vehicle would take far longer than you have. And the pirates are landing near the strange DropShip.

Your only choice is to ready your lance and try to stop those pirates—all by yourself.

Merry Christmas, MechWarriors!

GAME SETUP

BattleTech / Total Warfare

Put two maps together on their short sides, and keep two more maps in reserve for later.

Whenever the militia has collected all gifts on a map and has no more units left on that map, the map is removed, and a new map is placed behind the map on the other end. If you have enough room to put down all four maps at the beginning of the game, the map still leaves the table, but do not place another one. All pirate 'Mechs on the removed map are considered destroyed.

Put 6 markers (wrapped chocolate, candy, or similar items) on each map, for a total of 24 markers. If you only put down 2 maps for now, keep the remaining 12 markers in reserve, to be put on a new map when revealed (6 markers per map).

The pirates start on the short edge of the second map (the third map will be put behind them), and the militia units start on the opposite side of the two starting maps.

Write all the Gifts on similar pieces of paper (See *Filling the Stockings* below) and put them in a hat or bag so you can draw them blindly.

Alpha Strike

Both players start on opposite sides of the playing field.

Six Gift markers are placed randomly across the playing field. Whenever a Gift is unwrapped, a new one is placed immediately (up to 24). The new Gift has to be placed away from the recently opened one and may not be placed "behind" the militia lines. Players should find a fair position to prevent the militia from "camping" on Gifts.

Suggested Starting Units

Although you can start the game with any units you like, the following suggested starting units, whose miniatures are available in the *Beginner Box*, *A Game of Armored Combat*, and the *Clan Invasion* box sets, will make it easy to jump right into the game.

MILITIA

Name	Model	Piloting	Gunnery	Skill (AS)
Warhammer	WHM-6R	5	3	4
Griffin	GRF-4N	4	4	4
Phoenix Hawk	PXH-2	3	4	3
Locust	LCT-1V	2	4	3

PIRATES

Name	Model	Piloting	Gunnery	Skill (AS)
Mad Cat (Timber Wolf)	A	4	4	4
Rifleman	RFL-5M	5	4	4
Catapult	CLPT-C4C	5	3	4
Shadow Hawk	SHD-12C	3	4	3

Filling the Stockings

There are a total of 24 Gifts that the militia can unwrap. The first 23 Gifts contain various Kits the militia can use to help find Santa and destroy the pirate forces.

When setting up the game, write the following Gifts on pieces of paper to be drawn at random during gameplay:

8 'Mech Kits
6 Skill Kits
4 Upgrade Kits
3 Repair Kits
2 Ammunition Kits (*BT/TW*) OR 2 Heat Kits (*AS*)

Santa

The final Gift contains Santa, who is angry at being shot down. He will join the militia in fighting the pirates when that Gift is unwrapped.

Santa pilots a *Daishi* (*Dire Wolf*) *Widowmaker* (or any other assault 'Mech of the militia's choice), with 1/1 Piloting/Gunnery Skills (*AS*: Skill 1).

VICTORY CONDITIONS

Militia: Unwrap all 24 Gifts, destroy all pirate units, and ensure Santa survives.

Pirates: Destroy all militia units. If Santa has been unwrapped, he has to die, too. He is too angry to let you go unpunished. Also, you are pirates, so killing Santa seems like a regular Monday.

UNWRAPPING AND USING GIFTS

The Gifts in the game are represented by the markers placed during setup and throughout the game. When a Gift is unwrapped, draw a slip of paper to see what the Gift contains.

Only militia 'Mechs may unwrap Gifts and use the Kits they contain. Since pirates are evil, they cannot pick up or unwrap Gifts, and they cannot pick up or use Kits. Pirates are definitely on Santa's naughty list!

To unwrap a Gift, you must end your movement in the same hex as the Gift (*AS*: within a 2" radius of the Gift) and declare immediately whether you want to open it. You can then either immediately use the unwrapped Gift, pick it up for later, or leave it for someone else.

You cannot make any attacks (weapon or physical) on the turn in which you open a Gift. Santa doesn't like violence!

Gifts and Kits cannot be destroyed or damaged.

KITS

Kits can only be used by the unit carrying them. Kits can be left in a hex and picked up by another militia unit, traded from one adjacent hex to the other (*AS*: units trading are within 2"), or thrown up to three hexes (*AS*: 6") if the 'Mech carrying them has two hands. If Kits are traded, left, or thrown, you cannot declare any physical attacks that turn. None of these actions require a roll.

Picking up a Kit in your hex (*AS*: within a 2" radius) requires no roll, but you cannot declare any physical attacks that turn.

To use a Kit from an unwrapped Gift, declare their use at the end of the movement phase. Only 'Mech Kits (see below) must be used immediately.

Upgrade Kit

Turn your 'Mech into any other variant of itself. This includes *all* canon variants, even uniques and different models: for example, you can change a *Mad Cat* (*Timber Wolf*) Prime into a *Mad Cat* B, or even a *Mad Cat Mk II, Mad Cat III* or Mad Cat Mk *IV*, or you can change an *Atlas* AS7-D into an AS7-K, an *Atlas II,* or an *Atlas III*, and so on.

This upgrade action takes up a full turn. Your 'Mech will be fully repaired and have its ammo reloaded; however, it will not cool down this turn, and destroyed limbs are not repaired.

During your upgrade turn, you cannot shoot, but you get a +3 Target Movement Modifier (*AS*: +1 to TMM) due to the 'Mech's suddenly changing appearance throwing off targeting systems. Upgrade Kits can be used directly when unwrapped, like any other Kit. The +3 will replace any movement modifier the 'Mech had.

Lost limbs stay lost.

Repair Kit

Completely restore armor and internal structure on a 'Mech OR restore a lost limb. If you restore a limb, no other location gets repaired, but the limb will be fully restored and repaired. You cannot make any weapon or melee attacks this turn. Weapons and equipment that have suffered a critical hit do not get repaired.

Ammunition Kit (*BattleTech / Total Warfare* only)

Restore all ammunition to full loads. You cannot make any weapon or melee attacks this turn.

Heat Kit (*Alpha Strike* only)

A 'Mech can use Overheat once, without suffering any heat effect.

'Mech Kit

Holy crap, a 'Mech came out of the package. And it starts moving.

You try to peek into the cockpit and see a small, green...something... with pointy ears that looks very angry. "Seriously?"

Anyway, whatever this strange creature is, it starts shooting at the pirates, so you really don't care right now...

'Mech Kits take effect immediately after their Gift is unwrapped. Roll 2D6 and place the resulting 'Mech in an adjacent hex (*AS*: within 2") and with a facing declared by the player opening the Gift; this 'Mech is under the militia players' control. If stacking rules forbid the 'Mech from starting in an adjacent hex, ignore them. It's a Christmas miracle!

Add the new 'Mech to the militia's initiative for this turn; it may move and shoot this turn.

Suggested 'Mech Kit Contents

All gifted 'Mechs come with a Piloting Skill of 4 and a Gunnery Skill of 3 (*AS*: Skill 3).

2D6 Roll	'Mech
2	*Stinger* STG-6L
3	*Puma* (*Adder*) Prime
4–5	*Ryoken* (*Stormcrow*) A
6–7	*Wolverine* WVR-9M
8–9	*Thunderbolt* TDR-10M
10	*Mad Cat* (*Timber Wolf*) Prime
11	*Awesome* AWS-9M
12	*Gladiator* (*Executioner*) Prime

Skill Kits

Improve Piloting and Gunnery skill by 1, each (cannot go below 0/0) (*AS*: Improve Skill by 1, cannot go below 0).

PIRATE REINFORCEMENTS

Whenever the pirates have two or fewer 'Mechs on the battlefield at the end of the turn, they get two new 'Mechs at the beginning of the next turn. If they have no 'Mechs and Santa has not yet been found, they get four 'Mechs. The new pirate 'Mechs enter from the edge of the last map on the table (in case you have all four maps on the table, they enter one map behind the pirate 'Mech the farthest away from the militia's starting map). All pirate reinforcements have a Gunnery skill of 4 and a Piloting skill of 5 (*AS*: Skill 4).

Once Santa has been found, pirates no longer get reinforcements.

2D6 Roll	'Mech
2	*BattleMaster* BLR-1D
3	*Commando* COM-2Dr
4	*Black Hawk* (*Nova*) D
5	*Shadow Cat* Prime
6	*Marauder* MAD-4CS
7	*Archer* ARC-6W
8	*Loki* (*Hellbringer*) B
9	*Wasp* WSP-1S
10	*Valkyrie* VLK-QD4
11	*Man O' War* (*Gargoyle*) C
12	Pirate players' choice

HAVE FUN!

The goal of this scenario is to have fun, so the gamemaster (or pirates player, if no gamemaster) is free to change the contents of Gifts to ensure everyone gets an enjoyable game out of it.

That goes for the Gifts as well as pirate reinforcements. The gamemaster may change an unwrapped Gift to something the militia has more use for at the moment the Gift is unwrapped.

Regardless of any adjustments, Santa should still be saved in the end, after all—or do you want all the children in the Inner Sphere to be left without Christmas gifts?

AFTERMATH

The next morning, you wake up half naked on the table in the mess hall. Your lancemates are on the floor in a similar state. Your head hurts, and you feel like you drank too much alcohol. The empty whiskey bottles on the floor are a certain testament to that.

Only a drunken dream.

One of your lancemates sits up and says:

"Did anyone else dream of Santa in a BattleMech?"

IF AULD ACQUAINTANCE BE FORGOT…
(A KELL HOUNDS STORY)

MICHAEL A. STACKPOLE

PART 3 (OF 4)

I

URSA ALPHA SPACEPORT
AK-DEUCE, DUBHE
SILVER HAWKS COALITION
FREE WORLDS LEAGUE
15 MAY 3010, 0500 HOURS, WESTERN COASTAL TIME

White lightning seared the sky, its brilliance muted by the rain sheeting down over the spaceport. Static sizzled through Patrick Kell's holographic display. Another curtain of water splashed against the *Thunderbolt*'s windscreen as the 65-ton 'Mech lumbered forward over the ferrocrete landing strip. The world melted for the moment it took for the 'Mech's sensors to clear themselves, sinking the spaceport into darkness again.

And part of that darkness is moving.

Patrick clicked the sensors over to magnetic resonance, and a *Vulcan* appeared as if by sorcery. The smaller humanoid BattleMech boasted little in weaponry to oppose the *Thunderbolt*, but the Spaceport Authority had never intended it for much more than crowd control. Its machine gun and flamethrower filled that bill well. The medium laser and the autocannon mounted in its torso could have amply dealt with armored vehicles, but the pilot had to know they stood no chance against the larger 'Mech.

But still they came, their anti-'Mech weaponry drawing a bead on Patrick's 'Mech. The autocannon's depleted-uranium slugs chipped at the armor over the *Thunderbolt*'s right hip. The medium laser slagged a jagged line across the larger 'Mech's left shin, but neither shot inhibited the *Thunderbolt's* ability to fight.

Patrick dropped his crosshairs on the smaller 'Mech and when the golden dot flashed at its heart, he tightened up on his joystick triggers. The large laser burned through the armor on the *Vulcan's* left arm, utterly stripping it of protection. The green beam burned through myomer muscles and gnawed at the ferro-titanium bones underneath. Of the three medium lasers he triggered, one missed farther left, but the other two melted into the armor of the 'Mech's left flank, denuding it of all shielding and warping metal.

Patrick drove his 'Mech forward, intent on looming large in the pilot's targeting display. He wasn't so much worried about the damage the *Vulcan* could do to him as he was intent on demanding the pilot's full attention. A backwater world like Dubhe wasn't going to be home to much MechWarrior talent, and even though the storm made most radio communication impossible, he didn't want the pilot even thinking about alerting anyone.

The Kell Hound also didn't want the *Vulcan's* pilot to pick up on the signatures of the other 'Mechs that had emerged from the *Leopard*-class DropShip. They'd brought the ship down as a hurricane blasted into the coast, forcing the spaceport's evacuation save for a skeleton crew of essential personnel. The second the *Leopard* had touched down, Patrick and three other mercenaries had deployed to take control of the spaceport as quickly as possible.

Patrick again targeted the *Vulcan*. He used the same array of beam weapons, valuing their relative silence compared to guns and missiles. The large laser's verdant beam slashed up into the 'Mech's left flank, coring it. The *Vulcan's* left side collapsed as molten metal oozed down over its hip, and the left arm dangled like a man on a gibbet, bouncing and the end of one slender artificial-muscle thread.

The medium lasers stabbed scarlet lances deep into the 'Mech's torso. They ate through its heart, ablating all the armor on its chest. Unspent, they melted the *Vulcan's* spine. Molten metal sheared off and the torso slid to the right. The 'Mech's lower half fell forward, and the torso back, steam rising toward the angry sky.

To Patrick's left, more lasers burned colorful holes in the darkness. A lightning strike froze running infantry for a heartbeat, then the Kell Hound soldiers continued into the spaceport. Muzzle flashes lit the darkened facility and spread out like fireflies moving on an evening breeze. Farther left, a cascade of explosions took the legs off a *Locust*. Nearby, a *Spider* had done its best to support the *Locust*, but lit off its jump jets to escape before the *Locust* hit the ground.

Where is that other Locust? Patrick swung his *Thunderbolt* right, heading south, to come around past the Customs House and push further east. A kilometer and a half to the south lay the Gold Coast Aeroport, and beneath his feet was the high-speed pneumatic subway that would speed passengers between the two facilities. As with the Spaceport, the Aeroport had been evacuated because of the storm and all local flights grounded.

A couple red beams lanced into the sky as Patrick's companions sought to bring the *Spider* down. He glanced in that direction, then caught movement out of the corner of his eye to the right. It showed up in the portion of his holographic display indicating it was in his rear arc. Before he could bring his *Thunderbolt* back around, a laser flashed.

The *Locust*'s laser slashed a red beam into the armor on the *Thunderbolt*'s right arm. A monitor flashed in the cockpit, shifting the outline of the 'Mech's arm from solid green to a paler version of the same color. The incoming beam had scored armor, but nothing more, with plenty remaining to protect the larger 'Mech.

The *Locust*'s pilot clearly had more heart than brains, because they drove the *Locust* in toward Patrick. Before Patrick could figure out what the pilot intended—*and perhaps before the pilot knew themself*—two large laser beams flashed. One swept over the birdlike 'Mech's heart. The ferro-ceramic armor melted like wax beneath a blowtorch, splashing into steaming puddles on the ground. The other beam melted the 'Mech's stubby right arm off entirely.

Two more incarnadine energy lances slashed the *Locust*, vaporizing its left leg. The small 'Mech, the momentum of its charge preserved, pitched forward and cast sparks as it slid along the ferrocrete.

Patrick keyed his radio. "Thanks for having my back, Four."

"I should have been faster, sir." Walter de Mesnil, piloting a *Blackjack*, sounded disgusted with himself. "I won't be so slow again."

"I'm not worried." Patrick flipped his radio over to the second tactical frequency. "Report, Mr. Frost."

"We have the communication center and flight operations secure. The facilities manager is negotiating hard."

Patrick frowned. "'Facilities Manager?'"

"Custodian. He and his crew say they're not going to clean up the mess we made unless we're paying double-time."

"I think we can do that. Tell them we'll supply meals while they're doing it, too."

"Yes, sir. But we are good for phase two."

"Thank you, Mr. Frost."

Patrick turned the *Thunderbolt* around to face back onto the landing pad where their *Leopard* DropShip waited. He powered a medium laser down and used it to create a direct communications link to the ship. "Get airborne and out of the storm. Let Morgan know we are good to go with Phase Two, and I can't wait to see him down here."

II

PLANETARY ORBIT
DUBHE
SILVER HAWKS COALITION
FREE WORLDS LEAGUE
15 MAY 3010, 0600 HOURS, WESTERN COASTAL TIME

Morgan Kell punched up the broad tactical frequency that linked all of the Kell Hounds in the DropShip's 'Mech bays. "Word from Ak-Deuce is we are good to go. We are going in hot in the middle of a hurricane and we could be facing hostile forces. You all know your jobs. Hit and hit hard. Good luck. Morgan out."

Dubhe was one of those peculiar solar systems that scientists debated for ages. They all agreed that it was a binary star, but some went on to insist that a third star that lazily orbited the primary made it into a trinary system. The problem there was that the third star should have made the whole system unstable, but didn't. It just made it *quirky*. That meant gravitational fluctuations produced shifting jump points. In addition, the low energy output from the primary star took forever to recharge Kearny-Fuchida jump drives, and the secondary star lay over twenty astronomical units from Ak-Deuce, so it took forever for DropShips appearing there to make the normal run in.

Quirky worked in the Kell Hounds' favor. While the *Leopard*'s JumpShip had jumped into the primary's nadir point, the rest of the Hounds had taken advantage of a pirate point almost on top of Dubhe itself. Using the hurricane to obscure their arrival, they waited there in orbit for word that Patrick's crew had succeeded in taking the spaceport.

This will work, I know this will work. Morgan sighed. *It has to work.*

The Kell brothers, in their efforts to create a mercenary regiment, had made some powerful enemies. One of them had kidnapped Veronica Matova, a woman Morgan had fallen in love with. Her captor, using an intermediary, promised to return her unharmed if the Kell Hounds would perform a few operations. The first had been to neutralize a criminal cartel on Zavijava, which the Hounds had managed to do in short order.

It had also been relatively easy because the Hounds had already been on the world, and were able to use the element of surprise to their advantage. But in assaulting another world, one within the Free Worlds League—with whom neither the Hounds nor their employer, the Lyran Commonwealth, had cordial relations—there really was no such thing as surprise. In almost all cases, DropShips carrying troops would take days, or perhaps the better part of a week and a half to reach the planet. If a planet didn't muster force to oppose the landing, it was not for lack of forewarning.

In studying their target, Patrick Kell had pointed out that the southern half of the sole continent on Dubhe frequently faced powerful tropical storms at this time of year. The locals had adapted to that by adopting thick walls, strong domes, and half burying most of their buildings. They connected them with tunnel networks, creating human hives that thrived no matter what seasonal catastrophe struck the city of Ak-Deuce. The summer storms caused frequent evacuations and disrupted radio communications, making them great cover to disguise the Kell Hounds establishing a beachhead. Most of the Akers got used to remaining in their subterranean worlds during the stormy season, and the Hounds intended to take full advantage of that.

Limits exposure, limits collateral damage. Morgan, tucked into the seat of his *Archer*, rode out the first bump of the *Overlord* DropShip entering the atmosphere. He glanced at the 'Mech's auxiliary monitor and the countdown timer. *Thirty minutes until touchdown.*

He forced his fists open. The mission, when viewed as an abstract holo, shouldn't have been a problem. The Hounds would land a reinforced battalion, which would outgun any unit on the planet— unless something unexpected happened, like the Free Worlds League having dumped a regiment on Dubhe for training. The chances of that happening were relatively slender, because the system's transport issues meant any unit might be stuck there for a long while, rendering it useless if someone attacked elsewhere.

But, if we don't get this right... If the Hounds failed, if they took too long, the likely outcome was that Veronica would disappear forever. *I will not let that happen.*

The little 'Mech icons lined up on Morgan's secondary monitor began to turn from a dark outline to yellow and green as the mercenaries all began to power up their 'Mechs. He smiled. He'd outlined the mission, told them what was at stake, and told them it was voluntary only, with no recriminations if anyone opted out. Everyone, from the transport crew to the infantry, had agreed to go along. As Walter de Mesnil had put it, "Ms. Matova is a Lyran citizen, taken from a Lyran world. Getting her back is why the Archon is paying us—you know, even if she doesn't know it."

The DropShip again shook as it entered the storm system blanketing the continent's southwestern coast. The battalion's 'Mechs had all lit up as green on his monitor, so he shifted it back to an image of him and his brother, smiling and happy, which Veronica had taken. It made him feel closer to her than any holo he had of the two of them together. *She has insights into me that I don't.*

Morgan keyed the radio. "Be ready for anything. You know your objectives. Hit them. Secure them. Then we move on. No unnecessary heroics, just efficiency. We do this right, people, and not only do we accomplish our mission, but we jack the price for our service to future employers."

He hesitated. "Good luck, and thank you one and all."

III

VILLA VINO VERDE
MOUNTAIN OAKS, DUBHE
SILVER HAWKS COALITION
FREE WORLDS LEAGUE
15 MAY 3010, 0700 HOURS, CENTRAL TIME

Veronica Matova hid her smile, happy she had guessed correctly. Upon waking and seeing the day bright and yet cool, she opted for hunt clothing. Her outfit consisted of a white blouse and tan riding pants, with knee-length riding boots in brown. She tied her golden hair back into a ponytail with a black velvet ribbon. It was a look her captor favored, second only to her adopting a shy librarian look, which translated into his mind to a secretary who had made some serious mistakes.

Veronica set her shoulders and entered the salon with her red riding jacket draped over an arm. "Good morning, Count Somokis. You are up early today."

Markham Somokis, a mouse of a man with thinning brown hair and luxurious mustachios that he'd taken to curling into circles against his cheeks, looked up from his noteputer. "Yes, indeed, I couldn't wait."

He brandished the tablet. "You'll recall I'd gotten notice of an update to *Twilight of the Ion Knights* yesterday? My copy refreshed, and it is quite a spectacular update. So many revelations. Who would have known all the things going on on Zavijava?" His eyes narrowed. "Of course, you knew them, didn't you, my dear?"

"Oh?" Veronica gave him a gracious smile, despite his shifting tone making her wary. In the months she'd been his guest or captive or companion—suiting herself to his moods—she had learned to read him. As with most diminutive men, they tended toward passivity when in the company of women they considered beyond their reach. When that was his prevalent humor, she would flirt with him, complaining he was being mean to her. He would exert himself to show that was not true, and then affect to prove it in more material ways. Ultimately, he would win her confidence, and then she would express her physical appreciation for his kindness.

But the book, which had become his obsession since its publication four months earlier, always empowered him. It both flattered and infuriated him. She surfed those moods, careful to bring him back to the center. If he gave into fury, he would vent it upon her cruelly. But if he remained even-tempered, or even pleased, he would become the aggressor and conquer her, having her as he wished, and always earning her breathless praise for his prowess.

Ultimately, she found him no different from any of the men she had known in her time as a courtesan on Galatea. The difference here was that he actually *did* hold the power of life or death over her, so playing him became more than a professional lark. *Read him incorrectly, and the results could be fatal*.

"Yes, Veronica, you know things you did not tell me. The update to this book, it reveals a great deal. First, we have solved the identity of the anonymous author. It clearly is Constantine Fisk, that wretched actor, whose inept plotting ruined the Zavijava raid. If not for him, the Ion Knights would have been wildly successful."

She tapped a finger against her chin. "Fisk, a taller man, largely unmemorable. I met him on Galatea, the same place I met you, yes?"

The small man smiled and stroked his mustache. "Yes."

She draped her coat over the back of a chair. "You knew him far better than I, darling. He was but background noise in the symphony that was the evening I first laid eyes on you."

"A sour-struck note, too, certainly. He reveals himself by announcing that this book has been optioned for a holovid by stating, let me quote, 'the *sine qua non* action star, Constantine Fisk, will headline a cast for the epic adaptation of this book.' Apparently, he will be playing your lover, Morgan Kell."

Veronica shook her head. "He has neither the chin nor demeanor for it."

"Yes, well, no one would attach him to the holovid unless his appearance was required for obtaining the rights to the book. And to enhance things, he suggests the Ion Knights got away with far more in the way of loot than we did. He especially paints me as profiting mightily from the adventure."

"You are quite generous, my lord." She spread her arms. "You told me this villa is the least of your holdings, and it is massive. You could house an army here, and the vineyards and winery produce enough to keep them all stupefied for decades."

"One thing has nothing to do with the other, my dear. And while I did get away with a few varietal cuttings from Zavijava, this book contends I stole petabytes of Lyran economic data to enable the family firm to break into the Lyran Commonwealth market. He alleges my theft is worth over a trillion C-bills, and suggests that the Sixth Marik Militia Regiment intervened to help me get away with that data."

"It may not be true, my lord, but clearly the man holds your intellect in high esteem, else he would not think you capable of such a coup." She crossed to where he sat and knelt at his feet. "But, my lord, this is nothing I have had anything to do with. How is it I have been holding out on you?"

"Asked innocently and disingenuously. I think *you* hold my intellect in contempt." The count's face darkened, his expression turning faster than she had anticipated. "How have you deceived me? It says here that it was not Morgan Kell alone who organized the defense of Zavijava, but that with him was Prince Ian Davion, the leader of the Federated Suns. You knew this, you must have known this."

Veronica swallowed hard. "I was sworn to secrecy, my lord, and I did not think that information would be of use to you."

"Of *no use*? You are a wretched, lying *whore*." He lashed out with a foot, kicking her in the stomach; stealing her breath.

As she fell back, Markham stood and slid his belt from around his waist. "You need to be taught a lesson, Veronica, a lesson you will not soon forget."

IV

FIRST URSA MAJOR MILITIA BASE
AK-DEUCE, DUBHE
SILVER HAWKS COALITION
FREE WORLDS LEAGUE
15 MAY 3010, 0630 HOURS, WESTERN COASTAL TIME

The First Ursa Major Militia Battalion, known colloquially as "the Plushies," had long been a volunteer organization in which members served for five years as a rite of passage. Annually, they organized a holiday toy drive which collected enough presents to warrant a BattleMech or two pulling dumpsters full of toys as reindeer might draw a sleigh for Santa Claus in a parade. In addition, the Plushies helped harvest surplus farmland and bring the crops to food banks as a hedge against disaster during the storm season. They were aided in this function by the fact that refurbished AgroMechs made up one whole company of the battalion.

Of the current roster, exactly three members, all brand new, had actually seen combat. This trio coyly described their combat experience, withholding details because "things are still classified." Still, they brought their own 'Mechs, which had clearly seen some action.

The pilots—two men and one woman—took up residence in the militia compound permanently, and kept largely to themselves. The rest of the militia in residence were a half dozen pilots on a two-week rotation which would consist of diligent inspection of the base for leaks as the season's storms rolled in from the west.

Morgan Kell's awareness of these facts came from a Lyran Intelligence report on Dubhe. What the report didn't mention was that the trio of newcomers had most recently been members of the Ion Knights. Why they chose Dubhe to run to ground on Morgan couldn't imagine, save perhaps that they chose it by random because the world's only virtue appeared to be its self-sufficiency. Dubhe's strongest exports were coins and postage stamps, which they produced exclusively for the collectors' market—a market which was as lucrative as it was small.

The circular base consisted of several ferrocrete domes, the largest being at the circle's westernmost point. It served as a windbreak for the smaller administrative dome and the half dozen service and residential domes which surrounded the perimeter. Unlike the large, solid dome, the smaller ones had retractable roofs that would let in sunshine during more temperate seasons.

As the Kell Hounds' *Overlord*-Class DropShip landed west of the big dome, two of its particle projection cannons hurled bolts of artificial lightning. The twin azure beams slashed through the base's external 'Mech bay door. They began its destruction, and the hurricane's winds swiftly finished it. Then a quartet of scarlet laser beams poured through the opening and took down the internal door.

Morgan's *Archer* lumbered out of the DropShip and sprinted toward the smoking bay doors. Despite the rain and debris swirling in the air, there could be no missing the *Archer*, with its torso, head, and arms bright red, and legs painted black, with a wolf's-head logo on the left breast over the LRM launcher cover. Cat Wilson's *Marauder* came up fast in support, while Tim Moriarty's speedier *Centurion* made it to the doorway before either of them.

Morgan brought the humanoid 'Mech into the large dome on Moriarty's heels. The dome capped a cylinder with a large, round lift plate in the center. The perimeter held a dozen 'Mech bays, each containing a BattleMech. A half dozen of those were AgroMechs still dirt-encrusted from their recent campaign harvesting penta-fonio. Three others—one *Whitworth* and a pair of *Hermes II*s—had a green-brown woodlands camo pattern, save for the pink plush teddy bear in its logo, which had likewise been reproduced in the center of the lift place.

The last three had the gray-blue camo of the stormy season painted all over, but only one had gotten the Plushies logo added. Those 'Mechs—a *Dervish*, *Wolverine*, and *Javelin*—appeared to be the newest in the hangar. Three pilots raced across the open floor, heading for those 'Mechs, when Moriarty's *Centurion* sent a hot, red beam burning through the logo on the 'Mech bay floor. The pilots skidded to a halt before the black scar and slowly raised their hands.

Morgan Kell flipped his comm over to external speakers and pumped the volume so he could be heard above the storm's shrieking. "Hands up, weapons down. No one needs to die here today. Some of you used to be Ion Knights, and those who were not, if you cause no trouble, will be only mildly inconvenienced."

The blocky *Archer* turned toward the trio of gray-blue 'Mechs. He dialed down the power on the medium laser mounted in the 'Mech's midline and played the red beam over the *Dervish*. The beam took off the most recent coat of paint, revealing the purple with silver trim paint scheme of the Ion Knights beneath.

"Now that color combination looks familiar." Morgan marched the *Archer* over to interpose it between the three pilots and their 'Mechs. "We have a very specific mission to accomplish, and your cooperation will help us a great deal."

The tallest of the three pilots placed his empty hands atop his bald head and sank to his knees. "We were told the raid on Zavijava was just for a reality holovid program."

"That's not what Constantine Fisk said. He's told us everything about the Ion Knights and the loot you stole."

All three of the pilots slumped a little. The woman sighed. "We only got away with our 'Mechs, nothing else. I guess Count Somokis got a lot, but we got squat."

"I'd have more sympathy for you, but I was on Zavijava, and helped chase you off." Morgan chuckled. "But I think we might be able to work out a deal. You help me, and I'll help you. I don't know if you know it, but you and Count Somokis ended up on the same rock. I want him as badly as you do—and I want you to help me get him."

V

VILLA VINO VERDE
MOUNTAIN OAKS, DUBHE
SILVER HAWKS COALITION
FREE WORLDS LEAGUE
15 MAY 3010, 0945 HOURS, CENTRAL TIME

Veronica lay curled up beside her bed, clad only in the shredded remnants of her blouse and one of the boots she'd donned earlier. Her hair hung over her face and the weals crisscrossing her flesh pulsed and burned, tiny thunderstorms of torment. She shivered, her body beyond her control, barely able to swallow past the constriction around her throat. The carpet felt rough against her left cheek, her breasts, her stomach and hip.

Somokis had been furious—more than she'd seen before or would have ever imagined. He'd wielded the belt with an angry precision he'd never exhibited before. In the past, his idea of punishment had been play-acting. When he'd punished the errant secretary, he'd never hit her full force, and had always appeared apologetic after. Then he'd do his best to soothe her when she begged him to stop—and both of them knew that while her flesh stung, she had not truly been *hurt*.

But this time he did not abate. When she asked him to stop, he didn't even slow down. When she *demanded* he stop, he just hit her harder. When she screamed, he hit her harder still. And while it was not the worst beating she'd ever received in her life, it was the most savage.

And somewhere in it, she had lost herself.

In the past, when clients had indulged themselves, she'd known they were never actually beating her. They projected on her the person they wanted to punish. For some it was an ex-lover. Or a parent, or child, or someone who had humiliated them in distant memory. She'd always been able to detach herself from that instance and, at some point realizing the charade, the client had stopped.

Somokis had pushed her beyond that point. Vicious lashes with the belt and venomous comments got inside her head. Every kindness he'd done for her, every luxury wine and spice she'd had him import became a sin she'd committed against him. And she knew his accusations were true, for as he had been using her, so she had been using him. If she was to be caged, it would be a gilded cage, and would be a cage from within which her captivity could go unnoticed. She thought she'd been deceiving him, but clearly he had known, and ridiculed her for it.

He'd hissed the one comment that slithered deepest into her brain. "It is not just that you are a whore, Veronica, but that you are a dirty peasant whore of no consequence, who, when you finally vanish, will be missed by no one. No one at all."

She'd heard same whispered in her ear in the heat of the moment by countless noble clients, but they'd known it wasn't true. She *was* someone simply because they desired her; and their carnal, venereal hunger pulled them from the lofty position in which they saw themselves down into the sweaty gutter with the rest of the animals. When they spoke to her it was not to degrade her, but a vain effort to deny that they had degraded themselves.

But Somokis had her. He *owned* her. She'd made him buy her things, telling herself that exotic imports could be traced to Dubhe. Morgan knew her well enough to know her tastes. He would trace such things. He would find her.

She realized however, in that very moment, that she 'd been fooling herself. Had she truly wished to be free, she would have extracted herself. She'd been using the necessity of her rescue as a way for Morgan to prove he loved her; and yet had not tried to truly rescue herself. Why not? Because, at her core, she knew Somokis was right. She was no one, no one at all. *And was foolish to think I might be* someone *to people of his station. People like Morgan.*

She lay there, capable of nothing more than feeling pain. Pain was all she was, all she had to fill the hollow inside her. She'd once believed that Morgan loved her. *I allowed myself to believe he loved me. A stupid, silly fantasy, a girl's fantasy. An infant's fantasy. I am not. I never was.*

More stars in the sky, more fish in the sea. And I am the fool who allowed myself to believe.

Veronica heard footsteps. The door to her room opened and breath caught in someone's throat. Then he knelt beside her. Hands on her shoulders he shifted her into sitting position. He loosened the belt that had been tightened around her throat. He brushed hair from her face and raised a glass of water to her lips.

"Shhhhh, drink."

She did as bidden, not out of any desire, but because that command became the only thought in her mind. She drank, the water cool, and yet it hurt to swallow. Somehow, she raised a hand to his wrist and pushed the glass away, feeling the cold water splash against her breasts and dripping down to her thighs.

Somokis again brushed hair from her face. "Shhhh, Veronica, it will be okay. I didn't mean…you shouldn't have made me do this. I wouldn't have. You know me. I wouldn't have, but you made me."

She managed to lick her lips, but even that exertion took a lot out of her. She sat back against the side of the bed and the soft sheets ignited her skin. "I know."

He took her head in his hands and kissed her lips gently. "I will make it better. I have that champagne you like, the *Xaros Brut*, already chilling. And that caviar from Marik, you must remember that. I have that for you. It will be better, Veronica. You will see."

"Yes, my lord…" She began to drift, but got a hand under her to steady herself. She felt the belt he'd used to beat her and tightened her grip on it. "Yes, it will get better. Soon?"

"Very soon, Veronica." Count Somokis kissed her softly again. "You'll see. I promise, you'll see.'"

VI

FIRST URSA MAJOR MILITIA BASE
AK-DEUCE, DUBHE
SILVER HAWKS COALITION
FREE WORLDS LEAGUE
15 MAY 3010, 0900 HOURS, WESTERN COASTAL TIME

Patrick Kell looked at his noteputer. "No, Morgan, nothing yet."

Morgan hung his hands over the back of his neck. "There's something not right. You don't think they worded anything in this message to tip him off, do you?"

"No, I'm sure of it." Patrick forced a smile for his brother. "He might be distracted by God alone knows what. Remember, he's an hour ahead of us, and still likely hasn't risen yet. When he gets his messages, we'll be notified."

"And you're ready to go."

"I could be in the air now, Morgan, and hit the second we're in and have scoped the defenses."

"No, we can't take the chance that he gets spooked and runs."

When Patrick and Morgan had taken up the issue of trying to find Veronica Matova, they agreed on a couple of working assumptions. The first was that she'd be in the company of one of the Ion Knights, or that the Ion Knights would know where she had gone. They based this on the fact that the traffic leaving Zavijava during the time of her disappearance had a lot of Ion Knights going along with it. Thus tracking the Knights would be the best way to find her.

Doing that would be looking for the proverbial white dwarf in a galaxy, and made more difficult by the white dwarf not wanting to be found. While Constantine Fisk was more than happy to give up as many names as he could remember, the Ion Knights would be irredeemably stupid if they didn't create new identities and flee to a variety of worlds. The brothers realized that while the Knights had no intention of being tracked, they had to find a way to make the Knights *want* to be tracked.

An old Terran saying had been "The most plentiful things in the universe are hydrogen and stupidity." The Kells knew that third on that list was *ego*. Morgan had found and hired a hack writer on Zavijava to create an overnight history of the Ion Knights and their raid, titled *Twilight of the Ion Knights*. They'd published the book immediately—having deliberately included errors to be corrected in updates and crafting a mystery around the identity of the anonymous author. They left breadcrumb clues indicating that the writer had to be Constantine Fisk, and had many quotes from Fisk in the book. He'd even actually said a few of them. And then every two weeks or so they published a revised version of the work, and those who had purchased it could download the amended version for free.

The Kells had no intelligence agency like the LIC to actually trace every copy. That would have required a network of spies on countless planets. The only organization which could boast of such an operation was ComStar, but they never would have undertaken espionage like that. It would have violated some sacred dictum uttered by Jerome Blake and exposed them to accusations of dabbling in politics.

What ComStar would happily do, however, was report back commercial data—including information about orders, sales, imports and exports. In the case of the Kells, who hid behind the shell of a publishing company that specialized in books of poetry by MechWarriors, this meant providing information on worlds to which updates of the electronic book had been transmitted through ComStar's network. Assuming that the vast majority of purchasers for *Twilight of the Ion Knights* were Knights themselves, the Kells were able to track the worlds to which their quarry had fled.

Morgan also requested and got the same data for a variety of luxury items that Veronica enjoyed, or items she knew would attract his attention. Looking for such things had worked for them before, and they hoped for the same luck going forward. Sifting through all of those things and the book updates, the Kell brothers had pinpointed Dubhe as a world of extreme interest. It was a perfect place to go to ground, and by digging through shipping records, they determined that Veronica was most likely in the company of Count Markham Somokis.

In an effort to confirm that idea, they'd included material in the latest update of *Twilight* which alleged that Somokis had made off with a veritable fortune. What they hoped for was seeing communications directed toward him from other members of the Knights, outraged with his profiting from their efforts.

But the interrogation of the three Knights who had joined the Plushies had proved less than wholly useful. The pilots had chosen Dubhe because the bald one had once dated a man from here. When they made landfall, he'd tried to make contact, and discovered that story had been a lie. They also discovered it cost a lot more to leave Dubhe than it did to ship in, so they quickly found work with the Plushies and started saving up for a ticket out.

Learning that Somokis was on Dubhe and had a lot of money did not please the Knights. They fully agreed with the Kells' request that they draft a demand letter and send it to the count. Patrick helped them, attaching a simple virus to the holovid they recorded to ask for money—threatening the count with exposure if he didn't comply. Once the count watched the holovid, the virus would enable Patrick to peek through the count's security system—if he had one—and see what they'd be up against as they went to pay him a visit.

"Still nothing?"

Patrick shook his head. "Morgan, we know where he is. I'll load up in the *Leopard*, we hook south and come into Mountain Oaks from the east. He'll never know we're coming."

Morgan's eyes tightened. "You do a pass. If it looks odd, you get out of there and let me know. There's got to be more than one way to skin this cat, and, you know, by the time you get there, maybe I'll have figured out what that is."

VII

VILLA VINO VERDE
MOUNTAIN OAKS, DUBHE
SILVER HAWKS COALITION

FREE WORLDS LEAGUE
15 MAY 3010, 1230 HOURS, CENTRAL TIME

It occurred to Veronica that Count Somokis still did not look as regretful as he normally did after losing his temper. He met her gaze directly and did not shy away. His shoulders didn't have the characteristic slouch to them, and he spoke in a normal voice, not the slightly hushed tones she'd heard before. *Something is disturbing him more than his actions.*

"Forgive me, my lord, but something troubles you."

Somokis looked up from his noteputer, then pushed it farther up the table and away from his plate. He very seldom brought it with him onto the veranda when they dined there. He'd complained the sunlight made it difficult to read and, regardless, he found it disrespectful to his dining partners.

But even as he pushed it away, he glanced at it with irritation wrinkling his brow. "It's nothing."

She knew that for a lie, but said nothing. Veronica had managed to pull herself together enough to join him for luncheon, but only just barely. She wore a royal blue silken dressing gown, loosely cinched with a golden sash which matched the trim at cuffs and hem. The slight breeze which tugged at it threatened to expose a breast, which normally would have been ample distraction for the count, but she only cared that the air soothed her burning skin. To wear anything heavier than the robe would have left her in agony.

"Yes, my lord." Veronica reached for a crystal flute and sipped the *Xaros* champagne, and had to use both hands to return it to the table without spilling a drop. "It is a beautiful day, a beautiful view."

The man grunted and gave the grounds a perfunctory glance. A vast green pasturage with a handful sheep dotting it spread out to the east. Above it, climbing to the top of the first crest of rolling hilltops, the estate's vineyard grew in neat, verdant rows. Below, near the winery dome, a *Wolverine* BattleMech started a perimeter patrol. Save for the presence of the war machine, the bucolic setting would have been ideal.

The noteputer squeaked and Somokis snatched it up, tapped the surface. His face darkened. "No, no, that will not do."

"Shall I leave you, my lord?"

"No, stay there. I need to think." The mousy man bared his teeth. "As misfortune would have it, a couple of the Ion Knights landed on this tiny rock and they believe the tripe being published in *Twilight of the Ion Knights.* Specifically, they believe I made off with a great deal of money and they want some."

"Are they threatening you?"

"Veiled now, but it will become more overt, won't it? Perhaps I should have you deal with them. Set a whore to catch a whore?"

Veronica looked down at her plate and the untouched triangle of toast with caviar spread on it. "I would do as you wish, my lord." She wanted to oppose him, but with his fury rising and her skin still aching, she couldn't muster the will to protest. *Who are you to think you could oppose him?*

"What I wish you to do, Veronica, is tell me *how* they discovered I was here." He pounded a fist on the table. "No one could have known I was here unless you somehow got a message out. Did you do that?"

"No, my lord."

"No? Are you sure? When you were playing the errant secretary, perhaps?" Somokis stalked to her end of the table and grabbed a handful of her golden hair. He yanked her head back, forcing her to stare up at his reddening face. "But you would have, wouldn't you, if you could have. Don't deny it."

His face blurred as tears welled. "No, my lord."

For a half second she feared he would smash her face into table, shattering the plate, breaking her nose, dashing out her teeth. His grip tightened, and she raised her hands to brace herself against the table.

Then he gasped. His grip slackened. He gurgled and ran back into the estate.

What? Why?

Tears poured out of eyes and her vision cleared.

Just as the *Leopard*-class DropShip swooped down and its 'Mech bay hatches opened.

Patrick Kell's *Thunderbolt* dropped from the belly of the *Leopard* eight meters above the meadow. The war machine landed heavily, narrowly missed squashing a sheep. The 'Mech's broad feet sank a meter into the ground.

The DropShip continued on toward the estate, sowing a dozen jump infantry on the ground, then curved around north to drop another three 'Mechs at the estate's 'Mech hangar and landing strip.

He guided the *Thunderbolt*'s crosshairs onto the blocky *Wolverine*'s outline. The gold dot at the center pulsed and Patrick hit his triggers, unloading with everything but his machine guns and the short-range missiles. Heat spiked in the cockpit as Patrick's weapons fired.

Fifteen long-range missiles rode argent fire out of the *Thunderbolt*'s left-flank launch tubes. They corkscrewed down into the *Wolverine,* pitting the armor on both legs and the left arm in a rapid series of explosions. The large laser's green beam tracked down from shoulder to wrist on the *Wolverine*'s right arm. Ferro-ceramic armor bubbled and oozed before dripping into the grass. Then the ruby spears of coherent light from the *Thunderbolt*'s trio of medium lasers melted more armor from the opposing 'Mech's arms and scored a black scar over the its heart.

The *Wolverine*'s pilot brought its weapons to bear and returned fire. The autocannon carried in its right hand lipped flame. A burst of depleted-uranium shells blasted armor from the *Thunderbolt*'s left forearm. The boxy missile launcher on the 'Mech's left shoulder sent a half dozen short-range missiles into the air. They peppered the larger 'Mech, chipping armor over the chest, legs and arms. Then the medium laser mounted in the *Wolverine*'s head plowed a furrow in the armor on the *Thunderbolt*'s left arm.

Less than half the armor remaining there, but still strong unless he gets lucky. Patrick started the *Thunderbolt* drifting south, away from the estate buildings. *Time to end this little game before someone really gets hurt.*

Veronica sat frozen for a handful of heartbeats. At first, she thought the Ion Knights had somehow tracked Count Somokis to the estate. Then, as the first 'Mech dropped from the *Leopard*, she recognized the black-and-red color scheme. She knew it was from the Kell Hounds, and that she should be overjoyed, but she envisioned Morgan Kell in a towering rage, somehow more angry with her than Count Somokis had been. *He will hate me and he will hurt me.*

And she knew she deserved his ire. She hadn't done enough to try to escape. There were times when she'd allowed herself to forget she was a captive. And even a few times when she'd actually been happy.

Fear seized her. She pushed herself away from the table and began to run after Count Somokis. She stumbled, skinning a knee, but scrambled up to her feet and staggered onward. She clasped the door jamb to steady herself, the plunged on into the parlor. She steered from chairs to tables and couches, then sank down as gunshots sounded below. She didn't think they had come to kill her, but she felt equally certain she would die.

Then Veronica saw him. Somokis ran through the second-story corridor, heading to his safe room. He'd showed it to her once while boasting of both his wealth and his brilliant foresight. From that room he could access a tunnel down to the subterranean transport tubes that would take him into the village of Mountain Oaks, and then he could escape from there.

She ran after him and caught up to him as he reached the alcove with the life-sized, gilded statue of Venus, naked, rising from a half shell. Veronica reached his side as he opened a small panel that would, in turn, grant access to the controls that would reveal the safe room's door. Crying, she fell to her knees and clutched at his pant leg.

"Take me, my lord...you have to take me."

Somokis tried to shake her off his leg, but she clung on all the tighter. Gunshots sounded closer. "Let me go!"

"No!"

Snarling, he tried to scrape her off his leg as if she was something he'd stepped in. "Don't touch me, whore. You are nothing!" He kicked her again and again, harder.

Pain shot through her and she lost all strength. Something had popped in her chest. Her grip failed and she rolled over onto her back, her hands limp by her sides. Completely vulnerable.

Hatred twisted the small man's features. "I only kept you because he demanded it, you know. He let me have you. Not because he liked me, but he *hated* you. He even said I could kill you, that's how much he hated you."

Somokis lifted his foot and poised it to stomp on her throat. "Diverting, yes, but you were never worth the trouble."

His foot fell.

The *Wolverine* pilot had to know they were outgunned, but that didn't deter them. For a fleeting moment, Patrick wondered if his opponent was some local kid Somokis had hired to provide perimeter security. Perhaps a kid who had daydreamed about 'Mech battles while piloting an AgroMech in the unending war against rodents and weeds on the farm. So many of those improbable stories ended up with "And then I got him with a headshot and taught him what it really means to be a MechWarrior."

Whether the pilot suffered from daydream envy, or just was braver than Somokis deserved his people to be, they fought well. The autocannon again unleashed a spray of shells that obliterated the Kell Hounds logo on the *Thunderbolt*'s left breast and armor beneath. Two-thirds of the short-range missiles hit their target, blasting more armor off the left flank and crushing plates over the 'Mech's centerline. The errant missiles sailed past, putting a significant dent in the estate's wine production for the year. And the medium laser's ruby beam sizzled low, liquifying armor over the taller 'Mech's thigh.

With heat swirling through the *Thunderbolt*'s cockpit, Patrick refrained from triggering the LRMs, but let go with his full complement of lasers. The large laser's green beam speared the *Wolverine* in the center of the chest, leaving a smoking hole. The 'Mech shuddered, then listed to the right, suggesting the shot had punched through flawed plating and melted a gyro. The trio of red beams carved layers of armor from the 'Mech's left flank and left leg. None of them got through to vital systems, but the loss of armor radically shifted the 'Mech's mass.

The pilot struggled to keep the *Wolverine* upright, but between the loss of armor and the damage to the gyro, they failed. What had started as a list to the right became a tumble, the 'Mech slamming down on its right arm. The impact crushed the *Wolverine*'s right hand. The autocannon bounced free, torn belts of ammo sprinkling shells over the pasture.

Patrick flicked his external speakers on. "Pop your cockpit hatch and just park yourself where I can see you. Do not force me to hurt you any more than I have to."

He waited for a minute and had begun to wonder if the fall had knocked the pilot out. But then the cockpit windscreen flipped up, and a gangly waif hauled herself up onto the *Wolverine's* chin. She pulled off her neurohelmet, tossing it back into the cockpit. The morning's breeze teased her copper hair.

I'm glad someone's seen sense. Patrick turned his 'Mech toward the estate. *I hope the same can be said for Count Somokis.*

A sharp *crack* filled the air.

The top half of Somokis' head exploded, painting an unfeeling Venus with blood and brains and a dappling of bone fragments. Everything, from the bridge of his nose upward, gone. Then his body, which had seemed to Veronica to have been balanced on one foot for an eternity, toppled backward and landed with a wet *thump*.

Two men, carbine muzzles smoking, hurried to her. One crouched at her side, gently closing her robe. The other swept the area with his gun's muzzle. "Clear."

The first keyed the communicator clipped to his combat vest. "Icon found. Moving to a secure location. Medic on me." He glanced down at her. "Ms. Matova, can you walk?"

Veronica tried to speak, but just made croaking sounds as tears streamed down her face.

"Don't worry. We got you. Just hang on. We'll get you clear, then get a medic to look you over." The man drew a knife and cut out a one-by-two-meter swath of the carpet on which she'd fallen. "It'll be a bit of a ride, but you're safe now."

Her hand rose to cover her mouth and she still couldn't speak. She nodded and the man gave her a thumbs-up. He grabbed the carpet and, as the sounds of gunfire and explosions grew distant, dragged her deeper into the mansion and out of harm's way.

VIII

VILLA VINO VERDE
MOUNTAIN OAKS, DUBHE
SILVER HAWKS COALITION
FREE WORLDS LEAGUE
15 MAY 3010, 1420 HOURS, CENTRAL TIME

Patrick Kell looked up from the holodisplay table in the center of Count Somokis' office as his brother walked in. The office had been in keeping with the villa's overall Tuscan styling, with marble pillars and ornate furnishings often gilded. Centuries-old portraits hung on the walls, and newer scenes rendered as frescos appeared as ancient scenes, despite having 'Mechs and aircars in them. No books, though, which surprised Patrick, because men who went to such trouble to decorate an office as a temple to themselves usually imported books to suggest they possessed a wealth of knowledge.

Morgan, his expression grim as he entered, relented and gave his brother the hint of a grin. "You did good work here. Thank you. What do I need to know?"

"Well, you're here, so you know they sedated Veronica. She's going to be okay, but Somokis worked her over."

"And Somokis is dead."

"Frost got him. He was going to kill Veronica."

"I would have preferred him taken alive but..." Morgan banged his fists together. "I probably would have killed him myself."

And I'm glad that wasn't something I had to try to stop you from doing. Patrick's fingers played across the holographic controls. File folders and ledgers burned to life above the holotable. "Somokis used touch-DNA devices in lieu of retinal scanners or lower level security. We put him to work post mortem, granted ourselves admin access to everything here. I can build you an account, too, if you want."

"I hope we won't be here long enough that I'll need access." Morgan folded his arms over his chest. "What have you got?"

"Apparently he or someone in his family set this place up as a bolt-hole twenty-five years ago. Given Free Worlds League politics and how the Silver Hawks Coalition is known for tangling with the central government, it wasn't a bad idea. When things blew up on Zavijava, he headed here. I talked to the staff and the security pilots. They said the villa was always known as the Empty House, since no one was ever in residence. When Somokis arrived and started issuing orders, they just obeyed. Seems the local managers had been cooking the books, so everyone was making plenty of money, and they assumed he'd go away again soon enough."

Patrick tapped one of the ledgers. "The winery actually makes a decent amount of money—more than enough to make this place self-sustaining. The profits went into accounts at a local bank. When Somokis arrived, he had twenty-million C-bills converted into bearer bonds, which he stored in a case in his safe room. We've secured it."

Morgan smiled. "You have access to the money in the bank as well?"

"As I explained to the bank's representative in Mountain Oaks, with the passing of my uncle there would be some minor changes, but for the most part we intend to keep things running as they have been, for the good of the community."

"He bought that?"

"She. I might have had the *Thunderbolt* in the background when I made the call from the veranda." Patrick shrugged. "Because I was in the system here, I sent her all the confirmation she needed with the proper codes."

"Good. Pull forty million and send it to Emerson Reynald on Zavijava. Tell him it's reparations for what the Ion Knights did in their little raid last year."

"Okay. And we're taking the bearer bonds?"

Morgan nodded. "Katrina never would have forbidden us from staging this little raid, but there is no way it will be politically convenient for her. That twenty million can go a long way to buying some good will with a host of politicians, smoothing things out for her."

"Agreed."

Morgan stroked his chin. "I know you've only begun to sort through things here, but do you think Somokis was the person relaying orders through Ryan?"

A shiver ran up Patrick's spine. "I don't see it. There's nothing here that connects Somokis with Ivan Borovsky. I'll look deeper, but Somokis and his businesses were largely clean. He underpaid his taxes, and probably has other bolt-holes like this scattered around, but I think his being a producer of holovids and then the Ion Knights thing, those were..."

Morgan smiled. "Those were his midlife crisis?"

"Seems like. And there's something else."

"What?"

Patrick frowned. "Household bills, groceries, what the staff said about his months here, they thought he and Veronica were having an affair. That, literally, the two of them had left unhappy situations behind, and were actually happy with each other."

Morgan's smile died. "Your point being?"

"That something changed. Something set Somokis off." Patrick got up and laid a hand on his brother's shoulder. "He lit into Veronica after he'd gotten the latest update to *Twilight*, but before he got the communication from the Ion Knights. If I had to guess, he heard from the person giving Ryan orders, and something that person said set him off. Maybe it was another of the Ion Knights, I don't know. But what I do know is that there is zero record of any communication coming in through the system here."

"So you think he had another device, another communication system?"

"I'll keep digging."

"You have to. If Ryan's boss entrusted Veronica to Somokis, he will be checking up to make sure he still has leverage. Once he learns we have her back, he'll vanish, and we'll never find him. Anyone we ever get close to will be in jeopardy."

"I know." Patrick nodded solemnly. "What happened to Veronica won't happen to anyone else again."

A light rap sounded on the door and Walter de Mesnil peeked his head in. "Begging your pardon, Colonel. Ms. Matova is awake. She asked to see you."

Frost and the tactical team had ensconced Veronica in one of the estate's smaller bedrooms in the east wing, giving her a view of the vineyards if she wanted to rise from the bed and part the diaphanous curtains. Morgan, as he entered the room, noticed she didn't even glance in that direction, but instead had turned to face the wall. That meant she also had her back turned to the door.

He studied her for a moment. Aside from the IV drip there was no indication she was in any distress. A white silk robe covered her. Despite being very light, its opacity meant he couldn't see any of the angry welts and bruises crisscrossing her flesh. He'd seen her lay in bed on her right side often enough to know it was her, and yet she lay there somewhat stiffly, making her hurt obvious.

He rapped on the door was he entered the room, then closed the door quietly behind him. "I have missed you."

Her body shook and her shoulders slumped. "Morgan, don't." Her words came punctuated with sobbing.

He wanted to rush to her and just hold her, but to do that would increase her physical pain. He hated Count Somokis with the heat of a thousand suns in that moment, but forced his fists open. He took the chair from the vanity and brought it to her bedside, sitting beside her, stretching his legs out parallel to her. "What can I do for you, Veronica?"

"Go away."

His heart began to ache. "Will you tell me why?"

"What difference will it make?"

"Will you even look at me?"

"You don't want to see me. Remember me as I was."

Morgan sat forward, elbows on his knees. The chair creaked as he did so. "I have so many memories of you. None of them dulled in the least by the last six months. The one that keeps coming back to me, though, is of the woman who gave me a silver frame with two holographs. One of my brother and me at his graduation from the Nagelring, and the other of us on Galatea, an image she made before she really knew either of us. Her insight in taking that shot and then finding its companion gave me another perspective on life, my brother, our relationship. I cannot thank you enough."

"You're welcome." She sniffed. "Let that be my parting gift to you. You should go, Morgan, just forget me."

"That won't happen. Neither of those will." He glanced at her. "We're not leaving you here. It's not safe. We're a month worth of jumps from the Commonwealth, and I don't believe Count Somokis was the person who set up your kidnapping. Until we find that person, you won't be safe."

"I don't deserve to be safe. I am a danger to everyone, Morgan. Just leave me."

"Tell me why you think that, and I will."

She shifted on the bed, but made no effort to look at him. "You will just tell me how I'm wrong. I know you. You will."

Morgan grunted and shook his head. "I won't. You tell me why you want me to walk away and I will. I'll go right out that door and you'll never see me again. I'll have Patrick set you up with enough of the count's money that you'll be fine for a long time. You have my word."

Veronica lay silent and Morgan imagined her calculating the odds of his going back on his word, trying to talk her out of leaving or even restraining her against her will. She had to know that making an important decision while still in shock made no sense, but he would do nothing to dissuade her if she chose to send him away. *I owe her and what we have had enough to do at least that.*

"I betrayed myself, Morgan. I betrayed you. I did what I could to try to escape, and then when Count Somokis took custody of me, I stopped trying."

"Veronica, you knew we would find a way to track your favorite things, your *Xaros* champagne and those chocolates from Tharkad. Those orders laid out a wonderful trail."

"Yes." She gasped as she repositioned herself. "And I may have encouraged the count to look for updates to *Twilight of the Ion Knights.* That had to have been you. Perfect bait for a man of his egotistical nature. Bravo. You never do anything halfway."

"Nor you."

"But I did, Morgan. I didn't even go halfway. Champagne, caviar, and truffles? Rats in cages make more determined efforts to escape. But I didn't, Morgan, I gave up. Not consciously, not with intent, but I did. Look at this place. I had whatever I wanted, when I wanted it, and more when I ran out. I slept on sheets and bedding so soft that it could cushion something falling from orbit. While here I had massages as I desired, I could go riding and were I to want for something, no matter how outlandish, Somokis would obtain it for me."

"But he was your captor."

"When have I *not* been a captive, Morgan? When I grew up in a religious cult? When I worked for pimps and madams? When my business thrived because I bowed to the desires of the clients, and paid bribes to countless people who would destroy me if I did not? Being Somokis' captive only meant I didn't have to remember a new captor's name every night of the week."

He stared at his open hands. "Did you feel you were a captive when you traveled with me?"

"Yes… No." Veronica rolled onto her back and gasped at agonies Morgan could only imagine. "Morgan, I waited and hoped you would find me. I did, I really did. But there were days when I even forgot there was a world outside Mountain Oaks. And then, this morning, bare hours before you arrived, Count Somokis broke me. I lost all hope, Morgan. I lost hope in you. All I had to do was trust you, and I failed. I thought I knew who I was, but that was all an illusion. I am no one, and you deserve more, Morgan. That is why you have to go."

His heart leaden in his chest, Morgan slowly stood and took a step toward the door. He stopped and did not look back over his shoulder. He kept his voice low and soft. "I will leave, and do what I said, but I would ask a favor of you. As I said, someone commanded Somokis to take you. That someone was using your captivity as leverage against the Kell Hounds. Neither you nor we will be safe until that person is found. With Somokis dead, we need help to figure out who that person is. Will you help us?"

"Yes, yes I will." An edge crept into her voice, a cold, sharp edge Morgan had never heard her speak with before. "Provided, when you find him, it's my hand that wields the knife when we carve his heart from his chest."

To be concluded in *Shrapnel* #4!

UNIT DIGEST: 138TH MECHANIZED INFANTRY DIVISION VETERANS ASSOCIATION

ALEX KAEMPEN

Nickname: The Chicago Division
Affiliation: Star League
CO: Lieutenant General Mary Kaempen
Average Experience: Regular/Fanatical
Force Composition: 1 'Mech battalion (1 company of *Crockett*s; 1 company of *Shootist*s, 1 company of *Thorn*s), 2 combat vehicle battalions (1 battalion of Demon combat vehicles, 1 battalion of Gabriel hovercraft), 1 motorized infantry battalion
Unit Abilities: The 138th is adept at underhanded tactics. At the start of any game where the 138th is the Defender, they may deploy one hidden unit out of every four they field. They may also substitute two 20-point minefields for any one of those hidden units.
Parade Scheme: Olive drab

UNIT HISTORY

The 138th Mechanized Infantry Division, known by its nickname as the Chicago Division, met a brutal death during the Liberation of Terra. Approaching Lone Star with the rest of XLIV Corps in 2772, the 138th died in deep space due to the Caspars defending Lone Star targeting their DropShips. Over 80 percent of the division was lost, with the remainders disbanded and spread out to reinforce other divisions. By all official accounts, this was the end of the 138th, but the official records did not account for the affection the Terran city of Chicago had for its namesake division.

The scars of the Liberation ran deep in Chicago. Amaris' forces had ransacked the city repeatedly over the course of the occupation. Industrial concerns were run into the ground then shaken down for their last atoms of value. Jacob Cameron's vast palaces and lakefront parks had been turned into prison camps and killing grounds. The

Liberation saw this damage exacerbated by the Famine of 2781, a bureaucratic disaster that led to tens of thousands more deaths. The city was shell-shocked, and into this mess jumped an idealistic young city official. Realizing that Chicago needed heroes, she worked with the SLDF to invite all surviving veterans from the 138th for a parade in honor of *their* division.

The parade, and all the buildup around it, was wildly successful. For the first time in almost two decades, Chicago had something positive to talk about. The city extended offers to them to stay and become something of a cheerleading team. Most of the veterans accepted, though with something else in mind. The presence of House troops on Terra and the rapidly deteriorating situation in the Inner Sphere made clear the need for protection. Two months after their parade, on 8 October 2782, the ranking officer among the 138th's veterans, Lieutenant General Mary Kaempen, announced the creation of the 138th Mechanized Infantry Division Veterans Association.

With no Star League to fund them, and not officially part of the SLDF anyways, the 138th drew on private funding, becoming a de facto mercenary unit controlled by the city. This freedom allowed them to negotiate with local defense industries. By the time Aleksandr Kerensky left the Inner Sphere two years later, the 138th was operating as a fully equipped combined-arms reinforced regiment. With the 138th's loyalty to the Chicago megalopolis firm, it seemed as though Chicago might be able to weather the coming storm. Alas, fate took a different turn.

At 0110 CDT on 26 June 2788, Colonel Colin Toenjes, duty officer for the 138th, noticed a large number of former SLDF units on Terra moving without announcement. Immediately suspicious, he called the 138th to alert status. By 0130 the unit was fully alert and moving to their assigned sectors across Chicago. The first ComStar-aligned units made contact with the 138th at 0150 on the southeast side of the city as the ComStar units, elements of the 197th Mechanized Infantry Division, moved in to secure the Torrence Avenue Assembly plant. First blood went to the 138th as Major Richard Christian, leading two companies of tanks, blocked their advance at Wolf Lake. Unfortunately for the 138th, his victory would be short lived.

As morning turned to afternoon on the 26th, more ComStar units approached the city. Other elements of the 197th approached the city from the west. Moving quickly, they made for the 138th's headquarters at North Park. The 138th attempted to block them with a company of Gabriel hovercraft supported by a mixed company of *Shootists* and *Crocketts* under the command of Colonel Toenjes. The 197th's *Flashmans*, *Excaliburs*, and *Lancelots* outnumbered Colonel Toenjes' detail three to one. Using their superior numbers, the 197th quickly trapped and destroyed that detail in the Norridge area. By nightfall the 138th's headquarters and support facilities were in ComStar hands.

Denied her headquarters, General Kaempen took to the field. She hoped to defeat the southern elements of the 197th, turn around, and roll them up from the south. She knew other SLDF elements were also resisting, particularly in South America. The hope was to hold out long enough for them to defeat ComStar. With this plan in hand, General Kaempen led the remaining 'Mechs of the 138th south.

The parks of Jacob Cameron still bore the scars of the Amaris occupation, and General Kaempen intended to use them as cover as she moved to rendezvous with Major Christian. Unfortunately, the expected rendezvous never happened, as Major Christian's force was still holding at Wolf Lake at daybreak. Overnight, the 197th's third force had arrived in the abandoned industrial sector of Gary. With the sun at their backs, they boldly crossed Lake Michigan and enveloped Christian, and his tank quickly succumbed to the 197th's superior numbers.

General Kaempen therefore found herself trapped along the waterfront. The northern force quickly fell on her rear guard, commanded by Captain Patrick Finnegan. In a matter of minutes, the two lances holding at the Chicago River were overwhelmed. Two regiments of the 197th then engaged the main body of the 138th in downtown Chicago. In an attempt to save some of the unit, she ordered the majority of the unit, under the command of Major William Gauthier, to break out westward while she covered their retreat. The 138th's sudden assault was successful; however, minutes after her unit escaped, General Kaempen was killed when her *Highlander* exploded after absorbing the combined fire of an enemy 'Mech company.

Major Gauthier sent the remaining *Thorn*s and infantry ahead to secure their escape route. The hope was to reach a DropShip at Midway DropPort or break out into the Saganashkee Wilderness Restoration Zone. They initially made good progress but were quickly checked by the 197th's hovercrafts, which harassed their *Thorn*s and slowly whittled the force down. By nightfall on the 27th, the 138th attempted to resupply at a former repair depot in the La Grange area. Those efforts were foiled by continuous raids during the night, during one of which Major Gauthier was killed.

On the morning of 28 June, the remaining members of the 138th resumed their breakout attempt, this time to the southwest. Colonel Leonard Bell, leading the southern ComStar force, saw their intentions clearly. Moving his mixed regiment up to the South Branch of the Chicago River, he provided a master class in denying an opponent a river crossing. This allowed the northern ComStar forces to pin the 138th against the river. Forced back toward the city, the remains of the 138th were destroyed just north of the river along an old industrial road named Cermak. The survivors, though few in number, were treated with magnanimity as long as they dispersed and forswore any attempts at further reconstituting the 138th. With that agreement, the 138th passed into the ash heap of history.

COMPOSITION

As the name states, the 138th was originally a mechanized infantry division based around three regiments of 'Mechs. The survivors who made it through the maw of Lone Star and the rest of the Liberation roughly mirrored that composition. When the 138th's Veterans Association formally organized, they were able to field a reinforced regiment of personnel, although equipment was in short supply.

During the few short years after Kerensky's Exodus, the 138th made liberal usage of Terra's weapons factories. Chicago's own Bowie Industries was more than happy to provide cut-rate price Gabriels in exchange for a security detail for its Chicago headquarters. Likewise, Ford, concerned about the Chicago Assembly, its Torrence Avenue plant on the Southside, made a deal to provide a company of *Thorns* straight off that line as long as they too had access to protection.

TALES FROM THE CRACKED CANOPY: THE RAZOR'S EDGE OF OPPORTUNITY

LOREN L. COLEMAN

At the Cracked Canopy, a MechWarrior bar on the gaming world of Solaris VII, a Memory Wall displays mementos of glorious victories and bitter defeats, of honorable loyalties and venomous betrayals, of lifelong friendships and lost loves. Each enshrined object ensures that the past will not be forgotten and the future is something worth fighting for.

Everyone is looking for something.

That's basically true of everyone, at all times. The only thing that changes is what we're looking for, where, and how much time we're willing to spend pursuing it.

When I kicked the cowshit off my heels on Issaba, I was looking for adventure and opportunity.

When I kicked the mud of a dozen worlds from my combat boots and cashed out of the AFFS infantry, I was looking for peace of mind and control of my own life.

And by the time I came to Solaris VII, I was back to looking for opportunity again.

Yeah. We are all, always, looking.

Doesn't mean we'll find it.

I was looking for trouble by the time I hit the door at the Cracked Canopy, a watering hole close to the Davion Arena on Solaris VII known for routine sightings of has-beens and might-bes and rowdy nights when hot tickets fought on one of its three wall-covering vidscreens. The place took up the building's entire lower floor and smelled of fried foods and metal polish; a not-unpleasant combination. I was an hour late for lunch and two hours early for happy hour; right smack in the middle of that desperate slog seen by all bars that don't cater to professional alcoholics, but maybe should.

The front window was darkened by cheap tint that had bubbled up, dried, and cracked in too many places. Afternoon sunlight shot through a hazard of small pockmarks like bullet holes, dust motes dancing from one stingy beam to the next. Sidewall booths were dark and closed off this time of day. Dim spots fell on a long line of four-tops (empty), a dozen tables (one occupied by a local bruiser grabbing a quick bite before clocking in as the afternoon bouncer, another by a pair of cheap suits trying to fake a power lunch) and a bar of polished metal fronted by backless stools covered in fake neoleather.

One man sat at the bar, near the tender. Ignoring the silent flatscreen flashing highlights from last night's title match at the Factory. Watching me from between tall bottles fronting the glass barback.

I paused just opposite the table with the bruiser to see how much action he was looking for. Maybe one hundred sixty centimeters, but built like an AgroMech—wide and heavy with large shovels for hands.

He was halfway through what looked like a damn good burger, stacked high, with juices dripping off the back side into a pile of wedge-cut fries. He watched me, chewing carefully. Hesitated before taking another bite, then nodded and set his burger down on his plate. With those large hands spread flat against the table, he pushed himself to his feet, scooting his chair out with the back of his legs. He turned for the door, leaving behind his plate and a half-finished schooner that still had a decent head of foam.

Guy didn't know me. Didn't want to.

In the trade, we call that a *career decision*.

What trade? Well, that's not so easy to pin down. Not anymore. Before the Word of Blake lit Solaris VII (and a majority of the Inner Sphere) on fire, I was a low-rent mercenary with access to a higher class of weaponry than most in my price range. For a short time I was a public relations agent with a specialty for dealing with the local tongs. Then I spent several years in the hero business with Erik Gray, organizing and leading local resistance against the machine-whisperers. Not bad for an ex-dirt farmer, ex-Federated infantry. I guess it's fair to say I've always kept an eye open for *upward mobility*.

My business card says only: *Consultant*. Besides the fact that I *have* business cards these days, it's a nice catch-all that lets me sit in on management meetings at DeLon Stables, where I still oversee Erik Gray's mid-level career (among other special projects for Thomas DeLon himself) but isn't out of place when spreading hard coin and contact info among the alleys and shadier businesses of Solaris City.

Unhooking my amber-tinted Tacticals, I tucked them into my breast pocket. As I so often did when neither bullets nor lasers seemed high on the menu options, I wore a silver-gray sportscoat over a tight, midnight-black t-shirt and dark gray slacks. A Nakjama Profile rode shoulder holster, the small weapon making a discreet bulge for those who knew how to look, but I didn't expect to need it. More of a habit than anything else. Plus, it went with the sportscoat.

Some guys wear bowties.

With measured steps and hands very obviously in sight, I swung around the table with the cheap suits and approached the bar. The guy swiveled lightly on his barstool, like he was relaxed, but he had tense shoulders, and I'm not sure he'd blinked in the last minute.

I didn't feel like crowding him—not yet—so I chose a seat with two empty places between us. Not hostile, but not discouraging easy conversation either. He had late-thirties eyes, but wore a blousy, banded-collar peasant shirt and jeans, a gold chain bracelet, and bark-brown hair in a shaggy mop; all a generation too young for him. He had a highball (no ice) in front of him—hard, for so early in the afternoon. His left hand curled protectively around the glass. His right was balled into a fist.

Maybe he'd heard someone was poking around. I hoped so.

I'd paid extra for that.

"Timbiqui Pale, tall," I ordered from the barkeep as I slid onto my stool, sending him to the forest of taps. "And don't fruit it." It was the latest urban-professional craze, adding fruit garnishes to a variety of beers. I'm not part of the "UP" crowd, and never wanted to be.

Nodding at my neighbor through the barback's smoked glass, I offered, "How's it going?"

"It's a day," he replied. Not looking for conversation.

"Yeah. Been there." And I let my gaze wander just enough to seem maybe-harmless.

The Cracked Canopy boasted quite the selection of MechWarrior paraphernalia. Mostly—but not all—from the arena games, and nothing so pedestrian as signed glamor shots or quick-printed selfies. Mounted over the barback was a Kallon Industries autocannon in full casing that had JUSTIN XIANG stenciled on it with red crosshairs painted over the name; supposedly from Philip Capet's ill-fated *Rifleman*. On floating shelves sat a fire-scorched plushy giraffe, a drinking horn fashioned from the tusk of some impossibly large animal, a limited-edition resin figure of Natasha Kerensky (the hourglass-stenciled black tank-top gave it away), and what looked like a second-place rugby trophy. I also recognized a shoulder patch from Waco's Rangers and another from the Combine's First Sword of Light. A tattered banner of the original Blackstar Stables. A jack of spades playing card, ripped in half. A MechWarrior's right-hand pilot's glove with *ad astra per infernum* embroidered at the cuff. And sitting all alone on the barback, a glass presentation case containing a blue-steel star edged in red enamel, with a shield gold-etched in its center.

Everything came with a story. Some legendary. Some forgotten.

It was one of the forgotten stories—that jack of spades playing card—that had brought me here today.

"Impressive," I said to the barkeep as he served my pale. It had a medium head of foam, as any good pale should. Bonus points for not serving it in a frosted glass. I hate those. I sipped, and it was light and hoppy and left a nice, nutty aftertaste. "The collection, too."

He smiled with a connoisseur's pride. "Ya knows it." He had a strong Solaris Outback accent, but was playing it up for the bar's character. "Not gonna find like on Solaris VII."

"Do you know all the stories up there?"

He waggled his head back and forth. "More'n most. Not's many as Leo. He's eve-nins."

Leo Sullivan. Forty-two years, one-eighty centimeters, ninety-two kilos. The Cracked Canopy's general manager, and a reputation as a hard case. Wouldn't be on until five. Sedge, the usual day bartender, on his day off. The part-timer today was Jonathan. He could be pushed.

I do my homework.

I tried a deeper pull of the ale, enjoying its nutty flavor. With the instincts of good barkeeps everywhere, the guy hung around, maybe sensing I had another question.

"So how does a ripped playing card end up on the same wall as a Blue Star of Kerensky?" I asked, catching my neighbor raising his glass in the barback mirror. If you weren't watching for it, you might not notice the hitch in his motion, the double-sip of someone no longer tasting his drink.

I was. I did.

The barkeep grinned. This was a story he obviously thought he knew. "Ya knows what's a Free Worlds League Showdown?"

I chuckled. "Marik-head Poker? Sure. Everyone draws a single card and you 'tattoo' it to your forehead. You know all the cards in play but your own." I took another healthy drink. "You are *not* going to tell me someone won their BattleMech in a showdown, are you? I thought those stories were all urban legends."

He laughed. Swiped the counter with a fresh polish rag. "Nah. Not the BattleMech. But won his place on a ticket, he does."

I gave the barkeep a sort of half-shrug and a nod. All the encouragement he needs.

"Mebbe three years before the Word-a-Blake ruckus? Wanna-be named Mikhail Webb slicked his way inna the big game run by Miranda Li. Scooped up a decent pile, story goes, bettin' like he had nothin' ta lose. Risks it all in Showdown, drivin' everyone out but Everett Kincaid a' Kincaid Stables, and Kincaid's best up-a-comer, Jake Fabian."

"And Mikhail won on the jack?" I asked. I knew better, but a little social lubrication is rarely wasted.

"Nah. He folds onna seven-a-somethin'. But first he bluffs Fabian off that jack."

"Diamonds," the other guy at the bar whispered. Then he shook himself. "Sorry. I think it was the seven of diamonds. I heard."

"That's it," the barkeep said. "Fabian, he was short a' Mikhail's bet, so Mikhail challenges him ta put up his spot on Kincaid's next ticket. Was over a hunnerd grand on the table, better'n his guarantee, but Fabian, he folds."

"Which left Mikhail and Kincaid," I said, keeping up with the game and the story.

"Ya. Kincaid was bettin' hard on his ten-a-hearts. Raises with a promise he'll put uppa ticket. Mihail lays down his card. Never looks at it. Says he don't mind facing down another MechWarrior, but he's not gonna tell a stable owner what to do. Kincaid, after seeing Fabian woulda beat him if Mikhail hadn't bluffed him out, hands Mikhail that jack-a-spades and tells him to suit up Friday night."

My neighbor pushed aside his highball, still with a solid finger of amber left in the bottom. "I think that's it for me, Jon, if you wouldn't mind—"

"No, freshen his glass, on me," I said. When everyone hesitated: "I insist."

It isn't easy to sound reasonable and dangerous at the same time. It's a gift.

My new friend settles back, tilts a hand in surrender. Jonathan shrugs and pours a quick splash of barstock scotch. It smells like paint thinner, and I take a sip of my pale to mask the scent.

"Anyways," Jonathan continues. "Izza rivalry tween Mikhail and Fabian from that day, and the card becomes a prize. Over the next couple years, the jack trades back 'n forth four, mebbe five times. Then Word-a-Blake sets everythin' afire, Kincaid Stables self-destructs, and people lose track. Lotsa fighting. Lotsa chaos. And after? Lotsa finger-pointing."

I sipped again, but this time I didn't really taste my pale. My friend in the barback mirror is only pretending to drink, Jonathan is hedging, and this is usually where things start getting interesting—and why I didn't want that bruiser around.

"Sounds like only half of the story." To be fair, there *was* only half a playing card.

Jonathan wiped at the bar, but his heart wasn't in it. "Yah. Well. We gots rules. No pro-jihad souvenirs or stories. That jack-a-spades walks a line with Leo. But if'n we don't know..."

...you can't prosecute *or* persecute. Part of putting the Game World back together following the jihad's seven brutal years was letting go of that past. The lawyers called it *pro forma amnesty*. Solaris VII called it business as usual. After all, most stables were made up of warriors with a past, often with war records better left unpublished (check your old allegiances and former rivalries at the DropPort). Those who'd fought in support of Word of Blake's stupidity—or just got caught up in the moment—weren't eager to revisit those years. They were looking for quieter days.

Didn't mean they'd find it.

"Nobody's quoting Jerome Blake here." I checked my neighbor in the mirror. "Right?" He nodded. "So what's the rest?"

"I really shouldn't..." Jonathan began, and his gaze did a fast tour of the main floor. Looking for the evening bouncer? Worried that Leo Sullivan would make a sudden appearance?

I smiled. The barback mirror promised we still had time. "I insist."

It's easy to just sound dangerous. Doesn't take a lot of effort at all, really.

"Look. We really don't know. That jack traded hands at least once during those years. Mebbe more. So, like as not, either Jake Fabian or Mikhail Webb foughts for the Wobblies. And somewheres along the way, the card's used ta secure a debt with the yakuza. It got torn in half, to act like a key. The other half? It remained with one pilot or the other. But whenna dust settles, Jake Fabian resurfaces and gets picked up by Lion Stables. He shows up here one night. Buys a round for the house. Pays for it with halffa the jack."

"So Leo knows Mikhail Webb fought for the Word?"

"Knows it? Nah. But this is the Game World. Winner takes all. Word-a-Blake is gone. Jake Fabian's still here. Maybe the yakuza knows better, but they ain't talking. Not really their style."

"No," I agree. I know it all too well. "Not really." I swirled the last taste of my pale around the bottom of my glass. The last drink is never as good. Warm. Flat. I'd be better off ordering a second. But I hadn't come here looking for a drink.

"No one will ever know," my neighbor said. He tossed back a slug of the cheap scotch. "Not for sure."

The barkeep gave us both an exaggerated shrug. "Just Jake and Mikhail and whoever has the other halffa that jack-a-spades. Mebbe."

Maybe. So much possibility, wrapped up in such a little word. I set my glass onto the bar's polished metal. Gave it a distinct push to one side.

"Guess I should settle up," I offered, reaching into the lapel pocket of my sportscoat.

"Cash?" the barkeep asked.

"Card," I said.

And placed the lower half of the jack of spades on the polished metal surface.

My friend in the barback mirror slammed down his half-full highball, and the barkeep jumped at the shattering of heavy glass against the bar's bright metal. I scented the biting aroma of cheap scotch. Watched the cuts on his hand bleed drops of bright red into the amber pool. Dipping my left shoulder down and forward, I opened up my left breast lapel to make a crossbody draw *that* much easier. If I needed it.

If I was wrong.

Because Jonathan was correct. The Word of Blake's jihad had been seven years of chaos and madness. Warriors, sometimes entire factions, shifting sides with the political winds, or to settle old grudges. A small, personal rivalry? Who paid attention? Sure, the yakuza knew who had used the playing card as a key (Mikhail), but that deal had never been redeemed. It had also left those of us fighting the resistance holding the bag on a particularly nasty drop, costing several good lives.

Technically, with the top half of that jack, the yakuza could be pressured to settle up on the old deal, but the war was over, and I wasn't looking for *that* kind of trouble.

Had Mikhail Webb sandbagged us, or had circumstance prevented him from finishing the deal? I'm not saying that honoring an ongoing duel in the midst of the jihad was helpful (or bright) by any stretch, but very few had been lucky enough to come out of that time clinging to their honor by their fingernails. I'd make a terrible judge, and an even worse juror. I wasn't looking for that kind of trouble, either.

It was in his eyes for only a second. The shock, the anger, and then a flash of hope. I could work with that.

One thing I'm good at? Collecting debts.

My kind of trouble.

Jonathan threw several polish rags into the pool of spreading scotch, found a clean cloth to help wrap my barback friend's hand. He nodded at the ripped playing card still laying on the bar in between us. "Don't ya know what that's worth ta Leo?"

"Less than it's worth to Mikhail Webb," I said. "Even with my management fee."

The second card I drew from my inside lapel was my much more standard *Consultant* card. This I pushed over toward my new client, never losing eye contact in the barback mirror. Left it sitting in the vacant position next to me. From my breast pocket I pulled out my Tacticals, hooked them back over my ears. "DeLon Stables will have you on a ticket facing Jacob Fabian in three weeks," I promised him, sliding from the stool. "Suit up."

Yeah, there was more to the story of that jack of spades that needed telling. Much more. But it wasn't my place to tell it. I'd come into the Cracked Canopy ready for trouble, ready to believe the worst in people, and I was leaving with a new client. My second. Such a fine line between hypocrisy and hope. The razor's edge of opportunity, if you're willing to risk looking.

Doesn't always mean you'll find it.

Doesn't mean you can't.

PISTOLS: UP CLOSE AND PERSONAL

CRAIG A. REED, JR.

Pistols have been a part of military life for fifteen centuries and are the most common firearms in human existence. Ranging from one- or two-shot Derringers to overhyped Sternsacht, pistols are used by officers, special forces, vehicle crews, MechWarriors, aerospace fighter pilots, and both civilian and military police. Over time, these pistols will drift into the civilian market, either legally or illegally.

This article covers only a few of the pistols available, as numerous planets have their own pistol manufacturers and models, with little to distinguish themselves from the majority.

Note: All stats in this article are for *A Time of War* (AToW).

HCK P-14 (LYRAN COMMONWEALTH)

Called the "social general's popgun," the P-14 semiautomatic looks sleek and elegant, but is heavy, inaccurate, and has an anemic cartridge. Officially in service for only three years in the early thirtieth century, the P-14 is more a status symbol than an effective weapon. Over the years, owners have turned their P-14s into display pieces, giving them exotic wooden grips and inlaid gold leaf.

> **Equipment Rating:** C/X-D-D/C
> **AP/BD:** 2B/2
> **Range:** 5/15/35/70
> **Shots:** 8
> **Cost/Reload:** 130/5
> **Mass/Reload:** 1.2kg/40g
> **Notes:** Range modifiers: +0/-1/-3/-5; -2 to all repair rolls; jams on fumble.

STURM EAGLE MK4 (LYRAN COMMONWEALTH)

The MK4 is a solid service semiautomatic used by both LCAF soldiers and Commonwealth police. Reasonably accurate and reliable, the MK4 can be found everywhere in the Commonwealth. The pistol comes in two different variants. The MK4M is the military model, slightly longer and lighter than the MK4P, the police model. The MK4P has a built-in laser sight (+1 to all attack roll modifiers*).

MK4M
Equipment Rating: C/X-C-B/B
AP/BD: 4B/4
Range: 5/20/60/120
Shots: 12
Cost/Reload: 120/7
Mass/Reload: 1.2kg/10g
Notes: +1 to all repair rolls; range modifiers: +1/0/0/-1

MK4P
Equipment Rating: C/X-B-B/B
AP/BD: 4B/4
Range: 5/20/60/120
Shots: 12
Cost/Reload: 145/7
Mass/Reload: 1.3Kg/10g
Notes: +1 to all repair rolls; range modifiers (including laser sight*): +2/+1/+1/+0

*Requires Micro-Power Pack to function: uses 0.1 points per hour of continuous use.

WOLF M30 (FREE WORLDS LEAGUE)

The M30 is a common sidearm in Free World League Military units, and has been for a few hundred years. The current version, the M30T, varies little from older models, being only a few grams lighter, and square-notched rear sights allows accurate shooting in poor light. It is not uncommon for FWLM officers to carry the same M30 their grandparent did.

Equipment Rating: C/C-B-B/C
AP/BD: 4B/5
Range: 7/30/60/110
Shots: 17
Cost/Reload: 250/7
Mass/Reload: 950g/25g
Notes: +1 attack modifier in low light; range modifiers: +2/+1/0/-1

LEMISON COMBAT REVOLVER (FREE WORLDS LEAGUE)

Based on an ancient design, the Lemison has two barrels. Its eight-shot cylinder revolves around a separate central barrel that can be loaded with a single 51 mm shotgun shell. A lever next to the hammer allows the shooter to fire either the bullets or the shotgun round when the trigger is pulled. Considered a second-line weapon at best, the Lemison has its fans, though it is heavy for a pistol and somewhat tricky to repair.

Equipment Rating: C/X-C-B/B
AP/BD: 4B/5 (Shotgun: 2B/5S)
Range: 7/25/70/100 (Shotgun: 5/12/35/50)
Shots: 8 (1)
Cost/Reload: 120/7 (Shotgun: 5)
Mass/Reload: 1.6kg/25g
Notes: -2 to all repair rolls; Simple Action to change between pistol and shotgun mode; range modifiers: +0/+0/-1/-2 (Shotgun: +1/+0/-1/-2)

DREAMEL J-4 DERRINGER (FREE WORLDS LEAGUE)

Considered by many as a "gambler's pistol," the J-4 is a compact two-shot pistol that is easily concealable and amazingly accurate for its size. Having two triggers and a hammerless design, the J-4 can be easily drawn, and both rounds can be fired very quickly. Either kept in a vest pocket or on a sleeve rig, this pistol is designed to leave no telltale bulge and to pass through metal detectors.

Equipment Rating: C/B-C-B/B
AP/BD: 3B/4
Range: 3/6/12/24
Shots: 2
Cost/Reload: 60/5
Mass/Reload: 200g/1g
Notes: -2 to Perception Checks (Sound/Vision); +1 to Prestidigitation/Quickdraw Skill; range modifiers: +2/+1/0/-1

YĂNJÌNGSHÉ (CAPELLAN CONFEDERATION)

The *Yănjìngshé* (Cobra) pistol is issued only to senior CCAF officers and Death Commandos while on guard duty. The officers model is designed to be both functional and elegant, with the Confederation's insignia on the handgrips and the Chancellor's name engraved on the barrel. To lose such a pistol is considered a major disgrace. The ones issued to the Death Commandos are less ornate but otherwise identical.

> **Equipment Rating**: D/C-C-C/F
> **AP/BD**: 4B/5
> **Range:** 20/40/80/140
> **Shots:** 15
> **Cost/Reload:** 300/15
> **Mass/Reload**: 1kg/40g
> **Notes:** Range modifiers: +1/+0/+0/-1

TYPE 74 PISTOL (CAPELLAN CONFEDERATION)

The best word to describe the pistol most Confederation police forces use is "adequate." It isn't outstanding in any way. It is somewhat accurate, somewhat reliable, and has some stopping power. The 74P is used by uniformed officers, while the 74D is used by detectives. The 74D is smaller, lighter, and has a smaller magazine than the 74P model, but is easier to conceal and draw.

> **74P**
> **Equipment Rating**: D/C-C-C/E
> **AP/BD**: 4B/4
> **Range:** 15/35/75/115
> **Shots:** 14
> **Cost/Reload:** 150/7
> **Mass/Reload**: 800g/1g
> **Notes:** Range modifiers: +1/+1/+0/-1

> **74D**
> **Equipment Rating:** D/C-C-C/E
> **AP/BD:** 4B/4
> **Range:** 12/30/70/105
> **Shots:** 11
> **Cost/Reload:** 140/6
> **Mass/Reload:** 700g/15g
> **Notes:** +1 to Prestidigitation/Quickdraw Skill; range modifiers: +1/+0/-1/-1

MÒMÒ DE BÀOYÌNG (CAPELLAN CONFEDERATION)

The "Silent Retribution" is used solely by the Confederation's Death Commandos. Designed as a stealth weapon, the Retribution has a built-in sound/flash suppressor and a laser sight. Along with special ammo, the Retribution is solely an assassin's weapon, for those times when the Chancellor wishes to show their displeasure with someone. If anyone who is not a Death Commando is found with this pistol, they are immediately executed.

Equipment Rating: D/X-E-E/F
AP/BD: 4B/6 (Special ammo: 5B/6)
Range: 15/30/60/90
Shots: 10
Cost/Reload: 275/10 (Special ammo: 25)
Mass/Reload: 1.1 kg/10g
Notes: -2 to Perception Checks (Sound/Vision)**; range modifiers (including laser sight*): +3/+2/+1/+0

*Requires Micro-Power Pack to function: uses 0.1 points per hour of continuous use.
**Regular ammo. If special ammo is used, replace the -2 with -3 to Perception Checks (Sound/Vision).

RFW GALAHAD (FEDERATED SUNS)

The Galahad is a common sidearm in the Draconis March. A large, heavy pistol that fires 11.5mm rounds, the Galahad is designed to be hard-hitting and rugged. Called the "Lead Pipe" by its detractors, it is legendary for its toughness under extreme conditions and its usability as both a pistol and an improvised melee weapon.

Equipment Rating: D/C-C-C/C
AP/BD: 3B/6 (1M/3)
Range: 25/45/90/125 (1M)
Shots: 10
Cost/Reload: 200/20
Mass/Reload: 2.1 kg/50g
Notes: +2 to all repair rolls; -1 to all melee attack rolls; range modifiers: +2/+1/+0/-1

SERREK 7994 (FEDERATED SUNS)

All models in the 7994 series can fire either a single round or a three-round burst with a pull of the trigger. With an extended barrel/muzzle brake and a foldable foregrip, the 7994 has little recoil when firing multiple rounds. The SF model is a common sidearm among AFFS special forces, and they are modified with a longer barrel, sound/flash suppressor, and a laser sight. 7994 SF models are not for sale in the civilian market, though some gunsmiths will make the modifications, for a price. The Raven Alliance manufactures 7994s under license for the Alliance police forces.

7994
Equipment Rating: C/X-C-B/C
AP/BD: 3B/3
Range: 20/40/80/140
Shots: 20
Cost/Reload: 300/15
Mass/Reload: 900g/40g
Notes: Burst: 3, Recoil: +0. Simple Action to change between single-shot and burst modes. Range modifiers: +1/+0/+0/-1

7994 SF
Equipment Rating: C/X-D-C/C
AP/BD: 3B/3
Range: 25/50/95/160
Shots: 20
Cost/Reload: 400/15
Mass/Reload: 1.1g/40g
Notes: Burst: 3, Recoil: +0. Simple Action to change between single-shot and burst modes. -2 to Perception Checks (Sound/Vision). Range modifiers (including laser sight*): +2/+1/+1/+0

*Requires Micro-Power Pack to function: uses 0.1 points per hour of continuous use.

AA GEMINI (FEDERATED SUNS)

An unusual design, the Gemini features twin barrels, triggers, magazines, and hammers, set up side by side and built so the shooter can fire each barrel singly or both barrels at the same time. The Gemini has a high learning curve for a novice shooter, but is effective and easy to manage for an expert.

Equipment Rating: D/C-C-C/C
AP/BD: 4B/5 (If both barrels fired at same time, 4B/10)
Range: 20/40/80/150
Shots: 8x2
Cost/Reload: 400/40
Mass/Reload: 1.5kg/100g
Notes: If Small Arms Skill is less than 3, -1 to attack roll; If Small Arms Skill is greater than 3, +1 to attack roll. If firing both barrels and attack roll is successful, both rounds hit the same target location. If the attack roll fails, both rounds miss. Range modifiers: +2/+1/+0/-1

NAMBU 380 AND 480 SERIES (DRACONIS COMBINE)

The 380 series is used by the DCMS, while the 480 series is the sidearm used by most Civilian Guidance Corps detectives. Designed to be manufactured with simple parts and as low a tech base as possible, the 380 and 480 are adequate sidearms. The 480 series is somewhat smaller and lighter than the 380, but has less range and a smaller magazine. Also, the 480 series has a barrel-mounted flashlight, while the 380 series has a laser sight.

NAMBU 380
Equipment Rating: C/D-D-D/F
AP/BD: 3B/4
Range: 30/50/75/120
Shots: 18
Cost/Reload: 350/20
Mass/Reload: 950g/40g
Notes: Range modifiers (including laser sight*): +2/+1/+1/+0

*Requires Micro-Power Pack to function: uses 0.1 points per hour of continuous use.

NAMBU 480
Equipment Rating: C/C-C-C/F
AP/BD: 3B/4
Range: 25/40/60/100
Shots: 14
Cost/Reload: 350/20
Mass/Reload: 800g/40g
Notes: Barrel-mounted flashlight (negates darkness modifiers up to 15m*). Range modifiers: +1/+0/+0/-1

*Requires Micro-Power Pack to function: uses 0.1 points per hour of continuous use.

MPH-45 (DRACONIS COMBINE)

Issued only to a few senior officers and selected members of the Coordinator's staff, the MPH-45 is designed and built as a highly effective work of art. Each one is assembled by hand, and to possess one is considered a mark of the Coordinator's favor. The pistol is highly accurate even without the integrated laser sight, and has exceptional stopping power.

Equipment Rating: D/X-X-E/F
AP/BD: 5B/4
Range: 40/65/105/140
Shots: 10

Cost/Reload: 500/30
Mass/Reload: 1kg/50g
Notes: Range modifiers (including laser sight*): +4/+3/+2/+1

* Requires Micro-Power Pack to function: uses 0.1 points per hour
  of continuous use.

CAMDEN HR-7
(TAURIAN CONCORDAT/CALDERON PROTECTORATE)

This massive revolver was designed for big-game hunters, with an integrated telescopic sight and long barrel. It is heavy, and an inexperienced shooter is liable to injure both themselves and their target when firing this gun. Broken wrists and concussions due to inexperience are common, and Camden recommends it only for experienced shooters with sufficient upper body strength. In the hands of someone who knows how to use it, the HR-7 is an exceptional firearm, able to bring down large prey. Oddly enough, the pistol has become a favorite sidearm of Snow Raven Elementals.

Equipment Rating: C/C-C-C/A
AP/BD: 5B/5
Range: 40/80/100/150
Shots: 5
Cost/Reload: 650/15
Mass/Reload: 2.5kg/50g
Notes: Minimum STR 5 to use two-handed; minimum STR 7 to use one-handed. -1 to attack roll for each point below STR minimum. On a fumble, or if firing while below the STR minimum, shooter takes 2M/3 damage. Range modifiers (including telescopic sight): +1/+2/+2/+0

ALAMO-17 (TAURIAN CONCORDAT/CALDERON PROTECTORATE)

The Alamo series of handguns are the most common handguns in both the Taurian Concordat and Calderon Protectorate. They can be found in military, police, and civilian hands. The only difference between the various models is personal choices about accessories: the Alamo can be equipped with either a laser sight or a barrel-mounted flashlight.

Equipment Rating: C/A-A-A/A
AP/BD: 4B/4
Range: 30/55/95/130
Shots: 18
Cost/Reload: 250/15
Mass/Reload: 1kg/40g
Notes: Range modifiers: +1/+0/+0/-1

WHISPER-4 (MAGISTRACY OF CANOPUS)

Built for and used exclusively by the Magistracy Intelligence Ministry, the Whisper is a pure assassin's weapon. With an integrated laser sight and flash suppressor, the Whisper is designed to be lethal, accurate, and silent. The biggest drawback is the small magazine, but this pistol is not designed for extended use in an active combat situation. The Whisper normally loads subsonic rounds, but it can use standard-velocity rounds if the situation calls for it.

Equipment Rating: D/E-E-E/E
AP/BD: 5B/4 (Subsonic rounds: 3B/3, -1 Perception Check to hear shot)
Range: 25/45/90/120 (Subsonic rounds: 13/23/45/60)
Shots: 6
Cost/Reload: 650/25
Mass/Reload: 1.2kg/50g
Notes: -4 to Perception Checks (Sound/Vision). Range modifiers (including laser sight*): +3/+3/+2/+1

*Requires Micro-Power Pack to function: uses 0.1 points per hour of continuous use.

DOC BENS

DAVID SMITH

FORTRESS-CLASS DROPSHIP FSS *ARTEMIS*
PLANETARY ORBIT, NOUVEAU TOULOUSE
FEDERATED SUNS
9 NOVEMBER 2790
T-MINUS 7 HOURS 32 MINUTES TO PLANETARY BARRAGE

Admiral Merris was about to enjoy his coffee when the main viewer suggested only despair. The upper orbit of Nouveau Toulouse IV was littered with Combine DropShips. Vector lines and targets sorted the enemy fleet, lighting up the main bridge screen like a complex circuit.

"How many?" Captain Howard asked.

An ensign scanned cycling data. "Two hundred thirty-eight DropShips...240,762 fighters and bombers. Two hundred fourteen are bombers."

Merris set his coffee down. He had lost.

A JumpShip ferrying six more DropShips for the Federated Suns jolted into position at its selected pirate point, adding to his fleet of thirty-eight, but they would never make it in time. Merris' DropShip led the puny fleet into position above the planet. He didn't bother to deploy fighters.

"We need to bug out...head back to our JumpShips. Just get the hell out." Howard was dressed neatly in command blues, scrubbed, ironed, and attentive.

Merris stared at the impossible odds on the viewer. *That's what they want,* he thought. A sane commander would simply retreat.

Instead, he breathed in. "Keep our position." Merris looked weary, with a bushy salt-and-pepper mustache. He brushed it with his hand as he thought.

"If we stay, we are as good as dead," Howard said.

"I have contingency orders." Merris said it like a death sentence.

Howard looked the man over, soberly. His mouth moved, but not what he wanted it to say, "All DropShips, form up in echelon formation. Repeat, all DropShips. Fighter escorts deploy. Await further orders."

"Aye, sir." The bridge was absolutely quiet except for fingers tapping on keyboards.

"What's happening on the surface?" Merris kept himself calm. "At New Light?"

A comm officer repositioned her monitor and scrolled through tabs, zooming into ground video. Smoke and laser fire filled the screen. The video was mute and mostly pixelated. "Intense fighting, sir, about three battalions of Combine forces are moving in. We have...less than one battalion at New Light."

Another comm officer piped in, "All six factory cities are under heavy fire. Our forces are outnumbered two to one. More Combine DropShips are reinforcing, five to one."

"How about Doc Bens?" Merris asked, "Is he still alive?"

"Searching, sir." There was a long pause. "Searching."

"We're being hailed, sir. Channel eighty-one, command priority alpha one. Colonel Paul Bens."

Merris grimaced. "Don't respond."

The radio popped and squealed. "Federated Suns Relief Fleet, respond." Static blared and echoed. "Federated Suns Relief Fleet, respond, goddammit!"

"Don't."

Howard watched the data cycle. "The Drac fleet is holding position."

"They're waiting for us to retreat," Merris said.

Deafening feedback screeched at them. The comm officer softened it.

"Federated Suns Relief Fleet, respond." Static. "Federated Suns Relief Fleet, respond."

Merris put a hand to his forehead and sighed.

"Who's up there? Rymei? Merris? If it's you, Merris, you owe me! Respond. It's you, isn't it, Merris? It's got to be. Respond!"

"Put me through," Merris said. He waited for the connection. "This is Merris."

"About bloody time! I'm sending drop coordinates." Doc's voice was raspy from yelling and screaming.

"We were having comm trouble—"

"Don't give me that line, Merris! Just drop those 'Mechs at my coordinates. We've got this!"

"Well...we're awaiting confirmation from Command. We've lost, Colonel."

"What? What?! Where's Rymei? Is he up there? Get me Rymei!"

"It's just me, Paul. We've lost."

"Drop at my coordinates. We still have a chance!"

For years, Paul Bens had been fortifying bottlenecks at each factory city to stand against overwhelming forces. He just needed to exhaust the Kurita forces to a costly withdrawal. What Doc hadn't planned for was the immensity of the fleet in orbit that could hammer him with waves of reinforcements after easily dispatching the smaller FedSuns fleet.

What the Combine hadn't counted on was the inhuman tenacity of Doc Bens.

An explosion and loud static cut in. "You'll be a hero, Merris," Doc Bens continued. "You know that's what you want. We just need to hold New Light." Distracted, he yelled, "Focus fire on that *Archer*! You got 'em! Fire! Take 'em! Hell, yeah!" A few seconds later he said, "Look, Admiral. They won't even remember me, but you...the savior of Nouveau Toulouse, bucking orders in a desperate gamble with a brilliant ground strategy that was too costly for the Combine... I've been planning this for years. I know how we are going to win this." A sharp *bang* and static stung the ears of the bridge crew, then, "Sonova—" Another loud explosion. Paul regained the comm. "I can't lose! That's why you put me here. Now *drop*!"

Doc Bens is right, Merris thought. He was a tactical genius and a charismatic leader. He led the Eighth Avalon Hussars' Second Battalion before serving as professor of military strategy at Albion Military Academy. He then switched to Sakhara Academy because he was too... *abrasive.* He preferred Sakhara for its emphasis on duty and personal honor, and his second wife Casandra preferred the people. He held a doctorate in military history, hence the nickname. He had enough field decorations to lead any kind of 'Mech combat training. Doc thrived and shook the chain of command; he had *opinions.*

He had served tirelessly until Cassie's unexpected death. Mourning had stoked his political irritations into flippant political criticism, which resulted in his political assassination by powerful cowards. Doc Bens was an anomaly, too talented to set to pasture, but too charismatic to keep visible—he was practically a cult leader.

Merris himself had offered Nouveau Toulouse to Paul. He would lead a regional training battalion away from the rhetoric on a semi-quiet world known for its manufacturing, and essential due to its proximity to Combine space. He was so successful that his single battalion grew to three, enabling the original veteran defense force, the Second Avalon Hussars, to be redeployed to other conflicts. Eventually, these three regional training battalions were renamed Doc's Scorpions.

No doubt Bens has likely rallied the whole defense force into a perfect, obedient machine, Merris thought. Paul Bens earned respect by tirelessly devoting himself to his soldiers and usually putting himself in the greatest danger first, the opposite of a typical military politician. He inspired his men to their deaths in a real, thankful dignity. That was why Command feared him. That was why he was stationed at Nouveau Toulouse IV. He was too good for his own good because he was envied.

Merris had served under him at New Avalon. Doc Bens was like a father. Hell, Bens treated him better than his real father... If anyone could achieve victory against incredible odds, it was Doc Bens. But like a father, Paul's opinionated shouting caused political embarrassment for Merris, which almost cost him his career. Merris had brooded about it over the years; Paul was right about his former accusations, truthful, but too idealistic. But Merris wasn't ready to throw his life away. The odds were too great. He lacked the patriotism, the will. He had a family on New Avalon, a life.

Merris kept silent.

"You're not going to give in to that psycho, are you?" Howard blurted.

"Oh? No. Of course not." Merris straightened his jacket. "Paul. We are still waiting on Command for the final word."

"You know what to do! Drop at my coordinates." A final crackle and sputter ended the conversation.

Howard watched Merris pace a bit, "What now, sir?"

"We wait for our final orders."

NEW LIGHT CITY
NOUVEAU TOULOUSE
FEDERATED SUNS
9 NOVEMBER 2790
T-MINUS 7 HOURS 2 MINUTES TO PLANETARY BARRAGE

Doc's head shook in his neurohelmet from a nearby blast that rocked his 'Mech, an *Awesome* 8Q. Sweat ran down the lines on his face and around a thin white goatee. His helmet was newer and painted with a laughing mouth with cobra fangs. His body was athletic for his age, shaved, dressed in biker shorts and combat boots. A wide, faded tattoo of a soaring crow flexed on his chest with each jerk of his control sticks. Under the wings, the tattoo read: *Live to Die! Scorpions*. He preferred the upstart crow image, but scorpions were more typical of the desert regions of the planet, and more deadly.

Doc's massive *Awesome* raised its arm-mounted particle projection cannon to fire a crackling lightning blast at a jumping *Griffin*. The forest-green 'Mech was hit dead in the torso, shedding armor and internal chunks in a blast of smoke and electricity. As the *Griffin* touched down, the weight of the collapsing torso tore through its pelvis and it hit the ground in a roaring black cloud. Doc's *Awesome* and his command lance ran past the downed 'Mech.

Beside Doc ran his leftenant, Rick Adams, in an *Atlas*. Running for an assault 'Mech was not that fast, but it kept moving and raining fire on enemies ahead. Rick kept to himself outside of battles, and before today, that was years of practical solitude. He talked to Doc all the time though, for orders and direction. Doc liked Rick. Rick was dedicated, focused, and dependable. Rick was curt around others and everyone called him Richard behind his back because he hated it—everyone, except Doc's command lance. They appreciated him for what he was: a professional killer, none his equal except the Doc.

Ahead of Rick ran Alex Kunze in his lighter *Archer* 2R. Alex fired three medium lasers at a sprinting *Wasp*. Two shots missed their intended target of the chest, but instead cleaved the head straight off, throwing the *Wasp*'s body to the ground in a heap.

The final MechWarrior, Rob Trent, trampled the lifeless *Wasp* in his charging *Warhammer*. The heavy 'Mech slipped on the robotic corpse, but recovered after a slight misstep and a loud *crunch*. Like the rest of his lance, Rob's 'Mech was painted in sun-bleached khaki with wavy strips of dark red. A black scorpion, outlined in white, rested on a thick red chevron on the 'Mech's lower leg, the emblem for Doc's Scorpions.

Doc's command lance continued down a corridor of burning industrial buildings in the planet's capital, New Light. Remaining civilians were mostly packed into APCs and troop transports, waiting anxiously in armored parking garages, ready to evacuate. Doc and his troops needed to thin the attack force, or the transports would be sitting ducks for the Combine. Doc was keeping the Draconis forces busy until his reinforcements would arrive, and it was working.

Doc's Scorpions had been drilling for this anticipated conflict since Kerensky's Exodus. Nouveau Toulouse was valuable and vulnerable: valuable for its six specialized 'Mech and weapons factories, vulnerable for its remote location near the Kurita border. The last four years of planning and training had consumed Paul Bens. In fact, he had expected this invasion last year. He was surprised it had taken the Combine so long to attack this low-hanging fruit.

But so far so good, he thought. The battle was going as predicted, with just a few more casualties than expected. Doc just needed those reinforcements. His three battalions were dispersed across the city: one under his command, and the other two optimally split between the other five city factories. New Light would see the heaviest fighting. That's why he led the battle. Other Albion instructors would reluctantly confess that Doc was practically an assault lance unto himself.

Almost instinctually, Rick targeted a distant *Longbow*, firing a salvo of long-range missiles. In sync with Rick, Doc fired two of his PPCs. Rob and Alex added their own fire as well. The *Longbow* was pelted with missiles and energy blasts while targeting another FedSuns lance with its own alpha strike. The Combine 'Mech staggered in plumes of flame, limping behind a hill before one of its missile pods tore loose.

"Great work, men." Doc kept his eyes ahead of him, approaching another enemy lance.

A squawk of the radio sounded. Chic Mattson spoke over garbled static, "Doc. We're outnumbered at Factory Two. They're targeting our DropShip. They're gonna take it! I'm down two companies. I need more 'Mechs."

Paul didn't take his eyes off his targeting reticles. His command lance was blasting an enemy medium lance. Two Combine *Shadow Hawks* were targeting New Light's *Union*-class DropShip *Amanda 4*, mostly its defense weapons. This alerted Paul. *Why would they destroy our DropShips? They're too costly to destroy intentionally and a much better captured asset. A diversion?* "Okay, Mattson. I'll send Javi's Company."

"I need *two* at least."

"Christy, what are their numbers?"

Christy sprinted her *Locust* around the perimeter of New Light with her recon lance. Her 'Mech's titanium chicken legs sped through a hillside, kicking up turf and rock in her wake. "Twenty inside." She meant enemy 'Mechs in the city. "And only a support lance outside with a fracked *Longbow*. Nothing else, currently. Three *Overlord* DropShips inbound, but we have a good twenty minutes before they deploy."

"Thanks, Christy. Keep it up."

Christy snorted. "Hey, don't we have reinforcements coming? Where are they?"

"I'm on it."

"I need more than Javi!" Chic whined.

"All right. Javi and Emerald Companies, join up with Mattson at Factory Two."

"You sure, Doc?" Javi didn't want to leave the Doc shorthanded.

"We got this, Doc!" Rick piped in.

Rick had never called Paul "Doc." He was always stiff and formal, respectful. Was Rick loosening up in his enthusiasm, or had he let it slip due to fear? Was it the fear of inevitable death that brushed aside formality? The Scorpions had held so far, but without FedSuns reinforcements, they would be overrun soon. Even with the reinforcements, they would still be terribly outgunned...

Instinct took over his thought process. "Hell yeah, we got this! Live to die, Scorpions!"

The comm erupted from his pilots: "Live to die! Hell yeah!" All except Mattson.

"Wren Company, remain at Nav Three. Enemy 'Mechs inbound."

Both Javi and Emi affirmed their orders and their respective 'Mech companies sprinted toward Factory Two.

Combine lances broke through a building perimeter and rushed toward Wren Company. A chaos of ordnance fired between 'Mechs. Concrete and asphalt blew like confetti until black smoke concealed it.

Paul hit his comm. "Merris, Relief Fleet, over?"

An ensign replied, "We have you, Colonel."
"Merris, have you heard from Command?"

FSS *ARTEMIS*

Merris was hunched over a terminal. "No word yet."

"Just send them, Merris. We don't have any time left. Chic is under heavy fire. We're losing assets."

"We can't win this, Paul. We're outgunned six to one. The Dracs have us. We're done." Merris winced, thinking he likely sounded more like a recruit than an admiral. "They aren't firing on us. They're waiting. If we act, we're dead."

"We can do this. It'll be costly for them. They don't have the stomach for it."

"It's six to one *now*!"

"I can win this! Did you look at my drop points? My numbers?"

"They're bold, Paul. Risky."

"But we can do it!"

"I'm... I'm still waiting on Command." Merris glared at his comm officer to disconnect.

NEW LIGHT CITY

Paul's *Awesome* crunched through a smoldering Manticore tank and paced around a corner with his command lance, cursing under his breath. His targeting screen lit up: an enemy lance was closing. Paul pushed through a plume of smoke. "Got a visual?"

Alex had it. "Assault 'Mechs, *Thugs*...four of them."

The four 80-ton 'Mechs smashed through broken buildings, raining glass, ferrocrete chunks, and twisted frames of metal. Each one was delicately illustrated with crimson and gold dragons on jade paneling. One *Thug* had obsidian paneling with a shimmering jade "helmet" and "gloves." They seemed too costly to risk in a battle, too immaculate and priceless.

"Oh. Royalty," Doc said. "Focus, fire boys. Crush their command."

Alex fired a volley of forty long-range missiles at the lance. Smoke blew from his *Archer*'s exhaust ports as Doc's lance exchanged PPC fire with the charging *Thugs*. The missiles pounded one of the *Thugs*, nearly toppling it, but it corrected its gait and continued.

Doc's *Awesome* took a couple hits to its torso, which resembled a giant apartment building more than a robotic chest. The blasts pushed the 'Mech back a step, with sparks and armor fragments spitting from the wound. Doc fired all three of his PPCs, all connecting on the center enemy 'Mech.

Alex, Rick, and Rob fired everything at the rushing lance in one glorious alpha strike as they paced through broken buildings. A storm of missiles and lasers lit the sky in fire and light, slamming the enemy 'Mechs. The center jade *Thug* ignited in flame and crumpled into molten slag. The pilot ejected from the shattered 'Mech "helmet" in a spear of flame

The return salvo of PPC fire blew the right arm off Rob's *Warhammer*. His right torso was also ravaged, but his armor absorbed it. The *Warhammer* lost its balance and smashed into an adjacent building, crushing it like a paper bag. The interior structure caught Rob's 'Mech enough for him to regain his footing and spin around to return fire. What was left of his armor paneling simply dropped off when he fired a volley of short-range missiles. Only a couple missiles connected, but it covered him enough to keep moving.

A second Combine *Thug* took heavy PPC fire from Doc. Its right arm was blasted off, and a direct hit to the torso would have caused an internal explosion if it hadn't had CASE. The enormous arm slammed to the ground, crushing a nearby hatchback like aluminum. Paul aimed and fired a double shot again, not too concerned about the rising heat his 'Mech was generating just yet.

Doc's men and the Combine command 'Mechs ducked and weaved through buildings, circling and taking shots of opportunity. Rick's *Atlas* fired everything at a wounded jade *Thug,* but it was the blast of his heavy Defiance 'Mech Hunter autocannon that punched it through a building, finishing it off with a ridiculous cartoon-like hole through the chest. An ejection seat shot out, but it collided with a floor of a broken building, ricocheted, and thudded onto concrete.

"Keep firing. We have them!" Paul was aiming and firing through debris and bent light poles. "Rob, get up!" He knew Rob was up; it was more of poorly timed joke than a command.

Paul nearly skidded on debris of a flattened building as he was lining up a shot, but he kept his pace. The Combine pilots were agile for assault 'Mechs, but not experienced. Perhaps they were sons of dukes or counts, allowed to play war and gain experience at killing in a controlled game. Perhaps pride kept them from waiting until they had two more battalions in front of them to soften their targets. The possibility of this bravery gave Paul a bit of respect for them, but they were no match for his veteran lance, and he would show them no mercy.

The remaining two *Thugs* ducked behind ruined buildings. Alex was cooling down his weapons while maneuvering for a better shot. His targeting system showed the Combine 'Mechs gaining distance. "They're falling back."

"Wren, you have two assault 'Mechs incoming. Give them hell," Paul said.

"Those enemy DropShips are landing," Christy's voice cut in. "Battalions incoming. I don't see our forces in the sky yet. Tell me something good, Doc."

"Keep running, Christy. Wren, get dug in. We can't count on Merris. He's not going to drop. He's a coward. He's willing to give this planet to the Dracs. But we're not going to give it to them."

"No, sir."

"We will protect *Amanda 4* and get as many civilians and MechWarriors on board to escape."

"Yes, sir. You can count on us, Doc."

"Christy, observe the enemy's routes into the city and fall back to my position when they get within two klicks. Your squad will be the first to board the DropShip."

"We can back you up, Doc, with hit and run attacks—"

"You will be the first. We will cover you."

"Okay." Christy said with disappointment. Christy was in her thirties, experienced and dedicated. She often shared Doc's stubborn resolve to do what was *right*. She was old enough to be his daughter if he'd had one. He was proud of her. But her heroic self-sacrificing talk was starting to piss him off.

T-MINUS 5 HOURS 37 MINUTES TO PLANETARY BARRAGE

"Engaging assault 'Mechs," Wren cut in.

Wren's command lance consisted of two *Griffins*, one *Wolverine*, and one *Shadow Hawk.* All were medium 'Mechs with jump capability and waiting on top of three buildings in sniper positions. Both enemy *Thugs*, jade and obsidian, entered long range and fired their PPCs at the snipers. Two shots hit the building, and two connected with the *Shadow Hawk*, nearly shoving it off the roof in an explosion of blinding light.

"Focus fire, the left one!" Both *Griffins* fired their PPCs along with autocannon and missile shots from the others. The jade *Thug* slowed and shed burning armor. The obsidian *Thug* maneuvered in front of the damaged 'Mech to shield it.

"See that? Keep firing on the damaged one!" Wren kept firing. His lance was taking devastating hits from short-range missile and PPC fire. The buildings were shaking around him and the *Shadow Hawk*'s building collapsed in smoke and debris. The *Wolverine* was lost in a plume of dust and ash.

"Jace?!" Wren called to the *Shadow Hawk*. There was no reply. "Keep firing!" he ordered the others.

Both Combine 'Mechs smashed into Wren's building, still firing missiles and PPCs at his lance. The damaged jade *Thug* was caught in the collapsing building, weakened by missile and laser fire. The Combine pilot ejected in a bright plume of rocket thrust.

Wren and his fellow *Griffin* hit their jump jets when their building disintegrated underneath them. Both landed slowly near the remaining obsidian 'Mech. It punched off the second *Griffin*'s leg at the knee with a calculated hit. The *Griffin* stumbled and smashed into asphalt, but Wren fired his rifle-shaped PPC at the *Thug*, causing it to evade to cover.

Wren's *Wolverine* pilot, Eddy, emerged on foot from a collapsed building, running and coughing. "Sorry, Commander!" he radioed.

"Maybe we can dig you out," Wren said. He watched his fellow *Griffin* steady itself into a kneeling position, ready to fight.

"Not a chance."

"Get ready for another attack!" Wren was watching the blip that was the remaining obsidian *Thug*. It was blinking away from their position. Dozens of new blips lit the circumference of his tac display... enemy reinforcements. The *Thug* blip faded and ceased.

"They ran away!" Wren said in disbelief, just as a volley of missiles rained down on them, igniting the whole street in pounding explosions.

Paul's voice reverberated. "Fall back to my position. Nav One."

"Two battalions of Dracs are on us! I'm falling back to you!" Christy sounded shrill and panicked. "The third Drac DropShip reinforced at Factory Two, but six more are inbound."

"Wren and Christy, get over here. Civilians are already boarding. We'll cover them and get the hell out of here. Christy will board first."

"They've got air support!" Christy reported.

"Just get back here!"

Wren took to his comm. "Wren Company, fall back to *Amanda 4*."

His other two lances emerged through dust and flame, having dispatched a Kurita recon lance.

T-MINUS 3 HOURS 16 MINUTES TO PLANETARY BARRAGE

Doc had just positioned his command lance around the giant spheroid DropShip *Amanda 4* when enemy missiles pelted them. A line of APCs and transports entering the DropShip were hit, throwing a supply truck like a toy, smashing it into another truck on its flank.

"Focus on those *Longbow*s on that ridge at two o'clock," Paul ordered.

Rick fired a salvo of twenty long-range missiles from his *Atlas* to combine with Alex's double volley from his *Archer*. The missiles joined the hazy sky of explosions and tracer rounds.

"We're falling back to you, Paul." It sounded like Chic.

"Who? Is that Chic?"

"Yes. We're falling back to your position."

"Negative, Mattson. Secure your DropShip. We're getting out of here. We're evacuating."

"It's *gone*, Paul. It's wrecked. We're falling back."

"What the hell are you talking about? Get Javi and Emi on the comm."

"They're *gone*. Everything is fracked!"

Paul aimed and sniped at approaching Combine 'Mechs. Missiles exploded on his *Awesome*, but he shrugged it off.

Christy's recon lance arrived and ran circles around the convoy, dodging enemy fire and taking opportunity shots at approaching 'Mechs. Paul couldn't even greet her, he was too busy with Chic. "Where's Javi and Emi?"

"They're *dead*, Paul! Half my unit is wiped!"

"You got them killed?!" Paul's mouth spit when he said it.

"We're approaching your position."

FSS *ARTEMIS*
T-MINUS 1 HOUR 17 MINUTES TO PLANETARY BARRAGE

In low orbit, Merris entered the bridge and stepped toward Howard. A huge, centered tactical display showed the position of the 200-plus enemy DropShips and their own thirty-eight. Merris' fleet was not surrounded, but instead faced an enormous wedge of enemy DropShips.

Six additional friendly DropShips from the planet had positioned themselves behind Merris' force. These carried civilians and equipment, typically for 'Mech redeployment, and had launched before the invasion. Enemy fighter wings flew between them, but did not attack yet.

"You received word?" Howard asked. "Are we getting the hell out of here?"

"Yes." Merris was somber. "We are ordered to bomb the factories to keep them from Combine hands. *Then* we are getting the hell out of here."

"So...Doc? We're leaving him and the civilians?"

"He has a couple of DropShips. They can evacuate."

"One, sir. Chic lost his."

Merris' face turned white. He exhaled. "They'll have to make do. Paul knows what to do."

Howard and Merris held eye contact, considering their course of action, their crime.

Merris broke the silence. "Ready AMW warheads. Target all six factories. Prepare for evasive maneuvers the instant we launch. We'll make a break for the JumpShips. Comm, hail our JumpShips."

NEW LIGHT CITY
T-MINUS 41 MINUTES TO PLANETARY BARRAGE

Paul's lance was pounded by missile and autocannon fire, but they stood their ground at *Amanda 4*, which was unloading its own massive amounts of defensive fire to help cover the defending 'Mechs.

Rick's *Atlas* had lost most of its armor in its torso, exposing internal components and myomer. He fired his ordnance carelessly in an attempt to deny the enemy a gratuitous ammo explosion. The assault 'Mech had also taken a direct hit to its right hip actuator, so Rick was circling even slower than normal around craters and broken-up roads.

Alex's *Archer* had taken some heavy armor damage, and his left arm was gone. Rob's *Warhammer* had taken considerable damage as well, with both arm cannons lost and most of his torso armor stripped clean. He had dumped his machine gun ammo to avoid a critical explosion and kept fighting, still able to fight at close range.

Wren still had his *Griffin* with minimal damage, and his fellow *Griffin* kept to a kneeling rifle position.

Christy's recon lance was mostly unharmed. She had taken some damage to the center torso of her *Locust,* but her accompanying *Locust* and two *Wasp*s had only armor damage, and were weaving in and out of the city ruins around the DropShip.

Paul counted ten green blips for his 'Mechs, but thirty-plus enemies closing in. Four other enemy DropShips were unloading their units outside of the city, unopposed. It was only a matter of time now. *Perhaps Chic could provide some much-needed relief…*

What remained of his third battalion was falling back via APCs, losing 'Mechs to protect civilians and ground personnel. They were supposed to rendezvous with *Amanda 5*, Chic's DropShip, but it was gone now. Perhaps they could make it to *Amanda 4*. They had done their part. They were isolated at Factories Five and Six, and their losses were expected.

"*Amanda 4* is taking damage," Christy reported.

"You're next, Christy," Paul said. "Board your lance."

He had lost over half of his civilian evacuees so far. The Combine forces were too aggressive and held little value for noncombatants. Despite fighting and coordinating the battle, Paul's conscience found a moment to blame him for their deaths. "We're out of time. We need to evacuate."

"Chic will have civilians with him. Shouldn't they have priority?"

Christy was right. Paul hated to admit it. He didn't want to lose anyone else. He had lost too many of his own troops already…and it was his duty to protect the people and his fighters knew it, Christy knew it.

"Okay, Christy. You're right. Let's cover them when they arrive. We have to keep the enemy off their backs. We don't have room for

'Mechs, but we'll squeeze in as many APCs and people as we can. We have to do better."

There will only be room for those civilians, Paul thought. His team would perish defending them. He hated the thought, it angered him. Not all of the civilians would survive to get on board either. There would be a pinch of room, though. He would order Christy to board. *She could make it.*

The thought energized him, gave him a little hope; he fought fiercer. The enemy was on them, showering them in death. He could barely think as his 'Mech throttled and burned.

"Live to die!" she said.

Everyone else yelled, "Hell yeah! Scorpions!" Even Paul whispered it.

They were surrounded, taking fire, limbs tearing. Rick's *Atlas* kneeled, critically damaged, but still fired steadily. Rob's *Warhammer* exploded into molten chunks. He ejected into a hail of fire.

Even Paul's *Awesome* was hemorrhaging armor and black smoke. He kept fighting, his heat levels maxing, almost at shutdown.

Paul read his tac displays; a full regiment of enemy 'Mechs surrounded him now. Something from orbit? Paul double-checked. A barrage of smart missiles? They were AMWs—Asset Management Weapons, enough to glass the entire continent. Why would the Combine...? No... It was *Merris*!

"Oh god!" Christy said it first.

"Get on the DropShip. Christy, your lance is first! *Amanda 4*, launch! Launch!"

"There's room for you, Doc," *Amanda 4*'s pilot said.

"I said *launch*!"

"I got them, Doc. Get on with Christy." It was Rick. Again, he called him Doc.

Is this the end?

"Launch! Keep firing!" was all Paul could say.

T-MINUS 8 MINUTES TO PLANETARY BARRAGE

"We're here," Chic interrupted. "Cut a hole, Harmon. Storm the DropShip."

Chic's Scorpions smashed their way from behind a lance of Combine 'Mechs, rushing the DropShip. Chic piloted a battered *Marauder,* trailing smoke and sparks. Enemy 'Mechs targeted them, sparing Paul's group a moment.

"Get your civilians on," Paul said. "We'll cover you."

"They're gone," Chic replied. "We couldn't save them."

"Where's Third Battalion's APCs?"

"They were wiped covering us."

"No they weren't!" Paul was dumbfounded. He couldn't believe it.

"They're gone. We're taking the DropShip. We have wounded."

"You monster! How dare you!" Paul aimed his PPCs at Chic. "Christy, get your lance onboard! There's no time." Paul's tac screen tracked the orbital barrage: less than seven minutes to impact.

Amanda 4 lit ten stabilizing thrusters. Smoke and debris flushed from the enormous sphere.

Despite heavy enemy fire, Christy's recon lance sprinted for the DropShip. Christy was last in line, of course, assuring her troops made it on first.

Chic's lance opened fire on Christy's. Christy stopped, surprised, and returned fire at Chic.

Doc stepped up next to her, also firing back. "You are dead, Chic! Dead! Get on, Christy!"

Christy's battered *Locust* turned to face the ramp, when a giant metal slab smashed down near her cockpit, missing it, and smashing her right hip to pieces. It was the arm of the obsidian *Thug.* Her *Locust* collided with the boarding ramp. Christy slid out through her 'Mech's access hatch and ran for her life, slipping on sweat and blood.

Alex fired lasers at Chic's *Marauder,* running toward the ramp Christy was scrambling up. Rob rammed the *Thug* with his weakened *Warhammer.* The obsidian 'Mech fired both short-range missile groups at the *Warhammer,* directly into its chest, causing it to explode. Rob's auto-ejection system shot him into a sky full of tracer rounds and laser fire.

Doc faced the Combine *Thug.* It was burning and smoking at the joints, wounded from battle. There was a delicately inscribed kanji on its forehead. *This must be an elite,* he thought. *A royal trainer? Are the jade Thugs piloted by his pupils?*

The obsidian 'Mech charged. Doc's *Awesome* grappled with it, battering it with its left arm and PPC barrel, pushing the smoking 'Mech away. Doc gained some distance as they circled, exchanging bright blasts of PPC fire. Rick shot his heavy autocannon and remaining medium lasers at the enemy 'Mech, shredding the *Thug*'s left arm and torso in the attack. Crazed, the obsidian *Thug* charged Paul again.

Combined fire from two enemy lances hit Rick's *Atlas*. It burst apart and exploded in fire. "Thank you, sir," was all he could say at the end. The auto-ejection system shot him into the sky, but there was so much enemy fire...

Amid the chaos, Paul realized Rick was dead and he was being charged. He fired everything, an alpha strike. Alex's *Archer* joined him with a burst of missile and laser fire.

The upper left half of the *Thug* exploded into bits, but the enemy 'Mech kept running, or rather stumbling, into Paul, arm raised, short-range missiles firing. The *Thug* took Paul's PPC arm in one brutal yank. The obsidian 'Mech exploded in blinding light, ejection seat spiraling into the red sky.

Paul's *Awesome* crashed to the ground. Wren had shot the *Thug* in the back, finishing it off. But more shots from enemy 'Mechs surrounding them hit Wren. His 'Mech staggered and exploded into flames.

Paul wrenched his *Awesome* back into a standing position while taking laser hits from nearby enemy 'Mechs circling him. He saw Chic's lancemates boarding the *Amanda 4*. Chic was distracted in hand-to-hand combat with two enemy *Wolverines*. Otherwise, he would have been the first one on the DropShip.

Paul's *Awesome* paced toward Chic, taking more hits from Combine 'Mechs, but not dissuaded. Alex's limping 'Mech joined him, firing what he had left at Chic until his *Archer* succumbed to enemy fire and he ejected.

4:13 TO IMPACT

The DropShip bay doors were closing as thrusters roared for liftoff. Chic's *Marauder* broke away from the entangled 'Mechs and leaped toward the shuttered door.

Paul charged the *Marauder,* colliding and pushing it from the ramp. Both 'Mechs crashed into city rubble.

Its doors finally sealed, *Amanda 4* slowly lifted off. A final burst of fire from the rising DropShip kept many Combine 'Mechs pinned.

3:31 TO IMPACT

Paul burned and screamed, lifting his *Awesome* from broken ground. Chic's *Marauder* kicked to flop itself over. Whoever stood first to fire...

3:04 TO IMPACT

Christy frantically strapped herself into an emergency launch seat, chest heaving. Too panicked to grieve, she was angry. Gasping, she yelled in frustration. She had survived!

2:14 TO IMPACT

Chic's *Marauder* stood, barely, aimed recklessly to fire first, a double PPC strike hitting Paul's *Awesome* in the right leg, toppling him.

Paul fired in mid-fall. His PPC shot seemed so slow in that moment, electric blue tangles rippling in intensity until it struck the *Marauder* in the cockpit, blasting it to metallic splinters and crackling sparks.

96 SECONDS TO IMPACT

Christy clenched her teeth as the g-forces increased. The loading bay shook and rumbled. Techs and support crew had also strapped into launch seats. They all focused on the unbearable pressure.

Someone caught her eye, a MechWarrior. It was Rob. *He survived.* He didn't see her. She would have laughed, but she could barely breathe...

67 SECONDS TO IMPACT

Paul's smoldering *Awesome* lay on its back, and he watched the *Amanda 4* approach orbit via a fizzling tac display. He tried to exhale, pinned to his seat with exhaustion.

The sky was red, dotted with incoming missile flares. They were strangely beautiful, like fiery flowers. Combine 'Mechs stood watching as well. Some ran their 'Mechs in a useless panic, while the rest just stood there, marveling at the burning warheads.

A soldier approached...no, it was Alex. *He made it.* Alex limped toward the *Awesome* and saluted, and then put his hand over his heart and pointed to Paul.

Another approached; it was Wren. *Incredible.* Wren saluted and smiled toward the downed 'Mech.

Alex sat first, cross-legged on the left of the *Awesome*. Wren saw him and waved. They laughed. Wren sat, knees up, then crossed his legs like Alex. Paul moved the remaining arm on his 'Mech to point to the sky, to show them that he was still alive.

They sat there watching the red sky, in awe of their fate, until everything glowed white and the ground shattered around them.

ASSASSINATION PROTOCOL: KATHERINE STEINER-DAVION

DANIEL ISBERNER

—Gladiator Gazette, July Edition 3144

Welcome back to "Assassination Protocol." Last month we covered none other than Kafka. This month, we have someone most people wouldn't directly call an assassin, but I would say that lies in the eyes of the beholder. The decision whether or not this month's subject can actually be called an assassin is up to you, dear reader: Was Katherine Steiner-Davion an assassin or just a murderous psychopath with lots of money and influence?

Contrary to our usual subjects, we actually know a lot about her background. The eldest daughter of Hanse Davion and Melissa Steiner, she was groomed to be the second in line for the throne of the Federated Commonwealth, after her brother Victor, but she was unhappy with just being second.

Her first known kill was her own mother, killed by a bomb in 3055, planted by the Dancing Joker (featured in our May 3143 issue), which set in motion not only her own rise to power but also the devastating civil war between the unified nations of the Federated Suns and Lyran Commonwealth that started seven years later. There are still rumors she used poison to induce the heart attack that had killed her father. And while they may seem to make sense, given that she had her mother killed, the lack of concrete evidence after more than ninety years can be considered proof that she was not involved in that particular death.

Her next target was her brother's lover, Omiko Kurita. Killed in 3064, once more by the Dancing Joker, whom Katherine hired. There are also theories she was behind the assassination of Morgan Hasek-Davion, who was poisoned in 3060 during Task Force Serpent's voyage to the Clan Homeworlds, but those have never been proven, and most modern historians dismiss them.

So far, none of the presented information should be new to anyone, as it is taught in history classes all across the Inner Sphere (depth and detail may vary, depending on where you live, dear reader). What follows is the true gem. It took almost two years of research to get a glimpse on her doings inside of Clan Wolf, once she lost the FedCom Civil War.

Over time, we were able to have multiple sources within Clan Wolf's civilian caste confirm the events after her move to Clan Wolf. As Katherine Wolf, she used her enormous political acumen to manipulate events within the Wolves' warrior caste. When Katya Kerensky left her post as Loremaster of Clan Wolf in 3083 to align herself with the Republic of the Sphere, trials for a new Loremaster took place. There were three promising candidates, two of which Katherine was seemingly unhappy with.

Our sources claim that one of them, Star Colonel Nathin Tutuola, suffered a fatal accident while cleaning his antique gun collection. Tutuola was well versed in Inner Sphere and Clan history and law. He would have been an ideal candidate, but was openly critical of Katherine Wolf's growing influence within the Clan. The nature of the cleaning accident has always been suspect, and there was evidence of someone making it look like an accident. The involvement of still loyal or retired Loki agents seems the most likely, not just in this case.

The second person considered for the Loremaster position was Star Commander Mike "Ragedog" Vickers. While he, too, was an enemy of Katherine Steiner-Davion, he was never as outspoken as Nathin Tutuola. His position was still well known. The week before the Loremaster trials, he was challenged repeatedly over minor differences. While he won all his challenges, he was exhausted when the Loremaster trial came around, and his *Mad Dog*'s cockpit was critically damaged early, costing him one of his hazel eyes, while his challengers all rose in rank shortly after losing their challenges against him. He always suspected Katherine's involvement in his trials but could never prove it.

The final winner of the trial was Ronald Ch'in, a supporter of Katherine Wolf's position within the Clan.

While there are further rumors that she manipulated advancements within the Clan over the next decades, it was only in the beginning of the 32nd century that we could find more than just rumors.

In 3110, Star Commander Nikolai Ward challenged her standing within the Clan. He demanded a Trial of Grievance after a raid on Pandora in late December 3109. He claimed the intel Katherine had miraculously provided had not only been faulty and cost the lives of three of his *sibkin*, it had also been fabricated specifically to allow the Lyrans to take the world only weeks later in early 3110, while the Jade Falcon defenders were still weakened. To the surprise of almost everyone, Katherine accepted, and the challenge was to be fought the next day.

When Katherine entered the Circle of Equals, Ward's *Mad Cat*, *Crowbar*, was nowhere to be seen. The wayward Star Commander was soon found dead in his bunk. Poisoned.

Suspicion immediately fell on Katherine, who was still in the cockpit of her *Griffin*, *Stiletto*. In the now pointless Circle of Equals, she swore to find out who robbed her of her chance to prove her honor in a Circle of Equals. She insinuated that he had poisoned himself because his charges against her were wrong and his incompetence had led to the defeat on Pandora.

Another known victim was Star Captain Martin "Dingo" Kerensky. What exactly happened to him is shrouded in mystery. In 3115 he was found dead in an alley on Tamar, brutally beaten and stabbed to death by what civilian forensics called "multiple very skilled opponents." His codex bracelet was missing, and it took authorities days before they could establish his identity. We were able to interview one of the investigators on the case. According to him, parts of a torn piece of paper was found under the body. "Come and take it [...] Katherine Stei[...]-Da[...]" was written on it, and everything else was illegible. The paper led to the identification of the Star Captain and to the warrior caste shutting down the investigation. The investigator still maintains that it must have been a blackmail attempt gone wrong, but with the warrior caste shutting the investigation down, he did not dare dig any deeper.

And what about Khan Seth Ward? His murder by a Loki agent paved the way for Alaric Ward to rise to the Khanship of Clan Wolf. Had she ordered one of her still-loyal Loki agents to kill the Khan of the Wolves, to allow her son to ascend to his position? There has never been an investigation outside of the warrior caste. And the only witness? Alaric Ward, now Khan of Clan Wolf. It would have been the perfect assassination, a perfect last act to cement Katherine's legacy before she was assassinated herself.

So, dear reader, was Katherine Steiner-Davion an assassin or just a murderous psychopath? We are open to discussion, and will present the results in next month's issue.

SCENARIO: ORDER THROUGH STRENGTH

TOM STANLEY

This scenario can be played as a stand-alone game or incorporated into a longer campaign using the *Chaos Campaign* rules (available as a free download from https://store.catalystgamelabs.com/products/battletech-chaos-campaign-succession-wars).

For flexibility of play, this track contains rules for *Total Warfare* (*TW*), with *Alpha Strike: Commander's Edition* (*AS* or *AS:CE*) rules noted in parenthesis, allowing the battle to be played with either rule set.

Blizzard Trinary will deploy along three locations. Alpha Star will deploy between the mountainside and the city, where we crush these surat Motstånd once and for all. Bravo Star will protect the city and the Dominion History and Culture Center, should any of them slip by us. Charlie Star is to scout the mountains for any signs of a base. Your speed will allow us reinforcements if needed, but should they run your way, you have my authorization to teach these terrorists that they have no homes here!

—Star Captain Alvar, Blizzard Trinary, Second Tyr Assault Cluster, Rasalhague Galaxy

Resistance groups attached to the umbrella of Motstånd have never really gone away in the Rasalhague Dominion. By 3125 their forces overplayed their strength in brief but brutal terrorist acts that were promptly put down in the mid 3120s. During 3125 the natives of Balsta faced such a form of terror as the First Snapphanar struck at various targets on the system in the hopes of showing that not all bend to the Dominion's knee. Any buildings exalting Clan Ghost Bear's supremacy were quickly targeted by firebombing, suicide attacks, or BattleMech raids; even civilian centers, such as hospitals named in honor of former Rasalhagians whose descendants serve the Dominion, were fair game.

SITUATION

COSON HILL
BALSTA
RASALHAGUE DOMINION
27 DECEMBER 3125

To the Clans, Star League Day, 27 December, is a somber "holiday," a day of reflection for the assassination of First Lord Richard Cameron in 2766. Hatred is inflicted upon the Inner Sphere, which is seen to be responsible for the destruction of the Star League. This holiday usually ends in violence between the Great Houses and the Inner Sphere Clans.

The First Snapphanar attempted to attack from Coson Hill, an ancient battle site during the Clan Invasion, into the nearby city. Their main goal was the Dominion History and Culture Center, a massive series of buildings created as a center of learning and history for the Rasalhague Dominion. Motstånd believed such a structure would provide ample distraction while other forces raided weapon depots far away, also a moral victory for their cause—at least until Clan Watch operatives found the plan.

Blizzard Trinary of the Second Tyr Assault Cluster was given orders to intercept and obliterate the raiding forces who dared assault the Center on such an important Clan holiday.

As the Dominion is a fusion of Clan and Inner Sphere cultures, more efforts were put toward education of former mistakes from the Inner Sphere. The DHCC was constructed as a project for such an outlet.

GAME SETUP

The Defender picks two maps and places them with the short edges touching, forming a long rectangle. The Attacker picks one side as their home edge, the opposite side becomes the Defender's edge.

The Attacker's forces may deploy up to 3 hexes (*AS*: 6") from their edge.

The Defender's forces may deploy up to 4 hexes (*AS*: 8") from their edge; the Defender may also hide one unit if desired.

Attacker

The First Snapphanar fielded only one lance of BattleMechs for this fight. Two MechWarriors have Regular skills while the other two have Veteran skills, with one Veteran given the Dodge SPA (see p. 74, *Campaign Operations*, or p. 95, *AS:CE*).

Defender

Alpha Star of Blizzard Trinary fields one Star of BattleMechs. Four MechWarriors have Veteran skills while one is Star Captain Alvar;

Piloting 2, Gunnery 3 (*AS*: Skill 2) and has the Blood Stalker PSA (see p. 73, *Campaign Operations*, or p. 93, *AS:CE*).

WARCHEST
Track Cost: 300 WP

Optional Bonuses:

–100 "We Wait and See" (Attacker Only): Attacker wins one Initiative of their choosing after Initiative rolls are made.

+150 Getting an Early Start on the Day: Apply Dusk/Dawn conditions to the fight. All units apply a +1 to-hit modifier to all weapon attacks. For every 25 points of heat on a target unit that tracks heat, apply a –1 to-hit modifier to any weapon attacks; conventional infantry ignore this modifier. Units with searchlights will not offset these penalties.

OBJECTIVES

Push Through: If the Attacker moves at least half the number of their starting units off the Defender's home edge, the Attacker wins the track. If the Defender cripples or destroys half of the Attacker's starting units before this occurs, the Defender wins the track. **[200]**

Hold the Field: If all units on one side are destroyed or withdraw from the playing area, the other side successfully holds the field. **[100]**

SPECIAL RULES

Forced Withdrawal

Defenders must adhere to Forced Withdrawal rules (see p. 258, *TW*, or p. 126, *AS:CE*), but Attackers will not due to their desperation to break through the enemy lines.

Clan Honor

Due to the nature of the Attacker's force, no Clan Honor rules are in effect.

AFTERMATH

The First Snapphanar was given a death blow at Balsta. The Second Tyr had too many forces and too many weapons trained on the rebellion for the First to even have a chance. The Second proved their prowess and bravery to their Clan brethren, and were given important garrison positions for their service. The Motstånd lost its leaders due to manhunts and executions, reducing its influence to meekly handing out propaganda as their members did long ago.

PRINCE OF SKYE

BRYN BILLS

Check out this message I got in the last courier JumpShip download. Is this legit?
—Kristian Frosig

Date: 10 June 3138
Subject: Urgent message from the Prince of Skye

Hello my frend,

My name is Sir Jack Wilson and I am a prince from the citey of New New Glasgow on the Planet of Skye. I know it may be a surprise for you to have a man such as myself reaching out to you but I wanted to talk to you about an amazing opportunity that could benefit both of us greatly. As a person of your inenlightenment of course knows the Clan attacks on Skye have had a major impact on us. My father, Sir Oliver Wilson, recently died fighting alongside Archon Trillian Steiner-Davion defending New Niw Glasgow.

Upon my father's death his inheritance, valued by the royal treasury at 50,000,000 C-Bills, was to go to the people of Skye in order to help them defend themselves as well as rebuild. However, the clan's stole all of it after their last attack, leaving the people of Skye with no way to help themselves. We spent months tracking down the inheritance in order to protect the people and we finally found it on the plant of Rasalhague. Unfortunately our current Jumpship can only make one jomp and Rasalhhuge is 2½ jumps away. In order to makes it we need to upgrade our Jumpship with the super new Kell drive, powered by an ancient mysterious Kell hound power source.

In order to do this we need 5,000 C-bells and that is where you come in my friend. If you can provide us with the money we will be able to take our Mech regiments and retake the inheritance. Attached to this document is the account information to transfer the investment to. In return for your help we would be willing to give you 22% of the inheritance for your troubles. We would also make you a member of the Wilson royal family and will send our Kell Jumpship to bring you and your family here to live with us. Finally, you will be made duke of New Nuw Aberdeen.

As you can see, this opportunity will no only save millions of lives but will make you a hero and bring you great reaches. Please respond back to me as quickly as possible as time is running out before the Clans people take the inheritance to their sanctuaries and it will be lost forever.

I know you will do the right thing my dearest friend.

Sincerely,
Jack Wilson

THE SECRET FOX

BRYAN YOUNG

POTSDAM TOWN
JERANGLE
13 MAY 3143

"I had the dream again," Katie Ferraro said, but she was sure Scarecrow wasn't listening.

Scarecrow wasn't his real name, but that's what everyone in old Potsdam called him. He wasn't terribly scary, but he did have the sharp beak and black, bushy eyebrows like you might expect a crow to have.

His hand was out, taking the wrench she held up for him. "The MechWarrior dream again?"

"Yes." She smiled, and her eyes focused in on the lumbering AgroMech they worked on, wishing it were a BattleMech. "I was piloting a *Catapult*, skipping along toward a battle. I felt like I *was* the 'Mech. Every move I made, the 'Mech responded. My legs were the 'Mech's legs. My arms..." She paused, thinking for a second. *Catapult*s didn't have arms, per se. "Well, my arms were just part of the 'Mech. I didn't need them. Why would I?"

"*Catapult.* That's an old 'Mech. Long time since anyone's seen one of those 'round these parts," Scarecrow said, his head disappearing behind the maintenance compartment as he went back to tinker.

"It's been a long time since anyone's seen *any* real 'Mechs around here, Scarecrow."

"True enough, that is," he said. "At least since the bombs fell. Don't expect to see any more, either. Least not ones that aren't already here. The old battered up 'Mechs that got left behind."

Those battered up 'Mechs, BattleMechs and WorkMechs alike, were the bread and butter of Scarecrow's service. Since they were all held together with spit and baling wire, Scarecrow's shop never wanted for business. And since he made the proverbial house calls, there was almost always something to work on.

Katie frowned. "I just want to be a MechWarrior."

"No, you don't. It's hot, messy work. Lethal, too. MechWarriors from backwaters never last long. You don't want to waste your life gettin' shot up as a mercenary for who-knows-what for not enough pay. You're young. Got your whole life ahead of you."

"I'm seventeen," she said, a sing-song trace of defiance in her voice.

"And how many seventeen-year-olds you know got themselves apprenticed to a 'Mech tech?"

She toed the metal scaffolding grate in front of her. Sheepish. Katie knew she should be grateful. Scarecrow wasn't just her boss; he'd taken her in the year before. After her parents had died in the accident. They'd fostered her dream of being a MechWarrior, and they were the ones who had arranged the apprenticeship. They knew how important her dreams were, and on Jerangle, they knew Scarecrow was the closest she could come to touching them. This was probably the closest she'd ever get to working with 'Mechs in the backwater of a planet that had been written off by the Inner Sphere. They both knew it.

She put her hand on the AgroMech's construction-yellow arm as though she were consoling a living, breathing person. If she'd been born in another time, then maybe she would have had a chance to live those dreams.

But not right now.

Not in the 3140s.

All the excitement and conflict of the Inner Sphere passed Jerangle by. At least since the borders were more settled, and everyone seemed to have their eyes on something bigger than the smallest holdings in the Lyran Commonwealth. And there didn't look to be any chance of that changing. Not any time soon.

The most she'd ever see of new BattleMechs would be the occasional mercenary unit that blew into town for the odd job here or there. But even those were few and far between. Rarer still were visits from the Lyran military. It was like they didn't even remember Jerangle existed.

No. Jerangle was quiet.

"Hand me that spanner," Scarecrow told her.

She knew which one he meant. Maybe she'd even guessed he'd need it soon, since she'd already pulled it from the toolbox and held it, waiting for his request. Handing it to him, she stepped around to watch him ratchet the bolts back on the assembly for the AgroMech's shoulder joint.

He must have sensed the unease in her voice. "We've got to get this 'Mech back together and out in the field before lunch. Maybe one day you'll get your dream. But it's not going to be today."

Katie hoped he was wrong.

Katie convinced Scarecrow to let her pilot the AgroMech back to its owners and then give her the rest of the day off. There weren't any 'Mechs left in the bay for repairs, and the next scheduled maintenance on anything wouldn't be until next week.

He'd been reluctant at first, just like when she'd asked to pilot the AgroMech, but he had a hard time saying no when it mattered.

"Just be careful. And don't do anything foolish while you're out there," he told her over the radio as she settled into the AgroMech's command couch. "Can't afford to have anybody thinking ol' Scarecrow's lettin' you out to take risks or nothing. They'll say I've lost my marbles."

"Maybe you have, Scarecrow," she said. She couldn't contain the joy in her voice as she strapped the helmet on and willed the 'Mech forward.

It was a short walk to the outskirts of town where the fields were. They cultivated all sorts of things on Jerangle where the soil was good. Near Potsdam, it was mainly rice. Further into the forests on the other side of town, where the rocky jungle took over, they grew coffee, vanilla, and cacao. The crops all did well in the heat and humidity.

Katie had learned to love the heat herself. She thought growing up in such a place would help prepare her for being a MechWarrior. All the stories she read talked so much about how hot 'Mechs got.

For the AgroMechs she was allowed to pilot, the warmest they got was the ambient temperature of Potsdam.

She was reluctant to deliver the 'Mech. Something inside Katie wished she could just keep driving it. Past the farm, past the outskirts of Potsdam. Past everything. And she'd just find a new life out there, with the AgroMech as her only constant companion. It would be a hard life, but she'd make it work somehow. And once she'd hired her and her trusty 'Mech out for enough work, she'd be able to sell the AgroMech and trade up to a proper BattleMech.

She dreamed of starting her own mercenary company.

One day. She smiled. *One day.*

Instead of fleeing into the sunset, she parked the AgroMech outside of old man Peabody's rice farm and let him know it was back.

"Scarecrow did a great job with it, sir," she told Peabody. "It's running like new again."

Peabody was grateful, of course, and told Katie that he'd settle up with Scarecrow the next day, which was fine by her. It didn't matter to her when Scarecrow got paid as long as he did. She'd get hers soon enough. All she did was save up her money anyway.

That 'Mech wasn't going to buy itself.

With the rest of the day off and only an empty apartment above Scarecrow's shop to go home to, she figured she'd go hiking. It would keep her mind off the yearning in her heart. And she wouldn't die of boredom. She'd read the same books and watched the same shows over and over and over again and they'd lost all their allure.

She began her hike into the jungle from Peabody's farm. She didn't know if it was actually a jungle, but it seemed jungle enough to her. Hot and humid, lots of broad leafy trees and a thick canopy. Vines everywhere. It changed a bit as the land got craggier and led up the mountain, but it was all still very dense. As long as she didn't get into any of the crops beneath the canopy, no one would say boo about her traipsing through the jungle. The kids of Potsdam did it all the time.

Seemed like every year or two, one of them would get lost, and there would be a search party. Katie wouldn't let that happen to her. She had an innate sense of direction. And, occasionally, she cut small marks in trees as she passed, just to be sure she wouldn't get lost.

But getting lost was a thought that haunted her.

She'd already been lost by everything she'd ever loved. She didn't want to get lost from everything else, too.

There were many trails that led to notable places. One led to a waterfall. Another led to a system of caves and an underwater river. Katie tended to avoid that one, though. There had been too many stories of kids swimming into the caves and drowning.

She couldn't drown.

She wanted to die in a BattleMech.

Well, she didn't really want to die at all. But if she had to choose her death, she knew she wanted it to be inside a 'Mech.

That was the only thing that made sense to her.

The hike would be good for her, but she wanted to stay away from the beaten paths. She didn't want to interact with anyone who wasn't a 'Mech or a MechWarrior. And she wouldn't be finding anyone like that on Jerangle, at least not near Potsdam.

Pushing on, she found an opening she could forge on her own. Taking a deep right turn into dense foliage, Katie kicked her way through and walked until she came to the steep gash of a ravine. She knew it to be where the Mindel River cut through the jungle as it headed through Potsdam and out to the sea. She'd never seen the ravine from this high up before. Usually, she'd hike down the other way and see the falls from below.

Perhaps there hadn't been trails up to this spot because people found it dangerous. She let out a series of shallow breaths, doing her best to catch it. After wiping the sweat from her face, Katie pulled her beat-up old canteen from her belt and took a long, cool draught of the water.

Cutting through the jungle without a machete was difficult work. And the bits of her exposed flesh told the tale. She'd been nicked and cut in a dozen places where sharp leaves cut her or branches snagged her. But she had no qualms with the damage. She'd nicked the trees to keep her trail as much as they had nicked her, so it seemed a fair exchange.

She was just grateful to be out. And alive. And alone with her thoughts.

In these quiet times, she daydreamed about BattleMechs as much as she'd dreamed of anything in her nights, and tromping through the jungles reminded her of everything she wanted to do with her life, only from the cockpit of a 'Mech.

Screwing the cap back onto her canteen, she hooked it back onto her belt and took a long look at the ravine before her. The edge stood a few feet from her and she couldn't see the sparkle of the running water below her at that angle, but she could certainly hear its forceful rush. It added a lovely background to the foreground noise of cawing birds.

She stepped forward, inching closer to the edge until she could see the current far below her. A narrow shaft of hot sunlight cut across the chasm and made the water sparkle below it.

Truly a beautiful sight.

She looked up and down the ravine, hoping she could place where along the path she was, but didn't recognize the curve. She might have from an aerial map, just not from her memory. She etched the curve into her mind, hoping to look it up later.

That's when the glint of something silvery caught her eye down below.

Just as the river upstream disappeared, there stood a copse of jungle trees on an embankment on the shore. The trees climbed up to the level where she was, and it would be a hike to get down there. But through those trees, the sun caught metal.

"Metal?" Katie said to herself. There shouldn't be anything metal out here at all.

But as the sun shifted slightly over the course of the minutes she'd been there, she knew her mind wasn't playing tricks on her.

Then her curiosity took the better of her, and she knew she had to investigate.

Looking around, Katie found a tree nearby to nick with her tracking mark and began the hike uphill around the lip of the ravine to make her way down to the trees below and whatever secret they kept.

She divided her attention as she walked between the trees ahead and her feet below. There were definitely parts of her makeshift trail that weren't as solid as others and she'd send rocks tumbling down into the water below. Other times, the path was nonexistent, and she would have to cut into the trees again and walk around and back to the ravine's edge.

Once she finally reached the trees, there was nothing of the metal she could see. The tree canopy blocked any view she would have had of the ground, or any metal objects or structures held within.

No. If she wanted to know what was down there, she was going to have to climb down and see for herself.

Lost in the excitement, she didn't even stop to take a breather or drink more water. She simply went to work scanning around for a way down.

With no obvious path, she knew she'd have to climb down. It would be difficult and dangerous. It was ten meters to the floor, easy. And she couldn't tell how soft the ground was, but she'd be working without a net in either case.

Fortunately, her belt was made of tightly wound cord. Scarecrow had given it to her as a gift.

"It's never wise to be caught without essentials anywhere around. Just cut the buckle and *bam!*—fifteen meters of cord for anything you need."

She hadn't thought it a particularly nice gift at the time. She'd needed a belt, true, and she didn't mind the utilitarian nature of it. It was the fact that someone had paid him for a repair with a case of the belts. He'd been wearing one himself when he handed it to her, and she saw them in their packaging, scattered all over the workbench.

She'd laughed about it later, but was grateful for it now.

Unspooling the cord, she didn't quite realize how much was hidden in the weave. Fifteen meters was a lot. But it would be perfect for what she needed to do.

Finding a sturdy tree, she looped the cord around it and tied it into a heavy knot. Then knotted it again for good measure. The last thing she wanted was to rappel down the side and fall to her death because she used the wrong knot.

Satisfied that the rope would hold, she tossed the rest of her former belt down over the edge. There was a narrow gap between the canopy and the rocky wall, so she wouldn't have too much of a problem getting down. She put on the tight leather gloves from her pack and wrapped the cord around her waist, ready to make the descent.

Taking in a deep breath, she hoped no harm would come to her, and that there was something really interesting hidden in the trees to make all the effort worth it.

If there wasn't, she was going to be mighty pissed as she climbed back up the ravine.

The first step over the edge when rappelling was always the most nerve-wracking. It was that first moment of truth that forced you to trust in the work you'd done and the physics of climbing and mountaineering. And the strength in your own arms and legs.

Katie took in a deep breath and descended.

She went slow at first, and felt the broad leaves of the trees scrape against her back as she came down. But she kept her focus on the rope and the rock wall in front of her. She didn't want to put her foot in the wrong hole or smush a snake or kick a bird or anything else. And she certainly didn't want to get her feet stuck. Falling from that height would be bad enough; doing it backward after breaking an ankle wasn't going to be good for anyone.

"You got this, Katie," she told herself.

And she had no reason to believe she was lying.

The ground came up sooner than she expected. She'd been so focused on doing everything correctly, she didn't realize how long she'd been doing it. When she finally took that step onto solid ground and was able to let go of the rope, she stretched her aching fingers, hoping to bring feeling back into them quickly.

Then she bounced on her knees a bit, too, just to get all the blood flowing in all the right places.

She turned around to finally sate her curiosity and wondered if she'd even be able to find anything in the trees. They'd grown into something like a solid wall, a dozen trees, all clumped far too closely together.

"Nuts."

She'd have to trudge further still to satisfy her curiosity.

"This better be worth it."

Katie walked around the immediate wall of trees and found an opening that would let her through. It was a tight squeeze, and she felt like she'd entered a different world.

Dark and swampy. She'd been accustomed to the humidity, but the darkness and proximity to the river and the soft ground had turned the place into as much of a bog as anything. The din of the river was loud, but the noises of the birds had vanished, replaced by the sound of skittering insects and their clicking calls to each other.

Her flesh crawled as much as she imagined the insects were.

Looking up, she tried to see any of the piercing shards of sunlight that had reflected the glint of metal. Pin pricks only, but nothing metal, no shiny reflective surfaces. She would have to delve deeper to find anything.

Winding through another grouping of trees, the light grew even more scarce here. She stepped forward, reaching out in front of her to make sure she didn't bump into anything. She hoped her eyes would adjust to the darkness easier, but she had no such luck.

Reaching out in front of her, she felt something. Smooth. Not like the trees at all, which were rough. And cool to the touch.

It seemed like all the trees and leaves, especially in the more humid pockets like this one, were hot and damp. But this one was cool.

Metal?

Maybe she'd found it.

What she was looking for.

Stepping forward carefully, the tips of her boots found the same thing. She wondered if it was some old, forgotten power relay or transformer box. Maybe it was the remnants of an old hydroelectric plant. Jerangle had been populated for at least six hundred years, and the folks that first settled here could have built anything. It could have been a hundred things, but she wanted to know which one thing it really was.

She felt around, trying to find the edges of it and found that it wasn't large enough to really be a building of any sort. It was too narrow for that, though it was big. And it had a base around it that was wider than that.

Legs?

Katie's heart skipped a beat.

Could it be...?

A 'Mech?

She wasn't that lucky.

But her mind raced with the possibilities. *What if it is a 'Mech? How would it have gotten here? Why would it have just been abandoned?*

Trying to find the edges of the 'Mech—she'd already begun to think of it as a 'Mech—she found that it did, indeed have two "legs." Sure, they could have been struts for some ancient treehouse, but how did that even make sense?

Then she wondered about what the spot would have looked like without the grove sprouting up around it. Perhaps, if the river hadn't changed course in a few hundred years and maybe it was some electro plant, this could have been an observation post where someone could have kept an eye on things in both directions of this bend in the river.

But she *wanted* it to be a 'Mech.

That would have been the best of all scenarios. Right?

When she finally made it to the backside and had circumnavigated the entire mysterious object, she realized that she was going to have to climb it.

Cursing under her breath, she wished she hadn't tied her cord so tightly around the tree. Still, she'd be able to get along without it.

Remembering she had a light in her pack, she pulled it out, cursing the whole time. She shone it on the metal structure, and it definitely had hand- and footholds, even though they were grimy with age and covered in moss.

A bolt of excitement jolted her heart.

She smiled as she attached the light to her head with the provided elastic band and began her ascent.

Every meter she climbed, the more the excitement swelled within her.

This couldn't be possible.

But every time her hands found a new hold and her feet pushed her up higher, she knew at least some part of it to be true.

When she reached the cockpit, the light from the trees filtered in better up here, and she felt much more comfortable thinking the word that had her so excited.

BattleMech!

From what she could see, the 'Mech had only limited arms. It was a squat design. She'd have to do more research to find out exactly what kind of 'Mech she was dealing with. But the torso was wider than the legs, and the arms were more weapon than arms. It definitely didn't have hands.

She climbed around to the hatch that would grant her entrance and hoped that she'd be able to get inside. "Open, please."

Her arms were tired from all of her exertions, and she wasn't sure she'd be able to just hang on, clinging to the side of the 'Mech without losing her grip and falling down.

A keypad on the side of the hatch would grant her access, and her heart fell. How could she possibly guess the code of the MechWarrior who had last piloted this gorgeous, if abandoned, machine?

First, she touched the keypad to see if it even still had power. The fusion engines that powered a 'Mech were supposed to provide limitless energy, but there had to be a reason this particular 'Mech had been abandoned in the jungle and overgrown with moss.

Katie smiled when it lit up at her touch.

Her fingers hovered over the keys, wondering what she'd input. But then she remembered a lot of these 'Mechs had maintenance access codes. And she'd studied plenty of those. On the off-chance she'd ever get a hands on an actual 'Mech.

They were long sequences, but she had forced herself to commit them to memory as part of learning 'Mech lore.

The first she tried merely caused the console to beep at her disapprovingly.

The second time yielded the same result.

"Damn it."

But the third time?

Well, the third time worked, and the hatch opened.

The smell was the first, worst thing she noticed. The worst thing her nostrils had ever inhaled. Foul was an understatement. Something must have died and rotted inside the humid heat of the 'Mech's cockpit.

And that made her just the tiniest bit afraid of going in.

The cockpit was dark. The only light came from her headlamp and the faint glow of the buttons and dials on the other side of the command couch.

With her arm and legs weakening, Katie didn't have much of a choice but to head in.

Somehow, being *inside* the cockpit made the stench even worse. She pulled a bandana from her pocket and wrapped it around her nose and mouth. It didn't do much, but it would help some.

She smirked, thinking she'd look like some sort of bandit raiding a 'Mech.

The ache of her muscles and the burning in her legs reminded her of just how much effort it had taken to get to that point, so dead animal be damned, she was going to figure out what was wrong with the 'Mech and take it for her own if that was even possible.

Stepping around the command couch, she gasped.

The woman sitting there looked like she'd been dead for no more than a few months, but, logically, Katie knew it had to have been decades. Her face looked gaunt and agonized. Her hair pulled back into a tight bun over the leathery skin stretched over the skull.

She had apparently mummified in her cooling vest on the command couch. There was a sizable hole in her shoulder, caved in. On her vest was a pin that might be some clue to the woman's identity, though Katie didn't recognize it. An inverted triangle with a black outline and a red field inside. Some sort of animal head, straight on and in black, stared forward in the center of the red.

Katie thought the woman was beautiful and haunting and was surprised at herself for being able to resist the urge to scream.

She'd never seen a dead body before.

"I'm so sorry," Katie told the mummified corpse. "I'll see you get a proper burial."

Katie vowed to bury the woman herself, fashioning a grave for her at the feet of the 'Mech. Since she had no idea who this woman was or where she'd come from and had no way of knowing where she'd *want* to be buried, that seemed like the most sensible option. Especially since leaving her in the 'Mech wasn't possible.

The 'Mech was Katie's now.

It was *her* 'Mech.

Katie smiled.

She had a 'Mech.

31 JULY 3143

"Where you goin' these days?" Scarecrow asked.

"Oh, nowhere," Katie said, doing her best impression of an innocent teenager.

"I see you leavin'. You're barely around. Unless there's a 'Mech to be worked on, you skedaddle right out of here. Everything okay?"

"Yeah, everything is fine. I'm just—wrapped up in my studies, I guess." She handed him a wrench for the joint motor assembly they were rebuilding in the center of his shop.

He took the wrench and narrowed his eyes. "You seein' a boy?"

"No."

"A girl, then?"

That made her blush. "No."

"Someone special at all?"

"No, Scarecrow."

"Feels like it's been months since we had a proper talk. You sure you're alright?"

"I'm fine. Better than fine, even. I promise."

Scarecrow smiled slyly. "Are you up to something?"

Katie did her best to suppress a smile. "Not... No. Not really."

Scarecrow went back to the work, which she watched carefully. There was more at stake for her to learn than ever. "Well, whatever it is you're doing, I hope you're bein' careful. I know I'm not much of a... well...a guardian or nothing, but I look at you like family, such as it is. I don't want nothin' happening to you."

Katie smiled. Genuinely. Honestly. Scarecrow was doing his best to reach out to her. To be there for her. But she still felt uneasy telling him about her little secret. "I know, Scarecrow."

"All right, then," he said, getting back into his work. "Just keep an eye out and learn what you can."

As she watched, she daydreamed about being able to go back into the jungle and work on her own 'Mech. She'd determined, to the best of her ability, that it was a *Kit Fox*. It was a Clan 'Mech, and she figured she knew how it got to Jerangle. One of the biggest clues about how the 'Mech had gotten here was the pin on the cooling vest. Apparently, the woman had been a member of the Kell Hounds, which was a mercenary unit Katie hadn't heard of, but now tried to read up on as best she could. How she got a Clan 'Mech away from the Clans in the first place was a mystery Katie wished to uncover. How she got to Jerangle, doubly so.

She was able to piece together how the 'Mech got left behind in this specific spot, though. There had been a record of a battle near Potsdam. A small one, but a battle nonetheless. The mentions were vague, but Katie's best guess was that the Kell Hounds were retreating, and the pilot had gotten stuck with an overheating 'Mech. She tried to stop by the river. Katie wondered if the pilot was going to try to dip in and cool her 'Mech that way, but she never made it. Stuck in the trees.

She'd been wounded; the cockpit had suffered a savage hit, and the radio was broken. She hadn't been able to call for help. The mysterious MechWarrior had cooked in the *Kit Fox*'s cockpit, waiting for help that would never come.

Katie did everything she could to give the woman a warrior's funeral. To honor her for her sacrifice. To honor her for everything she had given to Katie, even if she didn't know it in life.

Because that 'Mech was going to change Katie's life. It already had.

"Katie...?" Scarecrow said, interrupting her thoughts.

"Huh? What?"

"I said give me the spanning wrench and the spot welder, will you?"

"Oh," she said. "Right."

"You're sure nothing's wrong? You got your head in the stars again?"

"Something like that."

"More dreams of bein' in a BattleMech?"

Katie smiled. "Is it that obvious?"

"Katie, sometimes I think if you don't get behind the cockpit of a 'Mech, you're liable to explode."

"You're not wrong." And what he didn't know wouldn't hurt him. She was as close as she'd ever been to getting the 'Mech back to the shop.

She thought she'd surprise him with it.

She hadn't dared move it, though, because she hadn't figured out how to get it out. With no jump jets, getting out of the ravine would

mean a dip in the river and she didn't know if the current would be too much for the 'Mech, or if the water would be too deep.

When she'd read about the Battle of Tukayyid, where the Prezno River had killed so many 'Mechs on its own, the last thing Katie wanted was to lose her 'Mech as soon as she had found it.

A low rumble shook her violently. Not just her, though: Scarecrow, the 'Mech joint assembly, and the whole shop.

"What in the hell is that?" Scarecrow asked, lifting up the goggles he'd been using to protect his eyes from the spot welder.

Katie shrugged. "I don't know."

The rumbling got louder.

And then there was the distinctive sound of laser fire.

"We're under attack," Scarecrow said matter-of-factly. He tossed the goggles and welder down and ran for the massive doors of the 'Mech shop.

Katie followed, surprised at how fast Scarecrow moved. She'd never seen him move *anywhere* that fast before. Possessed of some energy beyond him.

When Katie reached the doors, her eyes widened.

They *were* under attack.

It was a pair of 'Mechs, dirty and in disrepair, but functioning. They were painted black with red stripes. One looked like a barely-functioning *Crossbow* and the other an old battered *Sentinel*. Where they'd been dug up was anyone's guess. Probably from back in the time when the Lyrans had fought off some sort of attack on Jerangle or another. And the Lyrans had sported some 'Mechs that were already old even then.

She wondered how these pirates got them working. But they must not have been working very well. Both 'Mechs carried masked soldiers of some kind. They gesticulated with rifles and shouted wildly.

"What are they saying?" Scarecrow asked. His hearing wasn't as good as it used to be.

But she couldn't blame him. It was hard to hear *anyone* over the sound of a 'Mech tromping through a city street.

"It sounds like they're upset."

"I can see that."

Katie strained her ears, but still couldn't make out what they said any better than Scarecrow.

But when the *Crossbow* turned and punched the top of the bar, collapsing the roof in on itself.

"What the hell are they doing?" Scarecrow said.

"I hope you didn't need a drink today."

"Damn it."

Then, the *Sentinel* gestured with its right arm—the one that wasn't a cannon—and the MechWarrior inside (though Katie doubted he was a *real* MechWarrior) flipped on their external speakers. "Potsdam Town! We are the Red Stripe Raiders, and we declare you our subjects."

Scarecrow groaned. "These idiots are gonna get someone killed."

The *Sentinel* pilot carried on with their screed. "I have transmitted to you our demands. If the supplies we have asked for are not on the loading docks by tomorrow at sundown, we will tear this city apart."

For good measure, the *Crossbow* then kicked the building across the road from the bar. Katie couldn't quite see it. The 'Mechs were a couple streets away, and the only thing she could see were their torsos over the tops of the buildings.

With their threat transmitted and their timeline clear, they turned and left the town.

The idiots hanging on the tops of the 'Mechs, looking like they were ready to fall off anyway, hooted and hollered and fired their guns into the air.

It was an unmistakable show of force.

"What do we do now?" Katie asked.

Scarecrow shrugged.

Naturally, the whole town met in the municipal center. The mayor presided; a big woman with a fiery temperament and a last name she could never live down: Warhammer. Like the 'Mech.

Who had a name like Warhammer?

No wonder she kept winning elections in the town.

That, and no one really bothered running against her. Who wanted the job of administering a backwater town on a backwater planet?

It was a thankless job.

And now she had these so-called Red Stripes to deal with. They'd demanded money and crates of supplies. They must have a hovertruck of some kind to steal away with everything in addition to their rusty 'Mechs.

Scarecrow wondered out loud to Katie if, perhaps, they didn't have any ammo for their 'Mech's weapons, save for their lasers. The *Crossbow* should have had two mediums, and the *Sentinel* should have had a light one. But even those could have been stripped for parts a century prior, or sold for scrap at any point between then and now.

One of them had definitely fired a laser when they'd entered the town. That was what Katie and Scarecrow had heard that brought them out of the shop. Others had seen it. But beyond there, there was no guarantee that they had ammunition for anything else.

Mayor Warhammer stood at the front of the room, shushing the crowd. Her black skin served as a stark contrast to the white walls behind her. "Now we know what they've asked for, and I don't see as though we've got much of a choice but to give it to them."

"We don't have that many kroner," someone from the crowd said.

"Why would we turn them over, even if we did?" someone else shouted.

"But what else can we do?" came another voice.

Katie couldn't argue with any of their questions. But neither did she have any answers for them.

Mayor Warhammer didn't have answers for them, either. Despite her strength as a leader and as a person, she had no answers because the town was out of options. "Calm down, everyone," she said over the din of the townsfolk. "Settle. Settle down all of you. Settle."

But that didn't quite settle them down. A low roar of private conversation still filled the room.

That didn't stop the mayor from continuing. "We've been in tight spots before. And we've always come out on top. This whole world almost burned, and we're still here. Our grandparents and our great grandparents survived through the worst time in the history of our world, and we're not going to let a couple of jackasses with reclaimed BattleMechs threaten us or scare us away from what we need to do."

There was a modest cheer from the crowd.

"So," she continued, "I want ideas. I don't think we can just hand them our goods and our cash. But I'm also not sure we have a choice. The old defenses of the town aren't working, and we don't have anything but AgroMechs to field against them. Even if they only have one working laser between the two of them, they'd tear us apart and we'd lose even more."

The crowd murmured back and forth, some agreeing with the mayor, others dissenting. All of their voices, even in disagreement, still held respect for her.

"Anyone?" the mayor asked. "Does anyone have an idea?"

Katie did.

She raised her hand, sheepishly.

She wasn't sure she wanted to speak in front of such a large crowd. She wasn't always sure she wanted to speak in front of Scarecrow, let alone the entire town. This absolutely terrified her.

"You!" the mayor said, pointing a finger right at Katie. She made eye contact, and Katie almost withered beneath the mayor's gaze. For a moment, Katie forgot that she'd even asked to be recognized. Such was the power of a mayor named Warhammer.

Like the 'Mech.

That thought put a smile on Katie's face and she tried to speak in her loudest, bravest voice, though the results were mixed. "What if someone were able to chase them away...?"

The mayor laughed. "If someone could chase them away, I'd pay them half of the twenty-five thousand kroner these clowns are asking for."

Katie's eyes widened. "Seriously?"

"Absolutely. Now do you have any ideas for real? We know we want to chase them away."

"That's all I needed to know." And Katie turned, running from the room as fast as she could, leaving everyone to wonder what the hell all of that was about.

1 AUGUST 3143

The next day left the town of Potsdam in tense agony. As a collective, they'd decided they would pay the Red Stripes off for now, but they would also look for other means to destroy them in the future, even if that meant paying mercenaries. As it was, with communication across the Inner Sphere so slow, there was simply no time for them to come up with a better plan.

But they didn't know what Katie was up to, either.

She didn't want to tell anyone her plan until she was sure she'd be able to pull it off.

There were still so many unknown factors.

She'd spent the better part of two months fixing everything on the *Kit Fox* that she could. Every system relay, every bad batch of wiring. She'd even been able to patch a couple of pieces of armor with some sheets of metal small enough for her to carry out of the shop on her back. She'd brought more rope, too. And a rope ladder, so there had been less difficulty in getting down.

She did her best to keep the route hidden, though. And she didn't clear many of the trees in the copse that kept the BattleMech secret. She didn't want anyone to spot it like she did, if she could help it. Granted, no one had found it in maybe a hundred years, but once one person found it, the chances of another doing so skyrocketed.

She made a few last-minute checks of the repairs she made.

Katie was a good student, and Scarecrow had taught her well. Even if she'd never be a MechWarrior, she'd be a helluva 'Mech tech.

But why not both?

Settling into the command couch with the cockpit hatch closed and sealed behind her, it was time for the moment of truth.

Strapping the cooling vest—sans the aged company insignia—and settling the neurohelmet on her head, she was ready to go.

She placed her hands on the controls and started the ignition sequence. The old 'Mech hummed with power. "Okay, *Kagekitsune*," she told the 'Mech, "we're going to do this."

As if responding to her words, the console flashed to life, a constellation of lights and readouts.

A chill traveled up Katie's back and a tear rolled down her eye when the viewscreen came to life.

She'd never seen anything more beautiful.

The sun was still high in the sky, but falling fast. Dusk approached and she was running out of time and she hadn't even gone anywhere yet. She still had to get the 'Mech to Potsdam.

She hoped this would be the most difficult part of her day.

Taking a deep breath, she put her finger on the firing stud on the control stick, hoping one of the weapons worked. She'd not been able to test the integrity of any of the weapons, even the lasers, because she hadn't wanted to draw attention to her 'Mech. But now, she had no choice. And she wasn't going to make it out of the shadows if she didn't blow her way through the trees.

She hit the stud, but the only thing she heard was a horrible clicking.

Must be the short-range missiles, and I'm out of ammo.

On some level, she was relieved. The last thing she would have wanted was to cause an explosion of missiles that close to her 'Mech. Maybe she needed to do a little more research before she just started pushing buttons.

But there wasn't time.

Katie pulled the trigger on the control stick and her screen flashed a brilliant shade of green as the medium lasers fired, incinerating the trees before her in an instant.

Maybe she could have just stepped through the trees, but this seemed better somehow.

Before her stood only the river.

You can do this. You can do this. You can do this.

She repeated the mantra in her head as she willed the 'Mech forward for its first step. It wobbled a bit as it cleared the freshly-lasered tree stumps, but its chicken leg held firmly on the shore's bank. One more step, and she'd be walking into the river.

She'd studied the water depth on maps in the library, and found that it never got deeper than two or three meters. And the flow of water was brisk, but not insurmountable.

If the 'Mech held together and the walking was relatively even, she assured herself that she would be okay.

You're really good at lying to yourself, though.

Another deep breath, and then she moved forward into the drink.

The *Kit Fox* didn't so much step into the water, but hopped.

Katie thought that would be a better way to deal with the height discrepancy between the ledge of the river and the river itself. With her external mics on, she took in the sound of the rushing water. It changed in tone when the 'Mech changed the pattern of the water. It got louder, too. Maybe one of the mics was on the legs?

She took slow steps through the water, hoping she would be able to keep her balance and not drown in her 'Mech.

She smiled.

It didn't matter though.

She had a 'Mech.

And it worked.

She was going to be a MechWarrior.

She just had one last thing to do.

Mayor Marjorie Warhammer stood at the edge of town, watching the sunlight slowly dwindle during its golden hour, along with the chances of saving her village from the so-called Red Stripe gang.

These fools had cobbled together a couple of old 'Mechs and thought that was enough to scare the entire town. And, well, they were right.

As much as they wanted to resist, they simply didn't have the means.

No amount of pitchforks and threshers would stand up to the Red Stripe 'Mechs, no matter how righteous they felt their cause was. And no amount of strapping small arms on an AgroMech would help either. Again, their righteous fury meant nothing. There was a feeling unique to humanity that if people felt their cause was just, they would win no matter what the odds were. Since the dawn of humanity, they had told each other stories about good triumphing over evil and it made a lot of people make a lot of bad decisions.

Not that good shouldn't triumph over evil.

In the final accounting, it usually did.

But a lot of good people got killed going up against impossible odds because of that fire in their belly.

And the good Mayor of Potsdam didn't want to see that happen to any of the good people in her care.

Potsdam had been through a lot over the years, and she didn't want to see it go through any more hardship. The people around those parts were good, and they deserved some easy times, though since the war and the bombs, easy times seemed harder and harder. They were resilient, though. And as difficult as it was, they'd weather the Red Stripe gang, too, as frustrating as they were.

She wondered if it was some of the local kids who had found the 'Mechs, but then she realized how absurd that would be. None of the local kids had the know-how to repair a salvaged 'Mech, and these kids had a bit of a different accent. Maybe they were striking out on their own from one of the other close settlements. Arnhem, perhaps. Or even all the way from the capital of Snowy Monara, though that seemed like an incredibly far distance to raid a small town for a pittance of kroner and supplies.

As the sun dwindled further and the light turned from gold to gray, the mayor sighed.

The sound of the 'Mechs approaching came like thunder, a deep booming bass you could feel when they walked, right in the pit of your stomach.

It was something the mayor hadn't felt in a long time before these clowns showed up.

And she hoped it would be a long time still before she heard it ever again after their exchange.

The mayor walked down to the loading docks herself. It was just a staircase down from the rooftop lookout she'd chosen to watch the sunset from. She'd oversee the handoff personally. She didn't want to risk anyone else's life. And besides, she knew everyone in town. If she could make the handoff herself and they got close enough to do it, she might be close enough to recognize who they were and what they were up to.

The *Crossbow* and the *Sentinel* with the sloppy paint jobs and Red Stripe goons hanging off of them like they were a children's jungle gym sauntered toward the town's loading docks. Behind them was a hovertruck, just like the mayor had guessed would be there.

The mayor felt the rumble of each step of the two 'Mechs and it became more and more pronounced as they got closer.

On top of the crates of supplies they'd demanded, foodstuffs and medicine and technological components, was a bullhorn for the mayor's use.

She lifted it to her lips and spoke, "Red Stripes. This is Marjorie Warhammer, the mayor of Potsdam. We have everything you asked for. And a case full of kroner, in cash, since you weren't able to provide an account for transfer."

Mayor Warhammer raised the suitcase full of kroner to accentuate her point. She'd hoped they'd just give her an account number and they'd be able to trace these people that way. It would have been a lot easier to recover the money, even if the banks were dodgy themselves.

"We hope you'll take this and leave. Our business will be concluded, and we'll all go our separate ways."

The Red Stripe 'Mechs stood sentry on either side of the street as the hovertruck backed into the loading docks, ready to take their booty.

They didn't say anything, but they were going to have to come face to face with her to get the case full of cash. She wasn't going to just let them take it.

The driver and passenger of the hovertruck hopped out and approached. Maybe they'd gotten better uniforms since last she saw them, or knew they had to wear them more properly because they were going to be in closer contact with people, but both of them wore greasy-looking black jumpsuits that had a stripe of red painted along the front. It was as sloppy as the paint job on the *Crossbow* and the *Sentinel.* By the look of the stiffness of their fabric, Marjorie would have wagered it was even the same paint.

Real amateurs.

They wore masks that obscured most of their faces. Goggles and helmets hid the rest. They were taking no chances with their identities being exposed. And the mayor wasn't the best with voices, so she wondered if she *would* be able to recognize them at all.

"Give us the case," the driver said in a gruff tone that confirmed the mayor's suspicions. Indeed, she could not recognize the voices.

"Are you sure you want to do this?" the mayor asked, hoping that by getting them to talk more, she might get more clues about their identity.

"Of course we are. Now hand over the case and no one gets hurt."

The voice sounded gruff, but not terribly gendered one way or the other. Still not enough information.

The mayor tightened her grip on the handle of the luggage and hoped beyond hope things wouldn't be this easy for them.

And then her brow furrowed.

The vibration of a 'Mech moving rumbled through her feet and into her body, but neither the *Crossbow* nor the *Sentinel* were moving.

Both of the Red Stripe goons looked around, apparently wondering what could be going on, just like her. They seemed as surprised as the mayor was when they realized their friendly 'Mechs weren't moving either.

"What the...?" the driver said.

That's when the mayor saw it.

With the red paint and the mottled green moss covering over most of it, the old *Kit Fox* looked like something out of an ancient Christmas celebration. Part tree, part 'Mech.

Warhammer hadn't seen a 'Mech like that...well...ever.

Something about it told her it wasn't one of the Red Stripes though. Part of it was that the paint scheme didn't match. And as ignorant as these Red Stripe fools were, they at least had a dedication to their matching uniforms and paint schemes.

The other major part was that the *Crossbow* and the *Sentinel* both scrambled to get into a position to get the *Kit Fox* in their firing arc, all but ignoring the mayor and the promise of their loot.

There wasn't time for them to do much, though.

The mysterious *Kit Fox* opened fire with its green lasers, and blasted right into the *Crossbow*'s torso with a direct hit. The lasers carved off a massive chunk of the *Crossbow*'s middle, proving that the thing was weak enough to begin with, barely held together. The bandits hanging onto the *Crossbow*, not wishing to experience close laser fire a second time, leaped off the 'Mech as its ruined torso armor panel *clanged* to the ground. Those had hadn't injured themselves ran for cover, the others limped or crawled away.

Mayor Warhammer wanted to cheer at the mystery 'Mech drawing first blood. But she worried the *Kit Fox* didn't look much better and it was outmatched, two to one.

The *Crossbow* was able to twist around in and fire back at the *Kit Fox*, melting a fragment of its leg armor, but not before taking another laser hit that cut off one of its arms, sending it crashing to the ground.

For the *Sentinel*'s part, instead of firing back, it charged the *Kit Fox*, spilling its own riders along the way. Unfortunately, it couldn't close the distance in time.

The *Kit Fox* backed up and opened fire with a deafening double blast from its Ultra autocannon.

The *Sentinel* crashed into the ground, skidding on the pavement in front of the *Kit Fox*.

The mysterious MechWarrior that had come to the rescue of Potsdam aimed their lasers down at the *Sentinel* and fired them once more into the top of it, blowing a hole into it.

But that gave the *Crossbow* enough time to fire another blast at the *Kit Fox*.

Its first shot flew wide, blasting into the trees beyond it in the outskirts of town. The mayor hoped it didn't start a fire in the forest. That was the last thing she needed to deal with on a day like this.

The second shot hit the *Kit Fox* in the nose of its cockpit. The 'Mech was already mostly cockpit, a big, mean shell with spindly arms and raptor legs. Warhammer knew it was known for having weak armor in the head, and she worried that the mysterious benefactor wouldn't make it through this.

The *Kit Fox* took another step back and repositioned itself so that the *Crossbow* was back in its firing arc and fired again. Both lasers turned the center of the *Crossbow* into slag and it fell over.

The hovertruck driver and his passenger looked on in horror.

Then they turned back to the mayor, who only smiled at them. She dropped the case full of old C-bills and pulled a pistol from her hip, aiming at both of them.

The pistol didn't threaten them enough, though. They both ran, scrambling to get into the hovertruck, despite being empty handed. They didn't want to lose their lives any more than they wanted to lose their 'Mechs. But it had happened anyway.

The mayor fired a shot, but it flew wide.

The Red Stripe goons were able to get into the hovertruck, back it up, and attempt a reckless J-turn to straighten back out and escape.

The *Kit Fox* didn't seem to like that. It marched around the downed *Sentinel* and aimed its lasers down at the oncoming hovertruck.

It fired.

The lasers blew a hole in the road in front of the truck, and an explosion of dust and debris clouded much of the mayor's view. The hovertruck must have swerved to miss the pit, because the next thing she heard was a great crash.

The Red Stripes had collided into the building to their left. The pirates piled out of their wrecked vehicle and looked as though they were going to try to run, but the *Kit Fox* side stepped again to keep them in its firing arc.

Then, its external speakers flared to life.

"Red Stripe pirates," the voice said. It was the voice of a young woman straining to sound gruffer—and perhaps older—than she was. "Surrender or you will be destroyed."

Both of them cowered beneath the withering stare of the *Kit Fox*, their hands raised, granting the MechWarrior's wish. The rest of the bandits that had fallen or leaped off the two destroyed 'Mechs also raised their hands.

The mayor jogged toward them, leaving the bullhorn, but taking the case full of cash and the gun. She was going to arrest these fools herself and detain them with the help of the *Kit Fox* until the sheriff of Potsdam arrived to throw these clowns into the lockup.

"Hold it right there," she told them, leveling the pistol at them.

"We surrender, we surrender!" they said, flinching at the thought of being shot.

It was amazing what being robbed of your firepower and 'Mechs would do to the bravery of a person. It would reduce it right down to zero. These fools had nothing left and no power with which to bargain.

Only after the sheriff had arrived and hauled all the bandits off did the *Kit Fox* finally stand down.

"MechWarrior!" the mayor called up to the old 'Mech. "I'd like to thank you."

"Thanks aren't exactly necessary," the 'Mech pilot said through their external speaker, though they must have realized it was far too loud to hold a conversation that way. Unless they were trying to *remain* mysterious, there wouldn't be any problem with them getting out of their 'Mech and talking to the mayor one-to-one.

And that's exactly what happened.

The hatch on the back of the *Kit Fox* swung open and, just as the mayor had predicted, a young woman climbed out. She still couldn't quite tell who it was or if she knew the young woman, as her back was turned while she scaled down the side of the 'Mech.

"I think thanks *are* necessary. You saved our town."

When the MechWarrior spun around, the mayor was shocked to find that it was Scarecrow's grease monkey, Katie.

Katie Ferraro...? Yeah, that's it. She must not be older than sixteen or seventeen, tops.

"I mean, thanks are great and all, but I think there was something else." Katie had grease smeared on one cheek and her old and tattered cooling vest looked like it had been taken out of a museum.

"Something else?"

"You told me that if I could take care of these guys, I'd be able to get half of the money they asked for. So, I still think that's a pretty sweet deal." She looked around the street at the damage she had wrought and her eyes widened. Maybe she didn't realize how much destruction she could cause in a 'Mech when viewed from ground level. "Wow... I would, uh, also like to salvage their 'Mechs that I took down."

All things considered, Mayor Warhammer thought that would be a pretty good deal for the town. *Then Katie would be responsible for cleaning up the salvage and the street.*

She smiled. "I don't see why that would be a problem."

Katie toed the ground in front of her. Clearly there was something else on her mind.

"Was there something else?"

"Well, maybe, I was thinking..."

"Out with it, young lady."

"Well, I was thinking, what if you needed the services of a 'Mech to protect the town on an ongoing basis."

"You mean a contract?"

"Yeah, like a contract."

"That's something we could talk about, MechWarrior."

When the mayor referred to Katie as a MechWarrior, she saw the girl's eyes go wide and a blush come across her face as she smiled.

That was it.

She wants to be a MechWarrior.

Mayor Marjorie Warhammer returned the girl's smile.

A MechWarrior she will be...

BATTLETECH ERAS

The *BattleTech* universe is a living, vibrant entity that grows each year as more sourcebooks and fiction are published. A dynamic universe, its setting and characters evolve over time within a highly detailed continuity framework, bringing everything to life in a way a static game universe cannot match.

To help quickly and easily convey the timeline of the universe—and to allow a player to easily "plug in" a given novel or sourcebook—we've divided *BattleTech* into six major eras.

STAR LEAGUE
(Present–2780)

Ian Cameron, ruler of the Terran Hegemony, concludes decades of tireless effort with the creation of the Star League, a political and military alliance between all Great Houses and the Hegemony. Star League armed forces immediately launch the Reunification War, forcing the Periphery realms to join. For the next two centuries, humanity experiences a golden age across the thousand light-years of human-occupied space known as the Inner Sphere. It also sees the creation of the most powerful military in human history.

(This era also covers the centuries before the founding of the Star League in 2571, most notably the Age of War.)

SUCCESSION WARS
(2781–3049)

Every last member of First Lord Richard Cameron's family is killed during a coup launched by Stefan Amaris. Following the thirteen-year war to unseat him, the rulers of each of the five Great Houses disband the Star League. General Aleksandr Kerensky departs with eighty percent of the Star League Defense Force beyond known space and the Inner Sphere collapses into centuries of warfare known as the Succession Wars that will eventually result in a massive loss of technology across most worlds.

CLAN INVASION
(3050–3061)

A mysterious invading force strikes the coreward region of the Inner Sphere. The invaders, called the Clans, are descendants of Kerensky's SLDF troops, forged into a society dedicated to becoming the greatest fighting force in history. With vastly superior technology and warriors, the Clans conquer world after world. Eventually this outside threat will forge a new Star League, something hundreds of years of warfare failed to accomplish. In addition, the Clans will act as a catalyst for a technological renaissance.

CIVIL WAR
(3062-3067)

The Clan threat is eventually lessened with the complete destruction of a Clan. With that massive external threat apparently neutralized, internal conflicts explode around the Inner Sphere. House Liao conquers its former Commonality, the St. Ives Compact; a rebellion of military units belonging to House Kurita sparks a war with their powerful border enemy, Clan Ghost Bear; the fabulously powerful Federated Commonwealth of House Steiner and House Davion collapses into five long years of bitter civil war.

JIHAD
(3067-3080)

Following the Federated Commonwealth Civil War, the leaders of the Great Houses meet and disband the new Star League, declaring it a sham. The pseudo-religious Word of Blake—a splinter group of ComStar, the protectors and controllers of interstellar communication—launch the Jihad: an interstellar war that pits every faction against each other and even against themselves, as weapons of mass destruction are used for the first time in centuries while new and frightening technologies are also unleashed.

DARK AGE
(3081-3150)

Under the guidance of Devlin Stone, the Republic of the Sphere is born at the heart of the Inner Sphere following the Jihad. One of the more extensive periods of peace begins to break out as the 32nd century dawns. The factions, to one degree or another, embrace disarmament, and the massive armies of the Succession Wars begin to fade. However, in 3132 eighty percent of interstellar communications collapses, throwing the universe into chaos. Wars erupt almost immediately, and the factions begin rebuilding their armies.

ILCLAN
(3151-present)

The once-invulnerable Republic of the Sphere lies in ruins, torn apart by the Great Houses and the Clans as they wage war against each other on a scale not seen in nearly a century. Mercenaries flourish once more, selling their might to the highest bidder. As Fortress Republic collapses, the Clans race toward Terra to claim their long-denied birthright and create a supreme authority that will fulfill the dream of Aleksandr Kerensky and rule the Inner Sphere by any means necessary: The ilClan.

SUBMISSION GUIDELINES

Shrapnel is the market for official short fiction set in the *BattleTech* universe.

WHAT WE WANT

We are looking for stories of **3,000–7,000 words** that are character-oriented, meaning the characters, rather than the technology, provide the main focus of the action. Stories can be set in any established *BattleTech* era, and although we prefer stories where BattleMechs are featured, this is by no means a mandatory element.

WHAT WE DON'T WANT

The following items are generally grounds for immediate disqualification:

- Stories not set in the *BattleTech* universe. There are other markets for these stories.

- Stories centering solely on romance, supernatural, fantasy, or horror elements. If your story isn't primarily military sci-fi, then it's probably not for us.

- Stories containing gratuitous sex, gore, or profanity. Keep it PG-13, and you should be fine.

- Stories under 3,000 words or over 7,000 words. We don't publish flash fiction, and although we do publish works longer than 7,000 words, these are reserved for established *BattleTech* authors.

- Vanity stories, which include personal units, author-as-character inserts, or tabletop game sessions retold in narrative form.

- Publicly available *BattleTech* fan-fiction. If your story has been posted in a forum or other public venue, then we will not accept it.

MANUSCRIPT FORMAT

- .rtf, .doc, .docx formats ONLY
- 12-point Times New Roman, Cambria, or Palatino fonts ONLY
- 1" (2.54 cm) margins all around
- Double-spaced lines
- DO NOT put an extra space between each paragraph
- Filename: "Submission Title by Jane Q. Writer"

PAYMENT & RIGHTS

We pay $0.05 per word after publication. By submitting to *Shrapnel*, you acknowledge that your work is set in an owned universe and that you retain no rights to any of the characters, settings, or "ideas" detailed in your story. We purchase **all rights** to every published story; those rights are automatically transferred to The Topps Company, Inc.

SUBMISSIONS PORTAL

To send us a submission, visit our submissions portal here: **https://pulsepublishingsubmissions.moksha.io/publication/shrapnel-the-battletech-magazine-fiction**

LOOKING FOR MORE HARD HITTING BATTLETECH FICTION?

WE'LL GET YOU RIGHT BACK INTO THE BATTLE!

Catalyst Game Labs brings you the very best in *BattleTech* fiction, available at most ebook retailers, including Amazon, Apple Books, Kobo, Barnes & Noble, and more!

NOVELS

1. *Decision at Thunder Rift* by William H. Keith Jr.
2. *Mercenary's Star* by William H. Keith Jr.
3. *The Price of Glory* by William H. Keith, Jr.
4. *Warrior: En Garde* by Michael A. Stackpole
5. *Warrior: Riposte* by Michael A. Stackpole
6. *Warrior: Coupé* by Michael A. Stackpole
7. Wolves on the Border by Robert N. Charrette
8. *Heir to the Dragon* by Robert N. Charrette
9. *Lethal Heritage* (The Blood of Kerensky, Volume 1) by Michael A. Stackpole
10. *Blood Legacy* (The Blood of Kerensky, Volume 2) by Michael A. Stackpole
11. *Lost Destiny* (The Blood of Kerensky, Volume 3) by Michael A. Stackpole
12. *Way of the Clans* (Legend of the Jade Phoenix, Volume 1) by Robert Thurston
13. *Bloodname* (Legend of the Jade Phoenix, Volume 2) by Robert Thurston
14. *Falcon Guard* (Legend of the Jade Phoenix, Volume 3) by Robert Thurston
15. *Wolf Pack* by Robert N. Charrette
16. *Main Event* by James D. Long
17. *Natural Selection* by Michael A. Stackpole
18. *Assumption of Risk* by Michael A. Stackpole
19. *Blood of Heroes* by Andrew Keith
20. *Close Quarters* by Victor Milán
21. *Far Country* by Peter L. Rice
22. *D.R.T.* by James D. Long
23. *Tactics of Duty* by William H. Keith
24. *Bred for War* by Michael A. Stackpole
25. *I Am Jade Falcon* by Robert Thurston
26. *Highlander Gambit* by Blaine Lee Pardoe
27. *Hearts of Chaos* by Victor Milán
28. *Operation Excalibur* by William H. Keith
29. *Malicious Intent* by Michael A. Stackpole
30. *Black Dragon* by Victor Milán
31. *Impetus of War* by Blaine Lee Pardoe
32. *Double-Blind* by Loren L. Coleman
33. *Binding Force* by Loren L. Coleman
34. *Exodus Road* (Twilight of the Clans, Volume 1) by Blaine Lee Pardoe
35. *Grave Covenant* ((Twilight of the Clans, Volume 2) by Michael A. Stackpole

36. *The Hunters* (Twilight of the Clans, Volume 3) by Thomas S. Gressman
37. *Freebirth* (Twilight of the Clans, Volume 4) by Robert Thurston
38. *Sword and Fire* (Twilight of the Clans, Volume 5) by Thomas S. Gressman
39. *Shadows of War* (Twilight of the Clans, Volume 6) by Thomas S. Gressman
40. *Prince of Havoc* (Twilight of the Clans, Volume 7) by Michael A. Stackpole
41. *Falcon Rising* (Twilight of the Clans, Volume 8) by Robert Thurston
42. *Threads of Ambition* (The Capellan Solution, Book 1) by Loren L. Coleman
43. *The Killing Fields* (The Capellan Solution, Book 2) by Loren L. Coleman
44. *Dagger Point* by Thomas S. Gressman
45. *Ghost of Winter* by Stephen Kenson
46. *Roar of Honor* by Blaine Lee Pardoe
47. *By Blood Betrayed* by Blaine Lee Pardoe and Mel Odom
48. *Illusions of Victory* by Loren L. Coleman
49. *Flashpoint* by Loren L. Coleman
50. *Measure of a Hero* by Blaine Lee Pardoe
51. *Path of Glory* by Randall N. Bills
52. *Test of Vengeance* by Bryan Nystul
53. *Patriots and Tyrants* by Loren L. Coleman
54. *Call of Duty* by Blaine Lee Pardoe
55. *Initiation to War* by Robert N. Charrette
56. *The Dying Time* by Thomas S. Gressman
57. *Storms of Fate* by Loren L. Coleman
58. *Imminent Crisis* by Randall N. Bills
59. *Operation Audacity* by Blaine Lee Pardoe
60. *Endgame* by Loren L. Coleman
61. *A Bonfire of Worlds* by Steven Mohan, Jr.
62. *Isle of the Blessed* by Steven Mohan, Jr.
63. *Embers of War* by Jason Schmetzer
64. *Betrayal of Ideals* by Blaine Lee Pardoe
65. *Forever Faithful* by Blaine Lee Pardoe
66. *Kell Hounds Ascendant* by Michael A. Stackpole
67. *Redemption Rift* by Jason Schmetzer
68. *Grey Watch Protocol* (*Book One of the Highlander Covenant*) by Michael J. Ciaravella
69. *Honor's Gauntlet* by Bryan Young
70. *Icons of War* by Craig A. Reed, Jr.
71. *Children of Kerensky* by Blaine Lee Pardoe

YOUNG ADULT NOVELS

1. *The Nellus Academy Incident* by Jennifer Brozek
2. *Iron Dawn* (*Rogue Academy, Book 1*) by Jennifer Brozek
3. *Ghost Hour* (*Rogue Academy, Book 2*) by Jennifer Brozek

OMNIBUSES

1. *The Gray Death Legion Trilogy* by William H. Keith, Jr.

NOVELLAS/SHORT STORIES

1. *Lion's Roar* by Steven Mohan, Jr.
2. *Sniper* by Jason Schmetzer
3. *Eclipse* by Jason Schmetzer
4. *Hector* by Jason Schmetzer
5. *The Frost Advances (Operation Ice Storm, Part 1)* by Jason Schmetzer
6. *The Winds of Spring (Operation Ice Storm, Part 2)* by Jason Schmetzer
7. *Instrument of Destruction (Ghost Bear's Lament, Part 1)* by Steven Mohan, Jr.
8. *The Fading Call of Glory (Ghost Bear's Lament, Part 2)* by Steven Mohan, Jr.
9. *Vengeance* by Jason Schmetzer
10. *A Splinter of Hope* by Philip A. Lee
11. *The Anvil* by Blaine Lee Pardoe
12. *A Splinter of Hope/The Anvil* (omnibus)
13. *Not the Way the Smart Money Bets (Kell Hounds Ascendant #1)* by Michael A. Stackpole
14. *A Tiny Spot of Rebellion (Kell Hounds Ascendant #2)* by Michael A. Stackpole
15. *A Clever Bit of Fiction (Kell Hounds Ascendant #3)* by Michael A. Stackpole
16. *Break-Away (Proliferation Cycle #1)* by Ilsa J. Bick
17. *Prometheus Unbound (Proliferation Cycle #2)* by Herbert A. Beas II
18. *Nothing Ventured (Proliferation Cycle #3)* by Christoffer Trossen
19. *Fall Down Seven Times, Get Up Eight (Proliferation Cycle #4)* by Randall N. Bills
20. *A Dish Served Cold (Proliferation Cycle #5)* by Chris Hartford and Jason M. Hardy
21. *The Spider Dances (Proliferation Cycle #6)* by Jason Schmetzer
22. *Shell Games* by Jason Schmetzer
23. *Divided We Fall* by Blaine Lee Pardoe
24. *The Hunt for Jardine (Forgotten Worlds, Part One)* by Herbert A. Beas II
25. *Rock of the Republic* by Blaine Lee Pardoe
26. *Finding Jardine (Forgotten Worlds, Part Two)* by Herbert A. Beas II

ANTHOLOGIES

1. *The Corps (BattleCorps Anthology, Volume 1)* edited by Loren. L. Coleman
2. *First Strike (BattleCorps Anthology, Volume 2)* edited by Loren L. Coleman
3. *Weapons Free (BattleCorps Anthology, Volume 3)* edited by Jason Schmetzer
4. *Onslaught: Tales from the Clan Invasion* edited by Jason Schmetzer
5. *Edge of the Storm* by Jason Schmetzer
6. *Fire for Effect (BattleCorps Anthology, Volume 4)* edited by Jason Schmetzer
7. *Chaos Born (Chaos Irregulars, Book 1)* by Kevin Killiany
8. *Chaos Formed (Chaos Irregulars, Book 2)* by Kevin Killiany
9. *Counterattack (BattleCorps Anthology, Volume 5)* edited by Jason Schmetzer
10. *Front Lines (BattleCorps Anthology Volume 6)* edited by Jason Schmetzer and Philip A. Lee
11. *Legacy* edited by John Helfers and Philip A. Lee
12. *Kill Zone (BattleCorps Anthology Volume 7)* edited by Philip A. Lee
13. *Gray Markets (A BattleCorps Anthology)*, edited by Jason Schmetzer and Philip A. Lee
14. *Slack Tide (A BattleCorps Anthology)*, edited by Jason Schmetzer and Philip A. Lee

MAGAZINES

1. *Shrapnel* Issue #1
2. *Shrapnel* Issue #2
3. *Shrapnel* Issue #3

BATTLETECH